While the World Turns

While the World Turns

K. M. O'Neill

RESOURCE *Publications* · Eugene, Oregon

WHILE THE WORLD TURNS

Resource Publications
An Imprint of Wipf and Stock Publishers
199 W. 8th Ave., Suite 3
Eugene, OR 97401

www.wipfandstock.com

PAPERBACK ISBN: 978-1-6667-3169-9
HARDCOVER ISBN: 978-1-6667-2442-4
EBOOK ISBN: 978-1-6667-2443-1

| SEPTEMBER 28, 2021

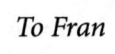

To Fran

Stat crux dum volvitur orbis.
—MOTTO OF THE ORDER OF CARTHUSIANS

CONTENTS

CHAPTER 1

SIXTEEN HUNDRED YEARS AGO, IN the days when the rich were gods locked in glass towers and countries had amassed themselves into bloated and rotting empires, Aitor saw God for the first and last time in his life.

He was just turning fourteen, and the heart of Andalucía sweltered, hazy and suffocated. Though it was the small hours of the night, the stench of heat-baked sewage and urine lingered in the streets, mixing with the tang of sea salt and garbage. The tall whitewashed apartment buildings glittered ghostly pale in the moonlight.

Aitor and his friends went first to the beach to celebrate. They splashed half-naked in the ocean at high tide, and scuffled in the cool sand, kissing and roughhousing. When they grew tired, they piled against each other, smoking in contented and lazy silence.

They were more than a little drunk. Later, Aitor would not be able to remember whose idea it was to break into the town's single movie theater. Two of them slipped away in the dark to find the projector room. The rest sprawled in the blissful air-conditioned blackness, trading crude jokes.

The movie, when it came on, was not in Spanish. They watched with creased brows, their alcohol-sleepy eyes struggling to focus on the captions, but one by one, they began to fall asleep, tangled up in the way of tired friends who are all a little in love with one other.

Only Aitor remained awake, his eyes as wide as they would go.

The people in this film were rugged adventurers, moving with a crisp and inexorable purpose. Everything they did was for one reason only: to ascend.

These people were on fire with a great excitement for the unknown. This, to Aitor, was foreign to the indolence of a dirty little coastal town—a place which had existed since the beginning of time, and which would always exist in the same sun-drunk apathy.

But these people—with joyful recklessness, they smiled, and saluted, and abandoned the face of the earth.

Aitor had never cared about space. There were other things to care about which were closer and more important. He had heard enough teachers' voices droning over slideshows of meteorites and gas giants—there were always facts to learn, and statistics, and wonders to describe. All noise.

But in this movie, as the people entered space, they fell silent.

Everything was silent.

The camera glided into the vastness of the void, its eyes following the sleek, blue-backlit vessels of the explorers at an impassive distance.

An occasional radio communication: terse, brief.

The darkness was hung with a million lights. Magisterial planets wrought with turbulent storms, faint and pulsing galaxies, dying stars flinging themselves outward and outward and outward until there was nothing left but rubble.

What fascinated Aitor the most, though, were the spaces in between. These spaces—these blacknesses—were not dead to him. Instead, he thought almost that they breathed with a secret life. Hiding there must be the strange and terrible knowledge of all things, seen and unseen.

The movie played out and the adventurers stepped onto their new planet. They planted their flag, and began a new life beneath the light of a pale blue-orange star. Astronauts hugged, shouted, clapped each other on the back. Credits rolled.

In the darkness of the theater, Aitor felt himself surrounded suddenly by something which watched him, everywhere and nowhere at the same time. This Watcher saw all things in totality: space and its plumes of nebula, its belts of desolate rock, its infinitely expanding web of galaxies and all acts of sin and grace which passed therein.

Aitor extricated himself from the sleeping heap and crept up to the empty projector room. There he put the movie on again, and returned to sit at the very front of the theater.

Here, it seemed that space had engulfed him entirely. He found himself inflamed with a rapturous desire to pull aside the veil and see the Watcher; at the same time, a staggering fear turned his bowels to liquid, shouted at him to run, to flee to the cold and wet hidden places where no eye could find him again.

Yet he could not leave, could not run. He could not understand it. He watched the film again and again.

In the morning, the owner of the theater found them and threw them out. He cursed them seven ways and threatened to call the policía, on top of a hundred other things.

The threats held no real weight, but they scattered into the back alleys regardless, laughing and swearing back. In the streets they said their goodbyes, and then Aitor was left alone.

He did not go home immediately, but looked up, blinking sleep from his eyes, to stare at the sky. It was early enough that the sun was rising, pushing off banks of mist from the coast, but even so, if he squinted, he could still see trails of stars winking down at him.

There were very few people out yet; a handful of old men sitting on their porches, ready to smoke and gossip the day away, and abuelas trundling away slowly to the local grocery, too stubborn to ask for help.

Aitor did not see them, though they stared. He walked with his eyes on the heavens.

The house was empty when he returned home at last. He climbed the stairs and into the small lightless room he shared with his brother, and collapsed into a weary stupor.

The next evening he went across the street to the little church where his abuelos had once taken him as a child. They were saying Mass, and against the heat of the afternoon, the doors were propped ajar. The chanting of the aged and the dying made a mournful and ancient counterpoint against the casual shouts of passing pedestrians and the whir of cars and motorcycles.

The priest there was not old. Aitor had not seen him before, though later he learned that his name was Padre Emilio Aguilera Alejo.

His voice as he prayed and sang was triumphant and bass and clarion as it issued forth from the church. But when he was not praying, he had the melancholic eyes of someone who is chronically alone, and the worn face of a man whose soul is far too old for its body.

When the church was slowly emptying and the priest emerged in only collar and cassock, Aitor was waiting to ask his question.

The padre told Aitor that what he had seen must surely have been God.

"But God is everywhere," Aitor said, remembering only vaguely what his mother had once whispered to him when he was very small.

"Yes," said the padre. "But perhaps that is where He is most, for you. It is very different for each person, where they find Him the easiest."

"Then I will have to always be very far away from Him," said Aitor.

The priest said, "When you contemplate Him, He will be near." His smile was patient, but tired.

"What if I am afraid?" Aitor said.

"What?"

Aitor had never been to confession, but this seemed close. To tell a priest that he did not like to be looked at by the Creator seemed like the highest blasphemy. "I felt happiness," he said. "But I wanted to hide."

The padre considered this. "What is it that you fear?"

"He saw me," said Aitor. And the seeing had gone down to the core of his being.

"To be loved, you must be known," said Padre Aguilera. "Is it not good, then, that He sees you?"

Aitor thought about it. "When I looked," he said, "I could not see Him back."

"Ah." And Padre Aguilera's eyes grew sad and distant and distracted, and he folded his hands together. "And so it goes," he said.

Aitor did not know what he meant, though, and said nothing.

"Be not afraid," said the priest, at last, looking again at Aitor, and this time it was his eyes that saw Aitor, and knew him, and understood him. "We must go forth blind. We may never truly see. But Aitor, do not be afraid."

And in all that time—sixteen hundred years ago—Aitor had not again feared.

He did not fear in the years he studied under the padre, and did not see God. For years he had knelt stubbornly at the altar of the small chapel each day. If the mystery remained, then so would he.

He did not fear on the day he snuck from his home and traveled into the city to be confirmed, receiving a new name as the bishop sealed his soul forever with the Holy Spirit.

Even when his father passed away and his brother abandoned him, he did not fear. He was not alone: Padre Aguilera came, and embraced him, and took him to the chapterhouse of the Order of St. Joseph of Cupertino.

There, he had ten fathers and there he fell deeply in love for the first time, the most terrifying of things that had ever happened to him. And in the end, he shed his ordinary life and gave up all his love, submitting his life to the mercies of a God whom he had never once seen.

But now, a millennium later, Padre Aitor Gómez Gomarra faced the vast and implacable beauty of space, holding his God in his hands, and he was afraid.

In the belly of a ship adrift on an endless circuit, standing at last in the heart of the endless and unchanging darkness, he was so afraid he could barely breathe.

This fear seized him the most often when he was enclosed in a windowless room. One day twenty years ago, he had opened his eyes to the low ceiling with its dim guidelights flashing, and had realized he no longer had hope or joy.

Decades had passed, and still he did not understand his God. He knew only this stifling fear which choked him, a fist rising up from his belly to strangle him from within.

For a long time, the chapel had been his refuge. Only recently had the fear begin to strike him as he was offering Mass in this, the last holy place in the universe.

The chapel had been built in the ship's nose, above the unmanned control unit. It was a cramped room which doubled as a sacristy on one side, containing the vestments, books, and a small plain chalice and ciborium.

To the right of the altar was the tabernacle, and its tiny artificial red candle. Beside that was the closet in which were stored thousands and thousands of vacuum-sealed wafers of unleavened bread for consecration, and dozens of racks of bottled wine.

The shipbuilders had not themselves been Catholic. The only concessions to traditional beauty in the chapel were the window, which took up the majority of the chapel's concave wall, and the crucifix, which hung eerily spotlighted over the altar.

The crucifix was not really beautiful at all. The priest who had carved it had said Mass in this chapel, once. His name was Mateusz Wojciechowski, of Knurów. He had put loving detail into the wounds of the Christ; he had spent years in suffering and then years of laying every ounce of that suffering into the wooden figure he had carved. He had been a friend.

The face of the man who had hung suspended over Aitor for so many years—so many long hours of every day—was written with visceral pain. Mateusz had lost his only family and stronghold, his beloved brother, in the early days of the starvations and the riots, when the idea of sending the Cupertinian Order to space was just a desperate fancy.

The lips of Jesus were twisted back in a ghastly cry; the eyes were open, and followed you wherever you walked. The flesh had been carved away in tatters from the wrists and feet where the nails had been plunged deep.

The carving was not quite human, but human enough that it made stomachs turn. On Earth, it had spent its days in a small side chapel at the Superior General's request, where visitors and discerning seminarians would not see it.

But the face of this suffering stranger was a face with which Aitor was intimately familiar. When he was not saying Mass in the old Latin, he spoke to the crucifix in Spanish, and there was a simple intimacy in this, cultivated from half a century together.

Behind the crucifix, the window spanned wider than a man's arms, and taller by half. It was not a real window—a digital screen, in reality—but when the ship was designed, one of the Brothers had requested it.

If a man was to spend his life in this one room, he had said, then it would be a kindness to give him something to look at.

"The only thing we need to look upon is Our Lord," said the Superior General. But he had been cut from sterner cloth than the rest of them, and he also would not join them on their ship for its long voyage. The window was constructed and rigged to cameras so that it looked out upon space as it slid by in an endless velvet river.

At last, Aitor had gone to the heavens to seek God. And here he looked and looked as he had as a boy of fourteen, only now he did not know what it was that he saw.

He wondered, sometimes, as he stood looking at the window, how many times it had saved the life of a Brother. It had saved his.

Aitor had begun his shift aboard *La Trascendencia* offering Masses in the Novus Ordo, facing the congregation. There were only three seats—formalities only—and when he consecrated the host, he presented it to people who were not there.

In the early days, he had pretended to fill the seats. He imagined his parents, his brothers and sisters and cousins, a hundred faces he had known and loved. Though many of them had not in truth set foot in a church in years, they bowed down before the Lord in his hands.

As the weeks turned into months and then into years, their faces gave way to others. He offered Mass for old classmates, and his fellow seminarians as he remembered them going through those long and difficult years of study.

Then it was Pablo, his best from childhood; the old men who sat on their patios smoking; the familiar but nameless vendors who sold fruit and vegetables at corner markets.

The day came that he found himself praying before people he did not know at all. Sometimes they faced the altar; other times, they drifted ghostly through the chapel, wandering through walls, looking at nothing.

They were sometimes strangers whom he had seen and helped during the Exodus. There was a woman whose baby was misshapen and deformed, who had wandered aimlessly down an empty street, both woman and child as voiceless as shades.

Once there was an elderly man who had sat by his darkened home, chanting *Ma'ariv* into the twilight. There was a family who had huddled under the shelter of a battered tarp strung between two cars, whose father had begged him for Last Rites, though Aitor had not then been ordained.

When the faces grew to be too much, Aitor had begun to offer the Mass traditionally, with his back to the seats. It did not help; he could still feel them watching him. Sometimes they joined in as he sang the hymns, and if he did not speak the proper congregation's responses, only listening, their melancholy voices filled the chapel.

Were they real? Or were they products of his fevered, lonely imagination? Only God knew, and God was not telling.

Aitor lowered the Host to the paten and began to consecrate the wine as well. He knew that as he spoke, his voice would be broadcast through the ship, his words falling on ears that had been deaf for centuries.

Take this, all of you, and drink. For this is the chalice of My Blood, the Blood of the new and eternal covenant—the Mystery of Faith—which shall be poured out for you and for many. Do this in memory of Me.

Aitor had embarked upon *La Trascendencia* with young hands, smooth and strong. They were age-ridged now, stiff and mottled. By the count of the screen beside his bed, nearly fifty years had passed since he had first been awoken to take up his duty.

Only twenty-one days left.

The command of the Superior General, given sixteen hundred years ago, still lingered at the edges of his thought. Thus it had lingered since the day of the Exodus, the Sundering, the End.

The brothers had stood thirty-three strong beneath the glistening gold-wrought baldachin of the cathedral. They crowded close in the small pool of light offered by the candles of the holy and sacrificial altar.

Thirty-three of them spent their last moments on Earth bent to hear the whispers of the Superior General as he blessed them and gave them their final command.

We must rebuild His people.

We will do what it takes.

May God have mercy on us all.

The Superior General had not boarded the ship with them. He remained, he said, to watch over what was left of the world, and to minister to his people. To preserve, as he could, the truth. But sometimes Aitor thought that he had just been a coward.

Only twenty-one days.

O Lord, Aitor thought, as he lowered the blood of his God to the altar, and looked into the chalice at the half-mouthful within. O Lord, once upon a time, you made a covenant with man that he would never again be destroyed forever. You died for our sake and said that the gates of Heaven were opened to us.

If all is forgiven, Lord, why is it that I am here, condemned for all my life to be here, alone? And when we go home, what will there be left?

If there was a stirring in his soul of an answer, he did not feel it.

If there was a Word, he could not hear.

CHAPTER 2

As he always did at the rising of the sun, Prophet spoke to the people of Saze.

Be strong and take hope, all you who hope in the Lord.

Once more, the voice rolled out across the city of Saze, crackling and staticky with its power, louder than the voice of any other living being.

Be strong and take hope, all you who hope in the Lord!

Prophet was a giant shining pole which rose from the earth. Four large boxes formed his heads, all of which were covered in glistening black panels.

The city rippled from Prophet as if he were a drop in water, the epicenter of a tumult of buildings and tarps, haphazard roads and animal pens. Beside him stood his church.

The church was the tallest building in the Saze, standing three times the height of any other building near it. It had been built before the Yellow Year, and yet it stood, weathering ages upon ages of the terrible dust storms which ravaged the land.

Talit thought that once the church must have been very glorious. Its beams and doors had long since crumbled away, but the rest of it was built from thick, strong stone and heavy pillars. It loomed uncannily above the city, a solemn alien monument displaced from its time amidst the chaos of the noisy Sazer city.

The voice of Prophet spoke a third and final time, calling the Sazers to prayer.

At the first sound of Prophet's wise and gentle voice, Talit was already inside the church. She liked to be the first one. It gave her time to think, to look at the pictures inside.

Some of the larger ones had long since faded and darkened, many of them lost. Here and there, Talit could make out a hand, a face, a gesture.

The pictures made of stone and wood remained. Almost all of them were of alien, colorless people with smooth, even faces, straight mouths, and piercing blank eyes. They were enormous, bigger even than Leader. Some were beasts unknown to Sazers, and they carried large symbols in their mouths or tails.

The city had been decorated by many generations—its walls and windbreaks and shelters bore murals of the Sazers' stories, tracing all the way back to the Yellow Year and the founding of the city itself. It was traditional to repaint the murals frequently, for when the dust storms came, they scoured away the images. There were many who dreamed of attaining the honor of becoming a storyteller or an artist, tasked with the preservation of legend and history.

But not even the work of those masters compared with pictures here. The carved clothes of the stone and wooden people draped as real cloth would, rich folds of fabric on fabric on fabric. The people themselves seemed almost to breathe lightly, their symmetrical faces downturned to observe those who walked below.

Their exotic beauty seemed fitting for this place, which even after so many years seemed divine and extraordinary.

This was where the Lord had once lived.

Long ago, he had gone away. For as long as the Sazers had known it, his home had remained empty—a black cove recessed deep in the wall, with a beam where he had sat to accept oblations and offerings.

Tradition said that after the Yellow Year and the destruction of the old world, the Lord had traveled deep into the hinterlands, abandoning his people out of grief and shame. As his people had forsaken him, so had he forsaken them in return.

For many years, though, there had been whispers that he had not left, but had been killed. There had been people, the stories went, who were angry, who blamed him for the Yellow Year, and they had taken him away and left him with no marker at his grave.

Talit did not truly believe that he had died, for the stories had all said that the Lord had died once already, and had risen again. But it was an easier truth to swallow.

If the Lord had died, after all, then it meant that he had not chosen to leave them forever. If he had died, then they could mourn him, and miss him.

Talit's favorite part of Prophet's Church was the belltower. She liked to think of it as her and Ziek's property. Of all the Sazers, only the four consecrated bellringers were permitted to ascend, with very few exceptions.

Talit and Ziek were the day watch, and had not seen the night watch since they had been consecrated and assigned their permanent duties. And so it was their haven, and theirs only.

They had spent countless hours here—what seemed like lifetimes observing, listening, practicing. The art of the bells was not just pulling at the rope. A bellringer had to know the sacred chants by heart, every foreign syllable.

But more than that: no one questioned the ascent of a bellringer, as theirs was a holy duty. And so many days, they had climbed to the top of the tower when they should have been studying, or at work. The loft was the best place not just for meditation or quiet contemplation, but also for lazy afternoons and silly conversations in whispers; for sneaking up to play games and share bottles of weedwine that would not be missed.

For Talit, the loft was home. Ziek was as much, and more.

The floorstones of the church were dark and cool when she entered. They had been swept to a glossy sheen in preparation for morning chant. As the day wore on, the wind would blow the fine orange dust of the desert into a thin film. Talit and Ziek, along with the other children destined for Consecration, had once been charged with sweeping it daily and keeping it polished until it glistened.

She had just set her hand to the first handhold of the long ascent to the towertop when a flash of white sped by her, laughing breathlessly. Ziek had beaten her to the climb.

Talit couldn't help but let out an inarticulate, indignant squawk as he surged past her, his lanky frame flinging itself recklessly up and away. But they had raced too many times for it to be a true surprise, and within a half a second, she, too, was hurtling upward, nimble and fast as a rat. The handholds were as familiar as old friends to her fingers and toes.

The exertion of a steep and difficult climb was welcome. Talit threw every inch of her energy into her movements, and was pleased by the smooth catch and release of her muscles. She would never have admitted it to Ziek, though he might have guessed, but she had spent many an early evening practicing without him.

The distance between them narrowed, then closed. Neither of them was laughing now, too focused on their competition to spare breath.

Talit waited to crow triumphantly until she had reached the towertop and hoisted herself onto the walkway. Even then, it was a small crow, for in the Church, sound carried, and both she and Ziek had been made aware several times, very sternly, that Consecrated bellringers were not to be racing or acting in an undignified manner within the House of Prophet.

It wasn't until she was standing there, poised to brag, that she noticed that Ziek was a good distance below her. He was moving, but more slowly than he usually did; his movements were lopsided and ungraceful.

Her words died in her throat. She leaned over the edge and reached out for him, and working together, they managed to get him hoisted onto the walkway.

Talit hovered over Ziek as he gathered his breath, his hand on his side.

"What, you're not going to make fun of me?" he said.

"What's wrong with you?" A feeling like frost had settled onto her skin. She stared at him intently, at how he hunched slightly, his breaths light and fast. For as long as they had raced, Ziek had always won.

He went to his place at the bell ropes, a grin lighting his face. "Come on, have your moment. It's not often I let you win."

"You didn't let me."

Ziek made himself busy untethering his rope, straightening; his expression was a familiar deadpan, now. "So you're admitting I'm faster than you, as a rule."

Talit spluttered and pulled away from him, heat flushing to her face. It was easy to forget her worry when he was teasing. "That's not what I meant."

"But that's what it would have to mean." Ziek could never keep from smiling too long, and she couldn't help but crack a smile in response.

"Shut up," she told him, without venom.

"I think I ate too much this morning. You won't get so lucky next time." Whatever had been bothering him before was gone now, and he was peering over the edge of the catwalk now, to the church floor far below them.

The faint chill of suspicion had not left—there was a fear trembling in her still, which she did not want to name—but now Sazers were beginning to enter the church for the morning chant, and reluctantly Talit turned away to go to her own bell.

There was no real chamber in the towertop. Instead, there was a ring about four hand-widths wide which enclosed the drop straight down to the floor below. There were two small platforms, one at each bell next to the heavy woven rope which rang it. The only thing separating them from a messy, bone-breaking fall was a rickety railing along the edge.

Long ago, though, Talit's fear had given way to awe.

Here at the belltower, the beauty of Prophet's church was breathtaking. The tile floors and old pillars in perfect rows stood in stark contrast to the chaotic sprawl of the city. The perfect alignment of shapes and colors made something click in Talit's head, and hum for joy.

Below Talit, the Sazers had begun to crowd inside, tiny pinprick figures compared to the grand stone people lining the pillars. Like her, they were all dressed in the pale colors of sand and sunlight, to better deflect the heat of the wasteland, and out of respect for the holiness of Prophet's Church, they wore veils to hide their faces.

There were a few Burdened, also, head-to-toe in swaths of tattered indigo cloth, the color of mourning. They wandered to the front of the crowd without resistance, where they stood, swaying in a dark mass, before the pulpit. Their face turned to the darkness behind the altar as if they turned to an invisible sunlight. Sazers pressed back instinctively to avoid their touch.

Talit crouched and pressed her face against the cold bars of the railing. The thrum of the Sazers' feet on the tiles below seemed to reverberate all the way up through the ribs of the church and into her cheeks.

Far below, Leader appeared from behind the altar. One of the largest of the Sazers, he looked massive even from this height. A breath, and then, his voice unerring and clear, he cried out, calling his people to prayer.

Leader's voice swelled in the Song for Protection; the Sazers responded, their tongues shaping the language of the ancients. None of the Sazers, not even Leader himself, understood what they sang. The songs had been passed down for countless hundreds of years, their meanings long lost, but the language had an eerie and foreboding beauty which fit the dark and solemn church.

For years innumerable, the Sazers came to the Church of Prophet seven times each day to beg the Lord for forgiveness, for him to return.

Prophet said that this was the price which was demanded of them: that they remain steadfast, that they cry out with unceasing voice.

This is what he had told them, when first he spoke to their people, a strange emissary of the ancients. Beg forgiveness and mercy without end. Offer your sacrifices with great joy. Wait.

And so in the tongue of the Lord, in the words which had once pleased him most, they waited, fulfilling their holy duty for years without end.

Some days, Talit felt that the Morning Chant lasted only a few beautiful and breathless moments, a rush of unknowable story and song. But today something was wrong. It prickled at her, the wrongness of it. The song was transcendent, exultant.

At first, she tried to squeeze her eyes shut to block out the light which streamed in through the open windows of the Church, to focus on Leader's voice. She envisioned her soul escaping her body, crying out to the Lord along with the souls of ten thousand others.

Today, though, the wrongness kept her grounded; she remained tethered, anxious, trembling.

She opened her eyes and looked at Ziek.

He was sweating, his veil clinging to his face and neck. His grip on the bell rope was slack and unsteady. It seemed almost that the rope supported him, and when he rang it, it was only because he dragged it down with his faltering weight.

The cold fear which had touched her before was back, clamping down on her so tightly that she could barely breathe.

She must not think about it. She must only focus on the sound of swelling, complex harmonies below her.

A verse ended. Ziek lurched, and Talit instinctively reached out as if she might steady him, even from across the air that separated them. Ziek's bell clanged into the stilted, awkward pause, even as he recovered himself and straightened.

Below, Talit saw heads turning upwards, veiled eyes searching for the sacred bellringers. Still, Leader continued to chant, his voice even and soothing. He gave no indication that anything might be wrong.

Ziek ignored Talit, his shoulders stone, his face turned away.

For the rest of the song—which now seemed to stretch interminably for years—he did not move a muscle except to ring his bell at the appointed time. He looked neither left, nor right; his gaze was fixed, as far as Talit could tell behind his veil, on the altar.

Secretly, very softly in her heart, Talit whispered an urgent prayer. She did not say it to the Lord. It was a blasphemy, although very small, she hoped, because she did not speak the words aloud.

Prophet was living and comforting and visible. He had never forsaken the Sazers.

He told them to pray to the Lord, to wait for the Lord, to hope in him. But the Lord had abandoned them, and so Talit hoped in Prophet.

Over and over again she murmured it to herself. She dared not give thought to the terrible thing that she prayed might not be true.

At last, the chant ended. Talit turned to Ziek, but he had already slipped away.

She descended the belltower faster than she had ever before. Before any of the Sazers had completed their meditations, she had already slipped through the church doors, unveiled, and was running as if dust-walkers snapped at her heels.

She passed a clump of Burdened who had drawn near, attracted by the sound of singing. They shambled too slowly to react, and she gave them a wide berth. As she passed, their heads beneath the heavy cloths turned. Invisible gazes followed her, and chills scattered up her spine.

Ziek was nowhere to be seen, though she ran faster than she had ever climbed in her life. The city blurred by her in a haphazard jumble of colorful mats and murals; the sounds of the city stirring drifted after her.

There were people setting to work, singing as they walked in groups, calling greetings. Dogs scampered through the labyrinthine maze of painted windbreaks, tussling with children in alleys, barking the world awake.

At the height of the day, the noise would be a cacophony of life and energy, twenty songs all rising at once from the dust bowl of the city—the shrieks of children, the braying of hungry animals, friendly banter shouted by workers across the way.

The city of Saze was a maelstrom of near-constant activity. To survive in a wasteland, eternally wracked by dust storms, every Sazer had to work, often to scrounge for a living. There were neither idle hands nor dragging feet.

Even amidst the chaos, an instinct born of long friendship carried Talit straight to Ziek.

The Sacred Archive lay beneath a hill to the east of Prophet's Church. This was a place of ancients, and out of respect, it lay alone and untouched by Sazer constructions. By tradition, only the Consecrated might enter.

Talit slowed automatically as she approached its heavy and foreign door. Once, legend said, it had borne a painting on the dull and battered triangular shape affixed to its face. If it had ever been there, it had long ago worn away. It had been repainted with the Mark of the Sazers—two intersecting lines of equal length, representing order and beauty in an irregular and violent land.

The door lay ajar. Talit had never had much cause to enter—she intended to train with Leader to become a warden of the city, a Consecrated soldier who fought dustwalkers and the other crooked creatures who stalked the wilds. She had had little need to struggle over the mysteries of the Archive.

Now she hesitated only briefly before plunging within.

The air below was dark and still. The purpose of the Archive was long lost to time, but here the touch of the ancients was visible. No Sazer hand had created the impossibly perfect shapes of the stairs which descended at sharp angles into the belly of the world. Nor had a Sazer built the odd rectangular constructions along the walls, which stood mute and motionless, nor left incomprehensible glyphs on every inch of the walls.

Ziek was at the heart of the Archive, hunched with manic focus over the Relic.

On the day that both she and Ziek had become bellringers, Leader had brought them here to see it. Here was the heart of all Sazer tradition, he had told them.

Made of many delicate slices of fragile material, it was covered in the same spidery glyphs as on the walls of the Archives. Hidden within lay the wisdom of the ancients, Leader said. It was thought that every scrap of legend which each Storyteller passed from generation to generation was contained within this sacred object.

Each member of the Consecrated took solemn vows to study it, to uncover its truths. But even in all these years, they had managed to uncover only that some of its markings were notations for the tones of the holy chants. Beyond that, nothing was known.

At first, Talit did not think Ziek heard her approach, so motionless was he as he bent over the Relic. Then he spoke without turning.

"I'm so close."

"So close to what?" She drew closer to him and saw what he was looking at. The Relic was opened to a section marked with the symbols that indicated song and changing pitch. None of it made a bit of sense to her.

"I have to understand," he said. Not once had he moved his eyes from the Relic. "There has to be something here—I have to understand—"

There was raw desperation, a feverish madness in his voice. He pawed through the Relic, heedless of its fragility, its unspeakable value.

Talit's breath felt as if it had been sucked away by a strong wind.

"Ziek," she said, gripping his wrists. He fought her wordlessly, but his expression was dead. It terrified her, but she did not let go. "Ziek."

With an effort, he calmed himself. Still he did not meet her eyes. "Go away," he said. "I have to understand. The Relic has the answers. If we could understand—"

Talit did not go away. The air felt very dry. She was afraid to ask if it was for certain—if it could be possible—if so, how long had he known, if at all—how badly it hurt. But all she could say was, "I can help," not knowing what it was that she could do.

"Talit, please, go away."

When she stepped closer and put her hand on his shoulder, tried to turn him away from the ancient artifact, he fought her. He was stronger, and taller. For a moment in the quiet of the Archive, they scrambled and struggled, him straining to break away from her, her fighting to support his awkward and thrashing weight. His flesh under her fingers was clammy and feverish.

"Don't touch me!—Don't come near me!—I won't let you get sick too—" he was shouting.

"I don't care! I don't care!" she shouted back, and their voices were thunderous in the small space.

Then she felt it blossoming on his ribs—a heavy, ugly distortion of flesh—and she let him go, terror numbing her.

Ziek tumbled from her arms and sprawled bonelessly on the hard floor of the Archive. He lay against the wall, no resistance left in him. He panted, his dark eyes staring wildly at nothing.

"It's over," he told her.

Talit's mind was filled with a blind white panic. The spongy, soft feeling of flesh-not-flesh under her hands. The alien swelling that threatened without words. "No," she said. "No." It was all she could think of to say, a dumb and useless denial. "Not you. It can't be."

But when she came near him to put her arms around him, she realized with hot and burning shame that she could not bring herself to touch him.

Ziek had mastered his face. It was blank and pale and stony now. "I've been studying the Relic," he said.

An unfinished thought. In it, Talit could see the ghost of what had once been his hope. She imagined Ziek creeping through the deadened streets of Saze at night, steeling himself to descend into the alien blackness of the Archive. She knew, without asking, how he must have spent long and sleepless hours here, hunched beneath the light of stolen candles, his eyes dry and reddened.

"How long?" she whispered.

A long pause. "Weeks," he said. "Ever since I found—" Again he did not finish his thought. "I thought there was a way."

Talit watched him stand, clearly drawing himself together until he was the Ziek she had raced to the top of the belltower these same last few weeks. He gave no indication of his pain now except for his drawn, tight face.

With new eyes she looked at him. She could not have said what her expression was, but as Ziek saw it, he looked away from her, and pulled up his shirt to show her.

It was there, the sign of Burdening already spreading across his ribs where they jutted out of his skinny chest. It showed as a darkening like a bruise, only it was a grotesque gray-purple, and lifted in a fist-like protrusion just beginning to emerge from his bones like a fish cresting from water.

Talit knew the signs of Burdening by heart; every Sazer did. But never before had she actually seen it. That was why the Burdened wore their heavy blue robes, so that the dignity of their flesh might be preserved.

This was the Sazers' payment for the sins of their forefathers; their curse for destroying the world. Here they survived in the desolate waste, generation after generation offered as reparation for the Yellow Year and the death of the world.

Long ago, every Sazer had suffered from the affliction. They had been lucky enough to grow old enough to bear a child before succumbing. And even so, the sickness had killed most children long before they reached adulthood.

Then, the Sazers had been a cluster of dwindling and terrified survivors. They bunkered down beneath the devastating dust storms and the unforgiving sun; they painted their history on the walls, praying that when they were gone, someone might remain to remember them.

Then they had found Prophet wandering in the desert. He had been an alien, of a different race. They had brought him peace offerings, and he learned their language. And when at last he had fallen in love with the Sazers and joined their people, he had become a pillar of strength in the wilderness. He became for them a holy desert mystic.

Under his word they had flourished. He had been their protector, and his word nourished them with hope. He taught them the ways of the Lord, which had long been abandoned. With him at their head, they declared themselves a new nation, natives of the endless expanses of this forsaken land.

When Prophet had seen the tortured suffering of the Sazer people, he had gone up to the places where the dunes became hills, and the hills grew larger than hills should be. There, he had communed with the Lord, and entered a deep trance.

The Lord had been pleased with Prophet, and had come down to speak with him.

In his state of immense holiness, Prophet had cast his soul at the Lord's feet, and begged for relief for the sickness which plagued the Sazers.

And slowly the Lord had answered. First it was every one out of three who fell ill. Then it had been one out of five, and one out of seven. The Burdening had eased, if only a little.

Still Prophet prayed, and the Lord was so pleased that he allowed Prophet to gather up the souls of the Burdened. Then while their bodies walked and suffered from crippling growths and rotting flesh, their minds and spirits fled to join also in the unceasing prayer.

It was said by the hopeful that the two of them—Prophet and the Lord—remained there on that great hill and would until eternity ended: Prophet on his knees in supplication, and the Lord, appeased, sat upon his throne with his eyes closed, listening, forever.

Many had been spared by the suffering of only one. It was well known that the Lord, in some mercy, Burdened only those who were deemed strong enough to bear it.

So it had been for many hundreds of years now, as long as any Sazer could remember. Each day they gave thanks to the Lord and to Prophet that they might survive another generation. They accepted their sacrifice, and toiled in the desert with joy.

It was because of Prophet that even though their bodies were cursed with unending plague and their home razed by desert storms, they rose still from the dust, rebuilt and survived, year after year, century after century.

They were the chosen people.

Talit had believed. It was a flesh offering, it was pain, it was great mercy; the Burdened were honored for their strength.

Until Ziek. Until him.

Talit's hands felt steeped in the touch-memory of being wrapped around his mottled, ridged flesh. She dropped them to her sides, where they betrayed her by balling up into fists.

Ordinarily, Ziek would have had some kind of casual joke to lighten the air. Now he only looked at the Relic and its untranslatable secrets, avoiding her gaze.

"Who else knows?" she whispered.

He dropped his shirt back over the ugliness, but she couldn't stop staring at the spot where the Burden lurked. "Just you, I guess," he said. "But they'll find out." His voice shook.

Talit knew what would happen. She had seen it happen before, and the thought of it now was too much to bear.

It *must* happen—

"I won't go." Ziek was no longer looking at her, but at the Relic, his eyes burning. "I won't."

But that was unthinkable. That was stupid. No one could hide the growth, the weakness, the deadening of the flesh and the mind. He would wander uncovered and blasphemous among the saved.

What if he infected a hundred others? What if Prophet was angry that his gift of leniency was rejected by someone who had been chosen as worthy?

"I don't want to be chosen. Why me?"

For a dizzying second, Talit was filled with anger and disgust—just as Leader would have been, just as every Sazer rightfully should be.

"You have been asked to sacrifice. What will happen if you refuse?"

But as she blurted out the accusatory response, it felt like stones falling between them, and she could not forgive herself for saying it. Ziek did not respond.

The question hung, threatening and ominous. Talit's heart was beating fast. She thought of Prophet's massive heads, which loomed, all-seeing, all-hearing, over the city of Saze. Did he watch their conversation now?

Prophet had spared them all the wrath of the Lord. But would he take back the Burdening, and let them all suffer under the sin of the ancients once again?

"I won't," Ziek said again, softly, and then more loudly this time: "I won't, I won't, I won't!" And he began to cry.

In that moment Talit knew she had only one choice, however futile it might be.

"I will help you," she told him, again, and finally she put her arms around him.

When his eyes were dry again, he put himself again to study the Relic, and Talit joined him.

For many hours they knelt there, poring over its pages, scratching with coal on the floor. Codes and puzzles, riddles and symbols—there must have been something there that would save Ziek, that would save them all.

But if there was anything, the two of them did not discover it.

And when they missed the midday prayer and then the evening prayer and there was no one in the tower to toll the bells, Leader came and found them there.

There, he stood before Ziek, and looked him in the eye. "You have been chosen," he said, in a thunderous tone, and Ziek had knelt before him, trembling, while Talit cowered near him, as if paralyzed.

She could do or say nothing while her friend huddled there, sick, his breaths coming fast and high.

"You have been chosen," Leader said again, into the Archive, ignoring the signs of their frantic and useless studies, ignoring the terror that made the air bitter with its stink. "Blessed be you."

He reached forth his hand, and Ziek took it.

"I accept my honor with joy," he whispered.

Leader smiled. He took Ziek away then, up and out of the Archive.

There were other Sazers there outside the door, waiting for them. To the sound of chanting they processed into the gathering night.

Talit could not follow them; the chant stuck bitterly in her throat. For a long time she knelt alone in the Archive, trying to decipher the glyphs of the Relics, trying to understand.

She knelt there until the torch had burnt itself out, and she was alone in the darkness.

And then still she knelt, her eyes dry and staring into nothing.

Ziek had been chosen.

Blessed was he.

CHAPTER 3

ON THE DAY BEFORE HIS release, Aitor's hands shook almost unbearably.

This was his last Mass adrift in the confines of space.

Tomorrow, he would be released from his prison, if not from his sacrifice.

He would see Jacob. He would go home.

He barely paid attention to his own words as he said the Mass. Today no hallucinatory figures stood before him, and he gave the final benediction to empty chairs.

Despite that, the empty space around him seemed filled up with his own thoughts. But if his thoughts were whispers, then the presence of the man who lay asleep in storage was a shout.

Sixteen hours, he told himself. Sixteen hours to fulfill the vow he made.

He had a light lunch from the dwindling rations reserve, and then went to his quarters. There he sat with his journal, where he had begun a tradition of writing down all the things which he had seen or heard during the Mass. In early entries he had been clinical, analytic, discerning what things might truly be visions and which might be the product of a fevered imagination. Over the course of fifty years, it had become the scribblings of a weary madman.

Today there had been nothing, though. He sat, staring at the blank page.

Again the message of the Superior General came to him: *We must build His church once more.*

Aitor's hand sat on the page for a long while before he wrote at last, in thick, shaking script. *Tomorrow, I can say: It is finished—*

He went for his exercise session. As always, he stayed longer than the mandatory two hours. The Father who had gone before him had told him that he must make routines.

"They may have told you that prayer is what keeps you sane," the priest said, "or God." Aitor remembered his creased, worn face, shockingly older than its seventy-five years, drawn and sagging and grayed like decomposing plastic. "But I say that God leads us only to holy madness. A death to the ordinary and everyday. What keeps you alive is doing the same thing, over and over, until you do not think about it anymore. That is the only way to pass the months, and remain in this world."

Fifty years had stolen away Aitor's ability to recognize the priest. Half a century ago they had been friends, brothers in Christ, who had shared a chapterhouse and prayed at one another's sides. But even his eyes had changed; they were alien, weighed with a million sorrows, a little insane. He had refused to give his name.

He looked at his journal, looked back through the hundreds of pages filled with his handwriting—once the firm uppercase of a young man in his early twenties, now the sloped and messy scrawl of a man whose hands were riddled with arthritis.

He had read the writings of those who had gone before him. Without fail they had descended, in one way or another, through agonizing aloneness, into acceptance, and at last into a tranquil madness that had consumed them as they waited for their end, alone amid the stars.

But Aitor had read them, each and every book containing fifty years of life. He had remembered them and honored them.

He ran his hand over the tattered cover of his book, smoothed its creased pages. Once the children of God returned to the Earth, would anyone remember him?

Would the last priest of the Cupertinian Order read his legacy, and know him as they had once known each other? Or would they be strangers now, with so many years driving them apart?

He opened again to the final page, and painstakingly, he signed it with his full name.

And then he went to storage.

He had not been there since the day he had been woken. Do not go, he had been commanded. This only makes the longing worse. You will want to undo everything for which so many have lived in sacrifice. You will want to die.

Perhaps other priests had also stood here at the heavy airlocked door, fighting for self control, wrestling against their vow of obedience. Perhaps others had broken that vow in a moment of weakness, keycoding themselves in, as he did now.

The chill of the air from the cooled room enfolded him as the door slid aside, and he stepped inside.

It was as he remembered it. The room was a mausoleum of long, dark boxes stacked in orderly rows like bunks all the way to the vaulted ceiling, separated by narrow walkways. The place was lit by bars of dimmed red lights in order to prevent tripping on the long snaking cables which ran along the floors.

Within those boxes lay the future of humanity: fifty men and women, to be woken when the time was right, if ever. And there had been thirty-three priests of the Order of St. Joseph of Cupertino sleeping, too, until their time to take up their vigil.

Of them, Aitor was the second-to-last.

When he had been awoken from his long sleep, there had been almost no noise but for the constant humming of the ship. Above him an old, hunched figure stood wordlessly, staring down at him. There had been walls in his eyes hiding thoughts that Aitor—young and disoriented—could not read.

Now the empty room thrummed with forgotten voices—distant, alien, prayers whispered from far away. The voices filled the air with a glamour that made it hard for him to breathe or to think.

He will bring you back—his hand will close your eyes—

Who sees us? Who knows us?—

From the city of one thousand, only one hundred remain—

Aitor's box lay open, its green signal light long extinguished. The imprint remained where his body had lain for centuries, pumped full of green fluid.

He went to it, but he did not pay it any mind. His focus was on the box beneath it.

Iakobos Masalis, O.J.C., Subject #33. Thirty-one years old. Birthplace Thessaloniki, Greece, hometown of Heraklion.

Jacob, brilliant, handsome, the luminary of the chapterhouse in Fisterra.

In the House at the End of the World, Aitor had been *El Fantasma*, the ghost. He had been quiet, skittish; he preferred to follow his calling without drawing attention to himself or his subpar English.

It had been difficult for him, in the clean and orderly chapterhouse with its well-educated, pious seminarians from Madrid and London and Berlin and Vienna, to shake the feeling that everyone could see the grimy streets of his home, the stain on his family. It had been easy for him to imagine that he had only been allowed to join in order to save him from falling into the life his father and brother had led.

In reparation, he was the model seminarian. He passed all his classes and spoke not one word more than was required, suffering without complaint through long, sleepless nights filled with metaphysics and theology and gnawing on pencil ends.

Jacob, though. Striking dark gaze, strong nose, loud voice, quick temper. Every eye had turned instinctively to him; everyone listened to him first. In discussion he was always the first to leap to some abstract and transcendent conclusion. He played Devil's advocate the most often, with great glee, poking and prodding at the defenses of the other students, to the delight of the Fathers who taught them.

He will be a saint, they had said of Jacob. He did not seem to have to work for anything, not even holiness. Philosophy and theology were, for him, as clear and uncomplicated as breath. In prayer he fell into such deep contemplation that his back arched like a bow, and his face would show the strain of it, as if he held tightly to a line straight to heaven—as if he could divest his soul of a body the way a snake sheds a skin, if only he tried hard enough.

On the first night he came to the chapterhouse with Padre Aguilera, they had prayed side by side: Jacob, eighteen and already wearing the robes of a postulant, and Aitor young and small and terrified, swallowed by the sound of Night Prayer.

That night, though, he had known no one, and the death of his father weighed on him like a stone. He had knelt with his head on the pew, his face buried in his hands, as the hymns of the Brothers mixed with heavy incense had settled the shadows into a velvet stillness.

Someone had laid a hand on his shoulder, then, warm and real. Aitor remembered turning his head to see that it was Jacob, his eyes closed as he sang from memory. With his chin upturned towards the tabernacle, his face golden in the candlelight, he had looked as if Heaven had already touched him.

After that it had been hard not to be drawn towards Jacob, his warmth, his light. Who would not want to be close to him? Who would not want to understand someone who seems to already understand a truth you did not know existed?

Then and all the years after, he had loved Jacob and what Jacob meant to him. In the end they became inseparable: the luminary and his shadow, the saint and the silent orphan.

And then the wars had begun in earnest, and there had been no more time for studies, or for talk of excellence. They had spent their hours ministering to those dying in the streets; in countless vigils, their voices breaking the tranquility of a hundred shattered nights. They had watched as city after city across the world fell to famine and disease and death.

They had been together as it was announced that the Catholic Church had come into possession of a ship—that their order was the closest, and that they would be the only ones who would make it in time.

The last time Aitor had seen Jacob had been at the drawing of the lots. Huddled together with the Superior General's final benediction hanging over them as a sentence, they had stood next to each other at the altar with their brothers. In the small light, surrounded by the blare of unholy klaxons and the rat-tat of far-off artillery, they waited anxiously as the Superior General allowed them one by one to choose numbers from a small metal bowl.

All of them had known that only one would draw the last number. Aitor had known it very well. He had already spent long hours reconciling himself with the fact that there was little chance he would be allowed to remain young, to fall under the long sleep with the hope of being able to walk the Earth again. He was the last to choose his slip.

Still, he had not expected the rush of shock that shook him when he saw that it had been Jacob who pulled the thirty-third slip—knowing that if he had chosen the slip which Jacob had held—he had been so close—it would have been him.

And when he drew his own number, he had seen only a shadow of what Aitor saw so clearly now—him standing above Jacob's box, old, spent, an entire empty lifetime between them—and he had mourned.

Under the watchful and sorrowing eye of the Superior General, the brothers had nodded gravely in affirmation. They would not walk away from the martyrdom which was offered them. They would enter *La Trascendencia*, and they would do their duty for the salvation of all mankind.

But these priests and seminarians who had once been drawn to Jacob with an inexorable and powerful magnetism had left him trailing behind them as they walked to the antechamber of the ship.

None of them looked at each other at all.

Aitor had felt their solitudes closing in over them even before they lay down in their gel beds, and the technicians began to prepare them for their journey. Every man walked in a shell, already untouched by the presence of others. They grieved for themselves in those few minutes more than they did for the entire world.

Aitor grieved too. But in his last hour awake upon the Earth, he had dared to look at the man whom they all had, for at least a single moment, hated.

Jacob had stood watching them all be frozen, one by one. He stood with his hands clenched up in fists at his sides, and he did not take his eyes away from any of his brothers with a frighteningly one-minded intensity.

One by one their eyes were sealed shut; they were jammed full of tubes, dehydrated, pumped full of preservative. Jacob's was the last face Aitor saw as, gripped by terror, he allowed the technicians to help him disrobe, and they poured the sealant over his eyes.

Jacob's face had been contorted, his frame wracked with sobs. "I'm sorry," he cried, "I'm so sorry, let me choose again. Please, no. No, *no*, *NO*—"

And then there was the sound of running feet, and a struggle, and Jacob's voice had gone away.

There had been excruciating pain, overtaken by a deep and numbing cold, which took root in the bone and grew into a house of silence around him.

Then, for a very long time, nothing.

Aitor laid his hand on the box containing Jacob. He let himself feel close to someone physical, as he had not for so many years. The closeness brought him to tears. He had hated the thought of Jacob waking, young and fresh, gifted with the world once more at his hands. Now he thought only of being near him again.

The clock said there were nine hours until the appointed waking time, the hour at which they had judged it safe to return to the Earth.

Aitor could try for sleep. He had vowed self-control and obedience, as was willed by God for all good and holy people. Already he had sinned enough by opening the vault to tempt himself.

He got down on his knees and pulled his Rosary from his pocket. He went around the beads once rapidly, and then again and again, chanting the words into the listening emptiness in a fevered hush. Though the room was cool, he sweated, praying in long streams without any real idea why. Maybe he prayed for God Himself to come to *La Trascendencia* to end his vigil. Maybe he prayed for the end of the world.

For a while he heard the voices of his family praying along with him in Spanish; he thought he might have heard a host of other voices echoing along with them. Whoever they were, he welcomed them.

He had no idea how many times he had finished the prayer by the time his voice dried into a hoarse croak. He could not say with certainty that the prayer had been received.

Four hours until the appointed time.

Aitor stood up, fighting the pain in his old knees. A hush had come over the universe.

He left cold storage, but he left the door open behind him this time. He made the long walk through the corridors past his chambers, the pantry, the lavatory, the library. He went to the front of the ship, where no one had set foot in many years.

For years he had dreamed of this walk. He had fantasized this moment: him sliding open the door to the control unit, walking to the glossy chrome control panel covered in meters, switches, and buttons.

On the floor at the foot of the console lay an upturned notebook. Someone had scrawled notes on it in a desperate hand. Aitor was able to read it, though the scrawl was angry, gashed violently across the page. In English, it said: *O God! Let me be free!*

The control panel's dim screen read coordinates and measurements of ship status. The only control which mattered now was the homing button which sat prominently at its center. HOME, it read, blinking through ten different languages.

Aitor took a long breath, let it out in an unspoken plea, and pressed the button.

There was a hesitation; the screen changed its display. CALIBRATING. CALIBRATING . . . CALIBRATION COMPLETE.

Aitor didn't know enough about spacecraft to understand the numbers and graphs flickering across the console. But he knew now that the signal tower that communicated with the ship still stood. A small miracle, a small sign that perhaps God listened.

And they were going home.

Tomorrow all the people in these boxes would awake. They would open their eyes and feel the blood rush back into their veins, and they would enter return capsules to make their descent. To them, no more than a day would have passed, no more than a long night's rest. But Aitor would see another human face for the first time in five decades.

Without thinking, he reached forward and pressed the softly glowing green button on Jacob's box.

He watched, transfixed. The box hummed and sang, its technology stirring. The digital pad beneath the button lit, and began to run through incomprehensible exercises, flashing numbers and code. A soft hissing filled the room as the box began to pump life back into Jacob.

Trembling and fear had overcome Aitor. For so long he had been alone, unjudged by human eyes.

And now Jacob would see him—would not know him—Jacob, whose memory of Aitor was so fresh, who would see him as he was now—a sad, desperate man—

The lid of the box slid open, and Jacob screamed.

The pain of reentering the world—of the blood rushing first sluggishly, then speeding through long-disused veins; of taking breath into stale and deflated lungs—it was agonizing. And yet, like the priest before him, Aitor did nothing to help, only stared.

Someone else. Another living human being. Jacob writhed before him. He no longer screamed, but his jaw was locked open in a rictus of terror and agony.

Was that how he had looked? Aitor no longer remembered.

For a long and drawn-out minute, Jacob pitched like a caught fish, his movements slowing, stilling as the pain eased. Finally he lay motionless, his dark eyes staring wildly.

He was as Aitor had remembered him for all these years. He was beautiful.

Aitor had seen beauty before, a thousand types of it in a thousand types of people. But Jacob was beautiful in a way he had never experienced before. As beautiful as he had been as he read, late at night, his head crooked intently as he thought; as beautiful as he had been when he lifted the host above his head, and the look of angels had made him otherworldly, inhuman—but this time there was something new to it. This time Jacob was beautiful also because he was young, and because he was the promise of the future of the world.

And he was all Aitor had left of the life he had left behind.

Jacob began to cry. He was bathed in sweat; he made no effort to hide his nakedness. He lay motionless now, his fists clenched as he sobbed, every muscle clenching and unclenching as he fought to regain control of his body. Between his cries, he called out in a strangled voice, perhaps in his own language, or perhaps without meaning at all.

Waking to the world. An end to isolation. Those were things that should have caused joy. Aitor stood captivated by the primal rage behind Jacob's eyes.

"How long?" Jacob's cries had taken on words now that Aitor could understand; he had seen Aitor, his eyes rolling as he tried to master his body again, to sit up. "How long has it been? When is it?"

Aitor found himself stammering over rusty English. "In four hours, it will be sixteen hundred years since the day we departed."

Jacob had fought his way up until he was sitting; he buried his head in his hands. His crying was gut-wrenching, now, but he no longer screamed. His shoulders shook.

Aitor went to get a blanket for him, half-running. When he came back, Jacob had not moved. He did not react when Aitor put the blanket around his shoulders, nor when he sat beside him.

They stayed there for a long time. Aitor thought of a thousand different things he wanted to say, all of them which meant the same thing. He thought about the half-century he had spent alone, circling the Earth in a soundless capsule, pretending this day would not come.

The thought came to him then, unexpected. *It could have been me. It should have been me waking just now, so close to the end.*

The stirring of that old feeling shook him. Fifty years, he thought, had buried it, that same twist of jealous rage that had seized him on the day of the lottery. But the ghostly hand of bitterness clutched his heart and squeezed, and it frightened him.

He stood abruptly, rushing over his words. "I woke you early. I did not want to wait any longer. I'm sorry. I thought maybe you would—wait with me."

Jacob did not answer him. But he got up with Aitor's help, and followed where he was led.

Aitor took him to get clothing. They had all taken so few belongings with them. There had been so little time.

Jacob asked no questions, did not say a word. He walked as if his soul were gone from his body, and he were a man-sized puppet. He took in his surroundings in a heavy stupor.

Aitor almost did not mind. The feel of Jacob's shoulder under his hand was real. The presence that walked beside him was real.

He led Jacob to the chapel. There, the screen displayed its void of stars looming behind the crucifix, turning slowly.

They sat facing the altar, and watched as, slowly and surely, the ship turned from its endless orbit to take a trajectory for return.

There, Aitor considered the anger that which now huddled, a small slick thing, within him. He understood it even less than he understood the devastating loss he had felt upon looking at Jacob's young and unlined face in those first few shocking seconds of awakening.

He looked instead at the face of the Christ who hung over the altar. Today, the tortured face brought him unease, as it had for many years now.

"Jacob," he whispered, almost afraid to break the peace. "It's me, Aitor."

Jacob turned and looked at him then. Still, he said nothing, but what Aitor found in his eyes broke his heart.

The chime of a bell rang through *La Trascendencia*. The ship spoke. SIGNAL ACQUIRED. PREPARING FOR RETURN.

It repeated itself in several other languages. Then again there was silence, even from the voices which usually filled the chapel with their secretive murmurs.

Aitor could not face Jacob's gaze anymore, the barely masked horror, the grief.

Together they watched the Earth turn slowly below them, their unspoken thoughts a wall between them.

CHAPTER 4

F IRES BURNED LOW IN THE city of Saze.

It was deep evening, the orange-blue sky darkened to a violent war of purples, fuchsia, and indigo. The moon hung heavy and ponderous over a bank of thick-hued clouds. The plumes of smoke from cookfires twisted up lazily to be caught by summer breeze, and dispersed.

The day was over; the Sazers had come back from their work in the fields and gardens, and rested. The air smelled of slowly roasting meat, baking flatbread, and the bitter tang of crushed spices. The Burdened had come in from their wandering, attracted by the sight of the smoke, and had gathered within city limits. They huddled, unmoving, among the living, huddled in dark corners, pressed into the corners of windbreaks.

On most nights there would be shouting and storytelling, and children racing about in play. But tonight, a hush lay over the city.

The people of Saze were going to the Church of Prophet to say farewell to Ziek.

The enormity of it hung over them. He was the first Burdened that they had seen in more months than usual; they had been beginning to hope. And for one of the Consecrated to fall ill—it was a terrible omen.

In small groups, the Sazers processed towards the heart of the city, carrying candles and offerings. They said nothing; there was nothing to be said.

Talit straggled behind her mother and father. They had eaten their evening meal without conversation, and now even as they walked together, there was a loose and shifting space between them. There was a presence which walked between them, pressing them apart, invisible, unspeakable.

Talit had not been born when her brother was taken by the Burdening. He had been young, not old enough even to have a work assignment.

Though her family had never spoken of Lanon, Talit had heard stories. He had been the first child in several generations who been taken by the Burdening. The tragedy of it had weighed the Sazers down. When they thought she was not listening, those who remembered him whispered of the hideous deformity that had mangled his small limbs, or the way that, even in his robes of the Burdened, he could be distinguished from the others because he was so little.

The procession came to a crossroads. Here was the Shrine of Lamentations for the Burdened, where sometimes devout families would leave out bread, prayer tokens, bowls of fresh water, woven mats and blankets. No one ever saw the Burdened take the offerings, but in the mornings, they were always gone.

Mother stopped, though many of the Sazers parted to go around her, and Father stopped with her.

Father was the first to lay his offering on the small pile. A token he had carved himself, and a blanket he had woven. He turned away. "He was a good boy," he said, and his voice was harsh with emotion.

After a moment, Mother added her own offering, a portion of dried meats. But she did not move.

"I saw him," she said. "Years ago, when I was hunting. By the river."

Talit, waiting behind them, went very still. They were not talking of Ziek, not now.

"He was standing there, looking at the desert. His back was to me." Mother's voice was choked. "So I called his name, and he turned. He looked at me. He heard me."

There was a pause. "A coincidence."

The Burdened heard nothing, saw nothing. They knew only the face of the Prophet, as they waited for a release to their sacrifice.

"He knew it was me." Mother was angry now, and Father did not respond to her. "He knew it was," she repeated. "He was bigger—he had grown." She began to cry. "Then he walked away."

Mother did not cry. She was the strongest of the family, stoic when Father raged and shouted and stormed; she was calm in the face of sandstorms, as she was stalked by dustwalkers in the wild. But she could not control herself now.

"He is not there. That is his husk. His soul is gone." Father's words were chopped and short. He did not turn to look at her.

"What if he is angry?" Mother's voice rose. "What if he hates us for abandoning him?"

"He is gone."

"He understood you?" Talit demanded.

"You saw his shell," Father shouted. "You saw a Burdened creature, a monster. My son was taken from us. Lanon is gone." He lunged, then, and with an impetuous gesture he struck the tall stone shrine, his flesh splitting open under the impact. "He was chosen. We must endure. To do anything otherwise is blasphemy."

His words were the Law of Prophet. But there was no force behind them, only brokenness. He walked away from them, rejoining the crowd of Sazers who walked on towards the church, towards Ziek's fate. He did not look back.

Talit had seen the Burdened who had once been Lanon, once. He had stood at the edge of the city, huddled with others of his kind. He had been like the rest of them: shuffling, mindless, shambling. The only thing to distinguish him had been the purple sash that Father had made for him.

It had been many long years ago. He had turned vaguely into the horde of Burdened who wandered the outskirts of the city, his head swinging aimlessly. She had not looked for him since.

No one kept track of the Burdened. They came and went, their fate directed by the Lord, and by Prophet. That was the law of the Sazers. What was claimed by the Lord was his, and he might do with them as he pleased.

Lanon was gone.

But maybe—

Mother had fallen to her knees before the shrine, and when Talit finally started to trail after Father, she did not follow.

The night bellringers stood at attention at the base of the tower. Since their commissioning, Talit had not seen them. They stared at her as she entered with morbid, open fascination. Everyone knew her face, and they knew that she had been with Ziek on the night he had been taken.

Talit did not meet their eyes as she veiled herself and ducked into the Church of Prophet.

It was different being down here; she had not seen the Church from its floor in many months. The press of Sazers around her was unbearably close and tight; there was no open space, only robed bodies, too much breath confined to one space. It was dark, but even in the gloom she could catch glimpses of the carved pictures of the ancients. From this angle they loomed huge and terrible, their smooth and alien faces leering vaguely at shadows.

She fought nausea, pushing her way to the edge of the crowd, towards the main aisle, where she could catch a breath.

The Church shifted, rumbled with the voices of whispering Sazers, and finally quieted. The midnight hour was coming. Here, in the fleeting, unreal spaces between dark and light, the person who was Ziek would be turned to a shade, and would slip away from this world to be forgotten in the wilds.

The bells rang. A shiver ran through Talit.

Leader emerged from the cloaked darkness, a veil hiding his face, and stood waiting behind the altar.

The Sazers around Talit drew back, forming a wide aisle from the entrance of the Church to the altar. There was enough space there for eight to walk abreast; Talit found herself crushed among her people as they pressed away from the figure who appeared at the doors.

Ziek wore his best ceremonial tunic, with dyed red slashes across his chest. Before him, he held a small tallow candle, whose unsteady and wavering flame drew every eye.

To the sound of silence—the voices of the bells lingering as an afterthought—Ziek processed alone through the sea of his people to Leader, who waited for him. He bowed, and placed the firepot at the altar. Then he stood, and trembled. He alone among the Sazers was unveiled, and naked before them all.

Talit's feet were rooted to the ground. So, it seemed, were the feet of every other Sazer in the Church. They were so still that they seemed carved of stone.

Leader placed his hands on Ziek's forehead and began to call out to the people who waited, who watched. Here was a Chosen One. Here was one who would accept the Burden of the Sazer people. Here was one who would offer his body as a sacrifice for others—

For long minutes, he spoke. Useless, ritual words, Talit thought. Words that stole Ziek's life from him, and turned him into nothing but a memory, even while he lived and breathed right in front of them.

She lifted her eyes from Leader and found herself staring into the cove behind the altar. Tonight it was a yawning black maw, stretching wide to swallow its victim.

Hello? she said to the hole. *Are you there?*

The hole loomed without response. Leader had finished his exhortation. Now Ziek knelt before him as Leader held the candle that he had brought, and extinguished the flame.

In the darkness, someone began to sing the hymn for the dead.

Around Talit, the others caught up the song. There was no harmony in this tune, only the stark acknowledgement of death. Someone nearby struck a spark; one by one, they began to light their little candles, so that the altar was lit from all around.

In their wavering light, Talit saw that Leader was arranging the dark blue shroud of death around Ziek's shoulders, so that it hid his figure from sight. It was almost profane to see her friend standing stiffly upright beneath the clothing of the Burdened, who hunched and shambled, weighted by their suffering.

Ziek did not turn his gaze from Leader's hidden face. Talit was selfishly glad that as he faced the altar, she did not have to see his expression.

As the song ended, Leader took up a bowl of spice-bittered water from the altar, and offered it to Ziek to drink. It was a symbolic death. As the water touched his lips, he would stop being a Sazer, and become Burdened forever.

Talit watched Ziek reach out and take the bowl. His shoulders were caved in on himself; his hands shook so badly that water slopped onto the tile floor of the Church.

As he drank, the bells began to cry out again: not in the steady, ordered manner of chant, but wildly, angrily. Their clappers clattered and their voices shuddered the bones of the Church in a cacophony of mourning.

Leader reached forward, and took the bowl from Ziek, setting it aside. Amid the clamor of the bells, he lifted the heavy blue veil of the Sazers, and slowly drew it over Ziek's face. Then he stepped down from the altar and joined the throng gathered at its foot.

The ceremony was over. Ziek was gone. From now on he was only a shadow, entrusted to the hands of the Lord to wander the desert as an offering.

In silence, the Sazers began to process from the Church. One by one, they bowed to the Burdened who stood, inscrutable behind its veil. Then they turned and slipped from the Church to disappear into the night beyond.

Soon only Talit remained, clinging to the shadows. When the last Sazer had left, she stepped from the pillar she had been hiding behind.

Ziek was turned away, facing the hole behind the altar. His chin was turned up, almost as if he saw something there now that she did not.

He was alone again, just as he had been on the floor of the Archive, and as he must have been as they prepared him for the death of his body.

"Ziek?" she whispered.

He did not respond. Still he looked up, his invisible gaze a force that was almost tangible.

Guilt and fear made every step closer to him as hard as if her legs were weighted down by stones. But she climbed the stairs until she stood next to him, a hushed, empty figure in blue, blending softly into the shadows.

She reached out, and felt for where his hand would be. Her fingers were cold and numb.

Are you still there? she thought, and was too afraid to say. Had his soul already left his body as a broken shell, and departed to be with Prophet?

She found his hand, and trembling, took it, and squeezed. "They wouldn't let me come see you," she said. "I'm sorry."

Beneath the heavy layers of fabric, a hand squeezed hers.

Something inside Talit that she thought might have been broken forever eased back into place.

Together, they looked at the cove, where the Lord had left nothing behind.

And as Talit looked at the hole, it seemed to dilate, and to enfold her in it; she was both outside and within it, and still as always it looked at her, empty, waiting.

Something else began to grow in Talit, then, as she held her best friend's hand.

She would not let him go off into the wilderness, to lose his own self, to be battered by fate. She would not leave him again.

For years untold, the Burdened had slipped into the desert, forgotten, to vanish. The Sazers had accepted their punishment wordlessly, and had not questioned.

But Talit could not accept it. There must be more to this; there must be some reason that even after generations, there was no respite to their suffering.

Surely it had been enough.

She must know. There must be a truth, and maybe it was that the Lord was gone, and the cure with him. Then at least she would know. At least it would be truth.

If there was anyone who could lift the curse from Ziek—from Lanon, from all of them—it would be the Lord. And if they found him, maybe he would forgive them, and end it forever and ever.

And if he would not—if the truth was vindictive, and his wrath eternal—then that, too, was a truth she was ready to face.

If the Lord was hiding, Talit was going to find him, and make him heal Ziek.

And if he would not, then she would find a way to kill him for good, so that he could curse them no longer.

The Burdening would come no more to the city of Saze.

CHAPTER 5

In the hour after being reanimated, Jacob had come to himself a little more, and had gone at last from the chapel to shower.

Aitor brooded by the room with the return pods, his heart racing. His feet would again touch solid ground. He would no longer be so near to the immense black eye of the Watcher—circling, always circling, skimming too close to its all-knowing nothing.

There had been days he thought that when his vigil was over, he would die of exhaustion, of simply existing. But it seemed that after all, he would be alive to carry out the order of the Superior General: rebuild His Church.

But this was not what occupied his thoughts now, as he paced restlessly between storage and the return room.

He thought now only of the men and women who lay in storage, and how they were young and strong. He thought of how it had felt to be touched again by a human.

Someone was approaching.

Aitor's heart sped at the sound, though he knew it was only Jacob. Or maybe because he knew it was Jacob. He turned slowly to face the man who was a ghost of his youth, and more.

Jacob was dressed in a fresh black cassock, but he had wrapped himself in a regulation blanket, and clung to it like a child.

"I must go home," he said.

"Yes."

A pause. "I do not have to go yet, do I?"

Aitor looked at Jacob's dripping hair, at the way his eyes were black and staring pits. He thought of his own awakening, and the terrible days that had followed.

He thought of the House at the End of the World, all those years ago, and all those times that he had thought of Jacob as his unshakeable rock, calm and steady-handed even in the face of war and death and dying.

"No," he said. "We can stay for a while."

Jacob stared at the return pods for a long time before turning away.

They did not go back to that room that day, nor the next. The pilgrims of *La Trascendencia* lay tucked away in their gel beds, dreaming of nothing.

Those first couple of days were spent without words. Aitor had not spoken to anyone in years, and he did not remember how to begin. Jacob walked as if he were a hollowed shell. He ate what was put in front of him; he followed Aitor like a voiceless shadow.

At night he slept upright in the reading chair in Aitor's quarters, and he twitched and trembled in his sleep. Often he called out in Greek, and Aitor, uncomprehending, held him down until he woke, blank-eyed and sweating, in the night.

Aitor still prayed and said the Mass. Though Jacob came and sat quietly facing the altar, his eyes were closed. He neither spoke the responses nor received Communion when it was offered.

As the days slipped by, neither of them mentioned the return pods, though the pantry's stock dwindled steadily.

Aitor watched Jacob unceasingly. To him it was as if a ghost had come back to life. Here was the chapterhouse's guiding light. Here was the hope and future of the souls of all of humanity. Here was Jacob, the one he loved.

Jacob did not look at him at all.

He had begun to recover his color. He ate ravenously, and his strength seemed to be returning, as well. When Aitor took his daily exercise, Jacob worked alongside him, grim and intense, and he began to stand tall, no longer huddled into himself, a hunched wraith of a man.

It was so easy to believe, seeing him now and remembering him as he was, that he could guide the people of God into a new life.

And even as he looked at him, Aitor was ever reminded that in that future, Jacob would not need him, an old man, made a stranger by time.

On the seventh night, they still had not spoken, though they sat finishing their evening meal side by side. Still there was too much history between them, too much unspoken grief for a past that was dead. The wall between them seemed both impossibly thick and tenuously thin at the same time.

Aitor could no longer stand it. He went to the chapel for night prayer, and got stiffly onto his knees before the macabre crucifix. Behind that, Earth continued to turn serenely; though the ship had not begun its return, it seemed closer now than it had ever been.

Jacob followed him, and slowly knelt at a distance. The air seemed so still suddenly that even the flickering of the little red tabernacle light seemed to cause the ship itself to tremble.

They were there for a long time. Aitor prayed: Where will I go, God? he demanded. What will I do? Will you take everything from me, again?

But he heard nothing, not even the voices which had haunted him in his chapel for so long, and so he gave up. For a while he simply knelt, and at least temporarily, he found peace.

When he tried to get up, his bones and joints and muscles fought him, as they often did these days. This time the familiar agony came with shame, because Jacob's hand was suddenly on his arm.

Despite Jacob's weakness, he lifted Aitor easily, his grip firm.

For the first time they sat, side by side, in the little chapel chairs. And for the first time, the distance between them seemed to close a little.

Jacob broke the silence. "They are all gone."

Aitor followed his gaze, where he stared beyond the crucifix at the false window, at their destination. "Perhaps something yet stands."

He knew without having to be told that their eyes searched the ravaged continents and unfamiliar seas for the same thing: the House at the End of the World. Fisterra, the chapel where they had left their hopes.

"Why me?" Jacob said, but the tone of his voice did not invite an answer.

The Superior General would have said something about the will of God being perfect. He would have lifted Jacob's spirits, told him that everything was being arranged for the sake of grace and salvation.

Aitor said, "Everyone followed you, Jacob. Everyone loved you. They will follow and love you now."

Jacob did not look at him. "Everything is different," he said. His tone had a distant finality that chilled Aitor, though he did not know why.

Abruptly, he stood. In the light of the sanctuary lamp, he was in silhouette, just as he had been on the first night that Aitor came, young and frightened, to the House at the End of the World.

He looked down so that they were only a few breaths apart. "Are you still Aitor?" he said, very softly.

Being named now felt shockingly intimate, as if Jacob had pulled apart his edges and stared at his bitter, feeble soul. Aitor could not meet his eyes. The name drew him, just as he wished that it were never his at all. Aitor was the name of a youthful and dedicated boy, brimming with a dogged, unrelenting fire. He could not dare to hope that Jacob saw that boy now.

"Yes," he whispered. It felt like a lie. "I am he. Still a servant of God."

Jacob's eyes searched him. In his gaze Aitor felt something terrible and manic and wrong. His fingers brushed Aitor's chin, turning his face to see it more clearly. "Aitor," he said, his voice tender. Naming him again. "What has He done to us?"

He turned away and left the chapel, his strides quick, as if something had settled in his soul.

Aitor followed him to storage.

The rest of the Travelers woke as Jacob had: in terrible pain, thrashing and moaning. Still, they recovered quickly, sitting up and shivering, stretching out their muscles with fearful hesitance.

All of them were young, so young. Aitor knew none of them. They had been signed on by invitation only, and had been housed by the ship itself, never visiting the Chapterhouse of the brothers. The men and women who had spearheaded the construction of *La Trascendencia* had chosen them, so that the Superior General would not have to be conflicted by the laws of God weighing on him as he weighed the lives of others.

There had been no room for mercy in the choosing. These were doctors, builders, soldiers, and hunters: young, strong, healthy.

They had been chosen, the Superior General had said, with dark circles under his eyes, so that they might survive. And if they survived with the guidance of the Brothers, then humanity would live another day to give glory to God.

Now they clumped in the dark storage room with its walls of boxes like frightened animals until they were directed to food and clothing. Then when they had dressed and eaten and gathered the supplies they would need, still they shivered and stared.

Aitor had imagined himself congratulating them on having survived the end of the world, on giving so freely of themselves. He had composed a speech where he exhorted them to do important things for mankind. To face the unknown, ready to create a new life.

In his head, it had been like the orations that powerful world leaders had given in those last days, on the brink of catastrophe. Then he would have ended with a prayer, and they would enter their pods with a song on their lips.

But he had composed the speech many years ago, when he was young.

He saw now the stark terror in their eyes mirroring his own. He saw that they mourned a world which had been dead to him for fifty years.

Aitor's words stuck in his throat. They all looked to him, even Jacob, who stood close by, his dark eyes flat.

"We will do the best we can with what we have been given," he told them. His tongue was dry.

The pilgrims loaded cargo and helped fasten each other into their pods in near silence. One by one the pods deployed from the bay of *La Trascendencia*, two to a pod. The trackers would take them towards the signal tower, which must stand where they had been abandoned.

When they had departed, only Aitor and Jacob were left.

The remaining pod contained the contents of the sacristy and the chapel. Aitor had broken it down on his own, refusing to let anyone else's hands touch the holy vessels until they were already wrapped and stowed.

The doors lay open, waiting.

Aitor took a step towards it, turned and looked back at Jacob, and saw at once that he was afraid of the box, of returning into darkness, sealed away from the eyes of the world. The look in his eyes was that of a wild animal facing a cage.

It was his turn to reach out for Jacob now. "I will help you," he said.

Jacob's face was waxen in the artificial light of the holding bay. He stepped towards the pod. He would not make eye contact; he trembled as Aitor helped him to fasten himself into the seat. When the pod slid shut around them, he let out a soft groan, and lay quiet.

Once again, Aitor was wrapped in darkness, just as the day he had entered the long sleep.

De morte transire ad vitam, the Superior General had said to them, on that day of grieving, as they prepared to begin their vigil. *From death into life.*

La Trascendencia had been stationed at a research base on the northwest coast of Spain, close to Figueiroa. By some miracle, the world powers had ignored its development. Perhaps their attentions had been too consumed by the Front.

It was possible also that they, too, had considered the end of the world, when they were not busy finding ways to bring it about, and had found it equally terrifying.

In the pastoral, misty green of Galicia, the aerospace center stood out like a futuristic monolith. The Chapterhouse of the Brothers, built on the cliffs overlooking the sea, had a clear view of its construction from across the bay which separated them, a mass of solar panels, trailers, speakers, and snaking wires.

Above all, there was the ship, rising from the morning mist like a strange and gleaming harbinger in a quiet, ancient world.

On the last day, the Brothers had taken the shuttle which the scientists provided for them. They prayed for the dead as they went; they were stopped at military checkpoints every three miles to be identified.

They had been honored, the Superior General told them. Theirs was a great and terrible duty.

Honor it might have been, but it was a grim one. They came in mourning. Even without many forms of communication available at the Chapterhouse, all that was needed to learn of the wars was to go out and minister to the people. In those days, death and sorrow had crept closer and closer until it knocked at their door.

The Brothers answered, and went out, and did what they could. But by then, all the Brothers in the world could not have done enough. On every tongue was news that the end was coming.

On that last day, someone else knocked on the door of the chapterhouse, and it was the government official who had come to tell them that it was time for them to go.

But as he saw La Trascendencia, Aitor's thoughts of death, of thousand-year condemnation, were momentarily stricken away. The ship was gorgeous. It was everything he had imagined, growing up with the memory of the American film vivid in his thoughts.

Everything, and more. Long, sleek, deep gunmetal gray; a phoenix in flight painted vibrant red across its hull, its beak open in an unheard shriek.

For only that second, Aitor envisioned with pride how he and the rest of his Order would look: gliding through space for a fraction of eternity, a blink in the eye of God, carrying the hope of all the human race.

That image had been lost to him in the moment he felt his body pressed into the cryobox, as dark and cold as the grave.

The return pods were even smaller than that box. But this time Aitor was not blind, and he could look out through a small panel into the airlock.

The bay of the ship looked back at him, gray and empty now.

They had not told him what would happen after this moment. It was Jacob, not him, who was meant to lead the children of Men back to their new home, to build the city of God again amidst the ruins.

There had been no time for anyone to tell Aitor his purpose, after the vigil was over. Or perhaps no one had known, either.

He had been eager to leave behind the ship, his prison. Now fear seized him, cold numbing his fingers and toes. What would there be left for him in the new world?

For he had now found God neither on earth nor in space, and there was nowhere left.

Be not afraid, he told himself, and pushed the deployment button.

The return trip would take roughly half an hour. Scientists had assured them that the homing mechanisms would return the pods roughly to the same location, grounding them all within a half-mile radius.

As they cleared *La Trascendencia*, for the second and last time, Aitor saw it from the outside.

It looked just the same as the day he had entered. The soft glow of the lights from the control cabin cut a faint path through the darkness. Perhaps even when the onboard power died and the insides had gone black and dead, it would still circle the world, and someone from another age might find it.

In that moment, he realized that, in a way, he already missed it.

Aitor's window faced what would become upwards; he could not see the earth. Here in the void caught between home and home, he felt as if time was also suspended. Even as he tried to count the minutes, he kept losing track.

There was a jolt. Terrific heat surged through the pod. He felt it through his suit and the capsule's padding, like he had been slotted into an oven. He had not experienced such heat since he was young.

The sky was fire.

It was so bright that it was blinding; even through his eyelids Aitor felt it piercing his skull. He found himself biting the inside of his cheek just to keep from screaming.

The light fade, and the inside of the capsule rocked and juddered. He squeezed his eyes shut.

There was sudden quiet. Then peace.

Aitor held his breath, and let it out slowly. Opened his eyes.

Earth.

Amen! said the voices of friends and family and strangers, a strong and unified shout that echoed as if through vast canyons.

Then again, silence.

The light that streamed through the pod window swallowed everything. It was ten, a hundred times brighter than any light aboard the ship, sharp and vibrant. He could see nothing past its brilliance.

Beneath him, he felt the pull of gravity. He could not move. Tears choked his throat.

It was Jacob who moved first, working the door's lock system, his hands scrabbling in panic over the unfamiliar mechanisms.

From now on, Aitor thought, frozen in a sort of stupidity, every moment they must now question if they lived, or died. If they would be struck dead by radiation poisoning. If there was life left; worse, if that life were even a life they would recognize.

The door opened, and they emerged into the world.

Aitor had known what had happened to the earth. He had read the logs. He had seen photos and videos of the planet engulfed in flame, then in heavy clouds of impenetrable soot, then cased in ice.

He had been at once both intimately chained to it, and incredibly remote, as if it were a foreign planet to be explored. He had thought many times of the American film he had watched: the triumphing conquerors, relieved to name a safe place home.

Seeing it now, he choked on a sob.

As his eyes adjusted to the light, he saw that their pod had landed at the heart of a city's graveyard. Now they looked up at the towering metal skeletons of buildings, half-caked in crumbling and blackened concrete. Seared, deformed, and rusted, they gave the impression of fingers clawing at a toxic sky. All the frames had been pushed outwards, leaning crazily where a blast had flattened them.

Corpses of civilization. This was all that was left to them. Much of it had already been buried, spurring upwards now from soft desert hills covered in sparse vegetation Aitor did not recognize.

The desolation that tore at him was visceral. *Kyrie eleison,* he prayed aloud, out of reflex.

Jacob had been staring at the buildings too, with a sick expression that Aitor imagined must mirror his own. But when he saw Aitor cross himself, he turned and looked at him, the sickness changing into something else.

"If there was a time for mercy," he said, "was it not sixteen hundred years ago?" His voice was gentle, hushed, almost pleading.

Aitor did not know what he asked. He said, "There is always mercy. We need it now more than ever."

But the question stirred an ugly feeling in him, and he could not tell if he was more disgusted with Jacob, or with himself. He did not finish his prayer.

The others had landed near them, miraculously unscathed. They gathered, carrying their supplies. Some stared, blank-eyed and incredulous, as if they were trapped in a nightmare. Others sobbed openly. For them, only a day before, the world had still existed. Blood-soaked and war-torn and full of corruption and death, at least it had existed.

Now it had been replaced with this endless nothing, this unsettling vision of apocalypse which lay unendingly before them.

It was not just that the vegetation they saw was different, that it was smaller and meaner; it was not that the sky was poisonously bright, and breathing had a strange metallic taste. It was not because of the bugs which had too many legs, or the choppy landscape pocked with craters and canyons, or the screeches and ululations of animals that had only distant relation with any animals they had known.

No, it lay deeper than that—not anything that could be named, though they tried.

Aitor felt it as an unidentifiable sickness in his gut, a paranoid feeling of an empty void yawning right behind him that, no matter how much he turned, he would never be able to see.

In unspoken agreement, the travelers turned their backs to the ruined city, walking with their heads down, packs pulled tight to their shoulders. They pressed close to one another, bumping shoulders, brushing hands.

Aitor could not have said who chose what direction in which to walk, nor who was leading whom. Jacob walked near him, his head up. He stared unflinchingly at the broken landscape with hollow eyes. The rest of the survivors trailed out in a long, bedraggled string behind them.

As they walked, some of them began to talk, exchanging names, countries, stories. A few of the survivors came forward to speak with Aitor and Jacob as well.

When they spoke to Jacob, it was with deference and anticipation. They knew their responsibilities; already they were shaping themselves to his will, looking to someone who would tell them that as they worked, it would all be worth it.

Jacob introduced himself as Father Masalis. Aitor saw that as the specialists came to him—discussing crops, and building plans, and water sources—life seemed to return to his eyes. His shoulders straightened; his face began again to take on its old expressive charisma. Already he effortlessly began to reclaim the man around whom others had rallied without question, thoughtful and imposing even in his youth.

Yet it was clear that the travelers feared Aitor. He saw that when they spoke to him they did not know how to speak of his sacrifice, his fifty years alone. They knew of it, and it weighed on them oppressively. But what words could you say to someone who has spent half a century in solitude for your own salvation?

He did not introduce himself, and they did not ask his name.

They thanked him, though, over and over, their voices hushed, their gazes downturned. Even so, he saw before they looked away from him that there was a reflexive disgust in their eyes: the aversion that youth has for the old, the immediate fear of decay.

Young and hopeful, they imagined themselves as Aitor was now. Stooped back, sunken flesh, spotted and feeble. Closer than death to life, he would not survive long in the wilderness.

But always they masked their repulsion, and Aitor was left wondering if he imagined the hurt he felt, the desire to hide himself from their eyes.

A pale-eyed woman introduced herself as Gisele, of Berlin. She had a cynical smile that seemed to defy the world around her, but her voice was gentle and kind. She took her pack from him and carried it along with her own.

"You have sacrificed much for us," she told Aitor. "We are grateful."

In her direct gaze, he saw more understanding there than he had in the eyes of most. He let her take his burden, nodding his thanks.

She struck up a conversation with Jacob, then, asking about his ordination, about the lottery. They spoke in low, grave voices.

Aitor did not have the energy or the will to add anything. Instead, he found himself falling further and further behind, until he walked near the end of the line.

The rest of the pilgrims made little effort to speak to him. But they put out their arms to help him, and as they walked they passed him between them, as if he were just another load of fragile cargo.

They walked until the sun was low and the day's heat had dropped to a sudden chill, as biting as the onset of winter, where it had been high summer only hours before.

Jacob chose the shelter—the ruins of an old building which looked as if it once might have been a strip mall—and they pitched their camp.

This was no place for a home, Aitor knew. A high wind had begun to blow, buffeting the survivors as they set up their tents in the crannies of building remnants, crowding out of its blast. They would have to go on in the morning.

He did not have to help set up; a tent was provided for him. Gisele was sent, she said, to tell him that he should rest, and that food would be brought to him.

But though his feet and body ached worse than he could ever remember, Aitor did not want rest.

"I need to be with them—" he said.

"With who?" She had her arm around him, trying to support him.

"With the people," he said, as she shepherded him to his tent. "I need to be with them—it is my duty. I need to help."

"You have done your duty, Father," she soothed him. The voice she used was the one with which you spoke to a child. "You have done it very well. Father Masalis will minister to the people. You need not worry. Rest."

Again and again she rose against his protests, her voice calm, her grip firm. Thank you, Father, she told him. You have done your duty. Thank you. But you look like death. Please rest. Please.

Her tone stirred deep shame in Aitor. He had seen how the old were treated; he had treated the elderly at the chapterhouse in the same manner. But he had not realized that this would be his lot, too.

He sat outside his tent with his hands folded. As she lay a blanket around his shoulders, he watched the others. They stoked fires, cooked, spread bedrolls. A few of them stood guard at the perimeter.

Jacob directed them. He walked here and there, issuing instructions, offering a helping hand here and there. Aitor's vision in the gathering dark was not good enough to read his expression, but he saw that Jacob walked taller than he had in *La Trascendencia*, that he had shed his weakness. Now he made himself into the man that the people needed.

When it was full night, he led all of them in prayer around the biggest fire. The travelers' voices were timid; many held hands.

Then Jacob spoke to them. His words were clear, concise, eloquent. He did not embellish or make false promises.

We are here only by God's grace, he told them. We have been spared. For whatever reason, the Lord has seen fit to allow us to live, to give us another chance.

This is an opportunity, he said. We may be the only ones left. It may be difficult. But now we can begin again, as it was meant to be.

Now we can build the city of God.

He encouraged them to build friendships, to trust one another. You will need to rely on each other in the coming days, he said. We are not individuals; we are not strangers. We are the Travelers. We are the last children of men.

And Aitor watched as their faces relaxed a little, and their shoulders lost some of their tension. They went back to share cookfires, to eat and talk quietly. They were safe, for now. They had a place to sleep, for now.

Some of them came to eat with Aitor, and talked without seeming to realize that he did not contribute.

But there was little for him to say. Their experiences were strange and distant to him, now. They spoke of the rising anxiety the wars had brought, of family and friends and homes they had lost.

All these things Aitor had known intimately for half a century. In his heart, he had already buried his dead.

He excused himself and went to his bedroll. There he lay, eyes closed.

It was not long afterwards that the rest of them went to sleep. He felt, rather than saw, the fires smolder low, and heard them rustling into their tents, zipping flaps shut.

The camp was still.

Aitor felt the tremor of footsteps near him. The tent flap opened, and even in the dark, he knew that the person who stooped to enter was Jacob.

He said, "Jacob—"

"We are to share," Jacob said. "This is our rectory." He had a tiny flashlight; Aitor opened his eyes to see him zipping the tent closed, his back to Aitor.

The weight of the years they had known each other and the years that they had lost lay between them heavily once more. So many summer nights they had snuck out of the chapterhouse together to go stargazing at the cliffs. They had fallen asleep under the bright golden eye of the moon, at ease.

It had been one of those breezy, warm nights that they discovered that the world might end in their time. Aitor thought of that night now, how they had huddled close to each other and watched the waves break white and glassy on the rocks. They had talked of very little, and understood more than words could say.

In that space between them had hovered the solemn chorus of the waves that night, the glistening of wet silver starlight against the spray on their cheeks. And there had been also something more tragic than either of them could express aloud. Together they mourned for a future they would never see.

Now and forever, that sad and gentle separation could never be crossed, nor acknowledged.

Aitor said, "I see." He settled back into his bedroll, and drew his blanket up to his chin, closing his eyes tightly against the flashlight beams.

"Goodnight," said Jacob. He moved around the tent briefly, making little getting-ready sounds. At last he folded himself onto the ground as well, and the beam of the light clicked off.

Aitor listened until his breathing had eased and become steady and deep. Still his thoughts were full of sea spray.

"I missed you," he whispered to Jacob, to the darkness.

Hours passed. Aitor began to doze, in the fitful sleep of the old to which he had become long accustomed.

When Jacob spoke, it startled Aitor's heart into an unsteady and achy gallop. "Tell me what happened to them," he said.

"What?" Aitor's voice came out too harsh, too sharp.

"What happened to them—the ones who kept vigil before you? Where did they go after they finished their watch?"

"I don't know what happened to them all. Only the one who went before me."

"And what happened to him?"

Aitor had promised himself that he would not think about it. But yet the thought had haunted him nearly every day of his watch for months, for years afterwards.

"For two days he stayed with me and helped me to recuperate. I gave him Confession. He made sure I knew my duties and what I needed to know to live on the ship. Then he told me that he was tired and going to sleep, but he did not walk in the direction of his room."

He had looked, Aitor remembered, as if the devil crawled within him. He had been short-tempered and cold. Aitor had been afraid to ask him questions.

"I followed him secretly. He went into the airlock without a suit, and ejected himself."

There was a pause. Then Jacob let out a sharp breath of laughter. It was so strange that Aitor felt a shock race through him, a tangible shudder from his head to his toes. He did not know how to respond.

Jacob fell quiet. After a moment, he said, "Do you think that he was rewarded?"

Aitor said nothing.

"After all those years of sacrifice, to end it all like that."

"Only God can judge him," Aitor whispered.

He heard Jacob turn over in his bedroll, pulling his blankets around him. From the direction of his voice, he was now directly facing Aitor. "Do you wish you were him?" he said. "Or me?"

A headache was taking shape, a storm swelling, angry and huge. "I wish nothing. I am only glad that we are here. Now."

"Why?" Jacob asked.

The silence stretched on and on. Aitor was so tense that he almost didn't realize when Jacob's breath finally slipped into the slow rhythm of true sleep.

Despite his exhaustion, Aitor remained awake. He missed the continual humming of the ship, and the feeling of invisible others walking with him. He had not realized how real they felt until they were suddenly not there.

There was shame and loss growing in his belly, and more than that, something he could not understand. There was jealousy, too. It twisted and burned, and it did not matter how much he curled himself around it, willing it to leave.

Some time passed. Finally he rose to his feet with some effort, and left the tent as quietly as he could, blanket wrapped around him, dragging his bedroll in one hand.

Just outside the tent there was a small patch of what might have passed as grass. He spread his bedroll on it and lay down again.

Above him, just as they had for so many years, the void of stars stretched as if he were looking down into a motionless sea, glittering and bright. His familiar eye picked out the old constellations one by one, and then the ones which he had invented himself.

And then, out of old habit, he found his gaze roaming the dark waters between the stars, wondering, as always, if he might find something there.

They were so far away now, and it strained his eyes to look. But however distantly under the domain of his old and constant friends, he felt himself come to an uneasy peace, and he slept.

CHAPTER 6

Hand in hand, Talit and Ziek crept from the Church of Prophet and into the city.

Talit did not know what would happen if they were caught. Exile—death—surely not death—

Regardless, the law was clear. What was given to the Lord belonged only to him. To speak to the Burdened, to touch them—to hope for them—was forbidden. It was blasphemy.

Not even for the sake of love must someone ever try to undo the Sacrifice of the Sazers.

They were heretics now, betrayers, sinners. The community would not let them go unpunished. They would not risk bringing down the wrath of heaven upon all of them.

Where were they going? Talit did not know. Ziek followed tamely, offering no advice. He had not spoken yet, but his grip on her hand was strong.

Her instincts shouted for them to run, to go helter-skelter from the city without looking back. But that would be the same as choosing death.

In the end she did not go home. She did not go to Ziek's home, either. His parents had both been at the ceremony. They, too, had given him away.

Instead her feet carried her towards the shrine of the Burdened, where the Sazers had left offerings. With every step, she felt her muscles winding tighter and tighter with fear. There must be something there that would help them. Food, clothing. Anything.

When they reached the Shrine of Lamentations, Talit found her mother.

She had not moved from where they had left her, huddled beneath the heap of stones. Her veil hung wildly around her shoulders, wind-blown and grimy from being pressed against the dust.

When she looked up and saw Talit standing there with Ziek, her eyes lit. She stood wordlessly and spread her arms to receive them.

Talit stepped into her mother's embrace. Always she had felt comforted by her tall mother's strength. Now it was strange to feel her trembling, quivering, as though a dust storm raged against her.

"He was alive," Mother kept repeating, and Talit knew that she did not mean Ziek.

Ziek stood a little way apart, where Talit had left him. Even now, he made no move to uncover his face. He seemed to look beyond them, head turning slowly, scanning for something Talit could not see.

Urgency made Talit finally break free from her mother's grip, pulling back. "I'm going to save him," she said. "We're going to find help."

Mother did not try to stop her, to convince her that it was death to try. She did not speak of exile, or punishment, or the law of the Sazers. But her eyes spoke the weight of a hundred griefs. She grieved for Lanon, and for Ziek. And now for Talit and for herself, for in her gaze it was easy to see that she knew what it meant to see her daughter holding the hand of a Burdened.

Instead she only pulled Talit close again, blinking her tears away, and said, "Wait."

Like a shadow herself, Mother disappeared into the maze of the city. When she returned, she bore two beastskin packs with her, heavy as Talit slung them over her shoulder. Her face was drawn and tight.

"Which way?" Talit whispered, squeezing her mother's hand. "Which way did Lanon go, when you saw him?"

A little hope returned to Mother's eyes—old and sad, but it was there. "West," she said, turning to look, as if she could see her son even through the many miles that must separate them. "Go west. Follow the river to the hills."

And Talit remembered the old stories. She realized now what Mother must have known for so many years. Lanon had gone seeking the Lord, too.

She reached out and took Ziek's hand again. In that moment, a shadow passed over her mother's face. It was in that moment that she left behind the city of Saze, perhaps forever.

Not forever. "I will come back," she said.

"Be brave," her mother answered, through tears.

When Talit got the nerve to look back over her shoulder, Mother was standing there by the Shrine of Lamentations, her arms wrapped around herself. Talit thought that probably she was there long afterward, even as they left the heart of the city behind and crept through the outskirts of the city.

Here, many of the huts surrounding them were falling apart, destroyed by the hard orange sun and reclaimed by the desert. The ashes from cooksites had long blown away and been replaced with dust, leaving only broken and blackened stone circles.

The moonlight did not seem to touch the earth here as strongly as it did in the heart of the city; the cold seemed bitterer. As they left their home behind, they could no longer hear the murmur of sleepy Sazers in their dwellings, nor the sputtering of smoldering fires dying for the night. Even before they had left behind the battered windbreaks and the ruins of the outer city behind, a solitude enfolded them like Talit had never known before.

But Talit realized as they ghosted through the alleys, ducking in and out of the shadows of ruined walls, that they were not alone.

In the shadows there were other shapes, barely discernible, tucked into corners and under overhangs, crumpled into heaps of garbage. Dressed all in indigo, they were misshapen, swollen lumps in the night.

Talit stopped, and Ziek came to a halt with her. She realized now what it was that he had been looking at.

The Burdened were all around them.

She felt her grip convulse, tighten on Ziek's. He did not react. He saw them, too.

"Hello?" she said, her voice too loud.

The heads of the Burdened turned towards her. But they made no effort to move, nor did they speak. A chill ran through her blood.

And then one of them raised a limb towards her—a hand?

Slowly, deliberately, it reached out. The fabric of its robes fell away and exposed a twisted, tumored claw, white-green and mottled with black, the flesh falling away in strips.

Shock jolted through Talit. She fled, dragging Ziek with her.

The Burdened did not follow them, but they ran until Talit's lungs burned and the ruins were long behind them.

For the first time in their lives, they stood outside the city that was home.

The river which fed the city and its sacred gardens stretched in a long unbroken line north and south. Around its banks there were long strips of thin gray-green forestation, and beyond that, only more desert.

Here in these wild places, the hunters roamed in heavily armed parties in hopes of felling fresh meat. And here also, creatures stalked the Sazers who entered their territories, just as much hunters as they were hunted.

Beyond the hunting grounds, only stories knew what lay there, and those stories were many hundreds of years old.

They stopped and looked back.

The giant heads of Prophet rose high from the center of the city—now an uncertain lump, backlit by hazy moonlight, glittering at its perimeters where watchfires burned. Did Talit imagine it, or did those gleaming black heads swivel in the night, tasting the air, sniffing them out?

The dark was eerie and filled with strange noises—a soft hissing somewhere, a rattle, a bird's shrieking and throaty cry. Further off, the long, drawn-out bellow of something in pain, maybe dying.

Tallit looked at Ziek, muffled beneath his ceremonial robes. She thought of the white and ghastly hand that had reached for her—she thought of what Lanon might look like now, if he lived—

Ziek did not move as she reached up, and pulled his veil away. It was her friend that looked back at her, after all. Pale, his eyes haunted. He smiled at her.

As if in response, a voice shouted from the ramparts of the city, distant and tinny. Another voice answered it, and then another, and another. The city of Saze began to wake.

Talit and Ziek fled into the desert. Behind them, the voices of the bells clattered the alarm, following them long after the city was out of sight.

CHAPTER 7

THE PEOPLE OF *LA TRASCENDENCIA* walked with the rising sun warming their right shoulders.

This was a world with no comfort. The landscape was desolate and unchanging, its colors too bright, its scents too sharp. Any signs of civilization they came across had long been abandoned or destroyed.

By necessity they became survivors, hunting the twisted and malformed animals that prowled the edges of their camp, fishing in the small brackish creeks.

Field medics and biologists worked alongside hunters and soldiers; there was no room for specialization, now. Together they grew tough and lean and hungry. On nights when there was no shelter, they slept pressed together beneath the bone-chilling winds until their skin was as chapped and tough as old leather.

Enough time slipped by that they began to feel as if they would wander the desert until they slipped one by one away, quietly, and were lost to the wilderness. No one spoke the fear aloud, but it filled all of their minds like a shout, and they began to call themselves the Travelers—a people without a home.

At the end of the first week, the linguist died quietly in the night. She was found lying with her eyes open, tear tracks running through the dust caked on her face. There were no marks on her, nor was there any indication of struggle or pain.

The rumor went around that she had died of sorrow, that she simply had not been able to go on. They dug her a shallow grave; there was little talk that day.

Aitor watched Jacob say a blessing over the body, and thought: *If she could give up now, why is it that I am still here?* And for his own selfish, prideful thought, he was filled with disgust.

On the sixteenth day they came across another city, as bleak and barren as all the others. On the outskirts, someone had built a towering cairn. If they had once left any sign to indicate who lay within, it had been lost; if the bones of its builder remained nearby, they had long turned to dust.

This was only the first of many cairns they saw built this way, massive hills heaped outside empty, forgotten cities.

Some of the Travelers whispered prayers as they passed; others said nothing. But they all went slowly, and looked where they walked, imagining the millions of bones that might be just below.

On the twenty-fifth day, the hunters shot a creature that did not fit any type of animal that had ever walked the earth: six-legged, its body crusted in chitinous shell, its bulging eyes the yellow of a biohazard sign. Its maw was filled with rows of serrated teeth.

Six of the hunters had unloaded their guns into it before it died; they tallied ten bullets of their precious ammunition. The shots' report echoed like an apocalypse in the dust-blasted valley.

Aitor was tired. He had little room for thoughts of anything, holy or profane. He thought only: I must go on.

Each night, the Travelers prayed for the angels to watch over them. Each morning, as they broke camp, they prayed for God to guide their steps.

And each night, Aitor fell asleep beneath the stars, staring up into the dome of the heavens. He imagined that he could see *La Trascendencia* pass over him again, and that the stillness of frozen, mindless transit came over him when he could see the neon glow of its pilot lights.

He had thought his waiting would be over on the day his feet once again touched the earth. But it seemed now that he waited still, only now it was violent, in sound and color and the voices of the living, the passage of time.

He had looked for God in the stars, but if He had been there, Aitor had not yet found Him. And now that he was home again, it seemed that each rotation of the earth spun him closer and closer to the earth, where he lay, beaten and weary.

But each day he put his head down, and walked, and prayed. He learned quickly to let the walking drive him into a stupor that left him conscious and fearful only in the deep of night, when he would wake suddenly, sweating, from dreams that he could not remember.

At last, as night fell on the thirty-ninth day, the creek they had been following grew into a stream, and from there, a river.

They walked always upstream—always uphill, their thirst alleviated if not their hunger and their bone-weariness—and at last they came to their new home.

Once it had been a compound of many buildings not too far from the river, surrounded by a concrete wall which age had broken down so that it looked much like a ruin from ancient times. A prison, probably, or a military base. It lay cradled in a windbreak, sheltered by thick shelves of rock on three sides. The buildings themselves stood half-intact, the rubble heaped untouched where it had fallen.

At last, many of them weeping with relief, the Travelers stumbled into the valley and laid down their burdens.

That night there was rejoicing and singing and praise around bright fires as big and cheery as beacons. There was little heed for safety; they were all too drunk on gladness.

The next day, they set to work. They sent scouts to scope the area, and began to reinforce the compound wall with mud and clay from the riverbanks. Many of the Travelers began to build permanent houses, shifting rubble, baking bricks in the hot sun.

Aitor rested for several days before joining them, and in that time, he began to feel again like a person.

No one asked him to join scouting parties, and he knew that it would be foolish to ask. Instead he helped with the construction, as much as he could. It was stiflingly hot during the day, and bone-bitingly cold at night. They worked through dawn and dusk, resting in the heat of the day.

There was much to do, and with only a hundred of them, the work slow and painstaking. Aitor was gifted neither in engineering nor architecture, and so he spent most of his time hauling materials, digging latrine pits, moving rubble out of the compound.

The simple work was grueling. Yet it reminded him of his days in the House at the End of the World, and it eased his anxiety. He pushed himself, praying the Litany of Humility under his breath as he worked.

Del deseo de ser lisonjeado, líbrame, Jesús . . .

Del deseo de ser alabado, líbrame, Jesús . . .

During the time he worked with them, Aitor grew to know the other Travelers. They had fallen into their work grimly, but as the settlement began to take shape, they had started to talk and laugh as they carried out their tasks.

Jacob was once again the charismatic seminarian whom Aitor had known, and yet he was not. There was the same just-beneath-the-surface torrent of energy which seemed to propel him forward as inexorably as a wildfire.

But there was a manic edge to it now. There was no more easy humor, no more claps on the back. He was focused, his questions curt and direct. His gaze was unnerving; it was like being opened with a knife. He knew the needs and wants, skills and weaknesses of each and every person without being told; he marshaled them all against the desert wasteland with a frightening intensity.

Survival, to Jacob, seemed to be a challenge, and he had chosen to respond with defiance, a refusal to be defeated.

Aitor understood that this man who had been chosen was the right one. Jacob effortlessly was counselor, mediator, delegator. The Travelers followed him without question. With his guidance there were organized watches and patrols, there was food and water for all, and the city had begun to assemble itself from the dust. He gave them a common purpose, and the will to live.

But Aitor avoided him. Jacob's gaze filled him with that terrible shame, that creeping unease. In Jacob's shadow, he was already forgotten, old and spent.

As the city grew walls and little homes took form, the mood of the Travelers lifted. They began to take their meals together, sitting around small fires to laugh and talk.

At first, they talked much about the time before the Departure. From their perspective, they had walked straight from a world full of death and chaos onto this vast wasteland with its violent colors, its too-sharp sky. Telling their stories rooted them to reality, bridging the gap between the old world and the new.

Not all of them were Catholic; many were not religious at all. Yet all of them had answered the call of the Superior General, putting their lives into the hands of the Cupertinian Order.

Construction workers, field doctors, engineers, hunters, agriculturists. They were some of the finest of their trade. All of them young, shell-shocked. Many of them had been born into the war.

Over and over they relived the gritty details of their last months on Earth, their expressions disbelieving horror. They repeated themselves until their words trailed off into mumbling, and someone put a hand on their backs to comfort them. Though they were quiet when someone else

was speaking, often their eyes turned inwards as they reflected on the terrible things they themselves had lived. Rather than listening, they waited
for a chance to tell their own stories, to unburden themselves so that with
the words spoken, it felt like perhaps help might finally come.

And then there was Noah, a tall man with distant, shadowed gray
eyes, who had been a second lieutenant in the British army. He had been
stationed at the Front, and deserted within the first two weeks to Spain
under a false name. Why the Superior General had selected him, he did
not say. He would not answer any more questions.

Aitor felt a sort of kinship with him. Both of them, he felt, had lived
through things that could not be expressed aloud.

In another lifetime, Aitor might have been friends with them. As
their talk drifted to lighter topics, it reminded him of days sipping a *tinto
de verano* at a bar looking over the Mediterranean, of shooting the breeze
with friends. He daydreamed often of ambling through the dusty, litter-
strewn streets of his pueblo at night when the cement had cooled, the
scent of sun and beer still lingering in every corner.

But it was different now. The Travelers did not dislike him, but neither could they understand. When they tentatively questioned him about
his time in the seminary, he could not remember, except in hazy and
fragmented snippets of beautiful things that could not be told. There was
no way to truly share the memories watching fog burn off the ocean each
morning, or how it felt to kneel in a chapel lit by a single candle, peace
assailing him in thunderous, unsettling waves.

When he was questioned about his time aboard the ship, he had no
answers for them.

"It was lonely," he said. "It was hard."

And they nodded, and murmured how terrible it must have been,
and thanked him for everything he had done.

"I couldn't imagine," they said to him.

"You could not," he said.

Perhaps they took the surety of his voice as confidence, perhaps as
arrogance. In any case, in those first few days, they uncertainly left him
in peace. Later, he regretted his shortness. It was not their fault they could
not know. But it was too late, and he did not know how to breach the
awkward space he had created. And in the end he could no longer tell if
they avoided him, or he them.

But with the growth of their new city, he had time to begin the task
to which the Superior General had set them. In the afternoons, when

many of the Travelers were going about their private business or dozing in the shade, he began to prepare a chapel.

He chose a building that was set somewhat apart, slightly above the rest of the compound, overlooking what had been designated as the main square. It had once been, he guessed, a gathering space, with a single room flanked by a hall and several smaller rooms. Much of the roof had caved in or had been blasted away; the main space had only three walls.

It took him only twenty minutes to unpack and set up. The small transportable altar, tabernacle, and crucifix went into the large room, and the containers of wafers, remaining wine, vestments, and lectionary into one of the side rooms.

The majority of his time was devoted to making it beautiful. The chapel was stark and ugly and broken, its walls grimy, the ground littered with debris and strange plants. He found bones huddled in one corner, and early one morning he gathered them up in a cloth and took them to the outside of the camp. He prayed the burial rite as the sun rose, and told no one.

The plainness of the chapel bothered him, but then again, Aitor had never been very artistic. His arrangements of the crippled and alien flowers he found struggling to grow were not symmetrical or aesthetically pleasing. He did not have cloth banners, nor candelabra, nor sacred artwork beyond the unattractive crucifix, whose presence made the dismal atmosphere even worse.

Still, Aitor and Jacob said Mass there in the evenings, when the work was finished, and the people were full from their evening meal.

The chapel became Aitor's cage. He cleaned obsessively, hauling water, scrubbing the floors and walls until they gleamed, but it was not yet beautiful. If anything, it grew more sterile, the meagerness of its decorations emphasized.

He worked, and worked, and agonized. It was the one thing left to him, and even this he could not get right. He forgot meals, lost track of time.

One day he came from his morning ablutions to find Noah there, working too. The tall soldier had carried broken stones into the chapel and was filling holes in the walls. He acknowledged Aitor with a nod, and did not comment when Aitor hesitantly came to help. At mealtime he went away again, and Aitor didn't follow.

When he came back, he had brought others with him. Gisele came, bearing armfuls of long reeds and grasses. She took a seat in the corner and began to plait neat mats for the floors. The engineers came and began to quietly talk of how to best reconstruct the building; a biologist came with an armful of colorful plants that might be flowers.

Jacob came, and worked with the same single-minded ferocity with which he did everything, these days. Though they did not speak, Aitor saw that Jacob watched him sometimes, his dark eyes unreadable.

Over the course of the day, all the Travelers lent their aid in one form or another, though they came and went as their other tasks demanded. No one told them what to do; Aitor wondered if they even knew what it was that they were building.

Only Jacob and Noah stayed with Aitor the whole day through. They did not speak to each other, either, but with their steady hands, the work went faster than Aitor could have ever managed on his own.

By the time the sun fell and it was time for the evening Mass, they had transformed the room. It was not necessarily beautiful, but neither was it barren and grim. They had shored the walls with stone and set them with mud that baked hard in the sun; there were decorative arches of cobbled stone on the interior walls, of a darker color than the rest. An altar had been constructed out of several slabs, and wreaths of vines and foliage twisted around the crucifix hung on the back wall.

Aitor rested. Gisele brought him food and water, the first he had had that day. The rest of the Travelers gathered around him as if he were an invalid, their faces speaking plainly that they were trying to solve a problem he could not see.

Noah crouched by him, put his hand on Aitor's shoulder.

"Thank you," Aitor told him. Then he put his face in his hands and sobbed.

That evening the hunting party brought back a strange-looking bird, grotesquely lumpy and uneven, its belly distended and wings bedraggled. They roasted it, and Aitor feasted with them. And while they treated him cautiously, he felt that he was, for now, a part of them.

Mass that evening seemed more like Mass. The solar flashlights they used seemed more like candles sitting in small woven greenery pots; the altar, now elevated on a rock platform, more grand.

It was Jacob's night to celebrate Mass, and his homily was exquisite. He spoke of the necessity of finding beauty in a ruined world. He praised the people for joining to transform the chapel into a house of worship. The people sat in rapt attention, gratified.

We are the Travelers! said Jacob. We are God's chosen people.

After the Mass, Jacob came to stand near Aitor in the sacristy as they removed and folded their vestments. It was the first time they had really spoken since they had begun to build the city.

"Thank you," Jacob said.

"It is only temporary," Aitor said. And for a moment he thought of telling Jacob everything—how he had wished it to make it grand, a great artwork like Catedral de Granada, or Basilica de San Pietro in Rome, the churches of old. Something lovely, a work of many years. But something stopped him short, and he only looked away, embarrassed.

"It is not enough for you?" Jacob said, but his tone did not hold judgment, only curiosity.

"The Superior General has told us to build the Church again." Aitor saw in his mind the towering spires the church would have, the wrought iron and monolithic pillars. There would be immense stained-glass windows filling every long aisle with jeweled light. "With nothing left, should we only survive, or should we build again, as you said?"

They would construct a tabernacle to hold the Host. And one day Aitor would open the door, and beyond it he would again see his God.

"It will be beautiful." Jacob turned and left the sacristy.

Aitor went back to the rectory-tent with a nagging discontent eating at the back of his thoughts. There he rolled himself into his blankets, thought of the stars, and slept.

He dreamed that he lay suspended in a bed of nothingness, far from the aches and pains of his body which had worsened greatly with work. He drifted over the Atlantic Sea, and far below him, he dreamed that he saw the space center on the coast of Figueiroa, his last view of Earth before the world had ended.

He dreamed the sound of footsteps echoing from another land.

"You poor fool," whispered a dream-voice, and Aitor was glad to hear it, an old beloved from a long-gone time.

The footsteps continued, and the world went quiet again.

In his dreams, Aitor was awash in voices. They spoke of the Travelers, recounting their sad stories, whispering unconfessed secrets. They told him of far-away lands he had never seen, recalling history he had never learned.

But when he woke to a bright cold dawn, he remembered none of it, and found himself troubled with a peaceless mind, a tired and fragile body. And so he rolled up his blankets, and went to the chapel to force himself to pray.

Jacob was already there. He stood in the aisle, looking up at the crucifix on the wall in all its ugliness. He held the gaze of the carving, unblinking, hands stiffly flexed at his sides.

Aitor drew closer, keeping to the shadows.

Those same shadows caught the hollows of Jacob's face and throat above his collar, a profile which had become rougher in the last weeks. They cast his eyes into heavy shadows, harshened his features, made him look older, crueler.

He was deeply in conversation—almost transfixed, Aitor thought. Somewhere, in a world far away, he was speaking.

The thought came to him that Someone Else might be speaking back to Jacob, with a voice that Aitor had not heard in many years, which he craved in a way that only addicts and dying men understand.

He did not know how long he waited. Jacob did not move for what seemed like eons, unchanging. There were tears standing unshed in his open, staring eyes.

When he moved it was like a statue coming to life. He turned abruptly away from the altar, and moved towards the entryway with a quick stride, his shoulders thrown back.

Aitor shrank into the wall reflexively, but Jacob had already seen him. He came close, and stopped only a breath away.

"Do you pray for me?" he said. The look in his eyes was wild and glossy. "Aitor, will you pray for me?"

Aitor opened his mouth, looking for words. He searched Jacob's face. It was the golden face that had once prayed in solemn rapture under amber candlelight, but the eyes were not the eyes of the boy he had adored.

His expression must have been answer enough. Jacob turned and left the chapel, walking towards the compound, and the fires where the Travelers were making breakfast. His cassock, dusty and ragged, billowed behind him.

Aitor watched him go. Then he turned and went deeper into the chapel. His feet sought the places Jacob had stood, and he turned his own chin to look at the crucifix. He contemplated it there, the way the wood was peeled back like flayed and living flesh, how it swelled and bulged in the imitation of grave injury.

He could not pray. Not for Jacob, not even for himself or for the Travelers. Instead, he thought: had Jacob heard something?

Had Christ delivered a message that He had not seen fit for Aitor to know?

He doesn't deserve it, Aitor thought, and he hated himself for it. If there is anything left at all, it should be mine. I have been faithful my whole life. I have given everything.

I will give everything.

He stared at the crucifix until his head pulsed with blinding white pain, and heard nothing.

This time he could not even cry.

CHAPTER 8

THE NIGHT WAS COLD—BITTERLY COLD, even with the animal skins that had been rolled up in the pack that Mother had given her.

They had been traveling for several days now, and it seemed that each night was colder than the last, that the further they traveled from the city of Saze, the more the heat of the world leached away. Even away from the coolness of the river and the heavy darkness of the trees, the sands felt like ice-slicked stone.

That first night they walked until long into the night, fueled by panic. Talit had imagined beasts or Sazers at every step; she had been too frightened to stop even when her feet started to drag and her eyes to close of their own accord.

Ziek, blue-lipped and panting, did not complain. It was only when his legs gave out and he slithered to the ground, panting, that they stopped. Talit made camp right where he fell, too mind-numbingly exhausted to think of the risks, her hands shaking. She blubbered incoherently as she worked, no words coming to mind, only miserable.

It was for nothing. There was no pursuit from the city. No one came, and Talit quickly realized that no one would. The Sazers did not need to punish them now. What violence they would not do, the wilderness would do for them.

The only certainty now was that there could be no return, not yet.

They had slept through the night, and the next day as well. When Talit finally opened her eyes, it was already evening, now darkening into twilight. Ziek lay as if dead beside her in their shoddy bedroll, only his slight breaths betraying the accursed life left to him.

Saze was far gone from the horizon, and their blankets lay on a sea of unknown wilds.

Talit looked at Ziek's sleeping face, very close to hers. "We're alive," she told him.

He woke slowly, and as the night fell they ate sparingly of flatcakes, sitting shoulder to shoulder to stave off the hugeness of the world.

When they had finished, Talit took the time to open the pack Mother had given her. Within there was more of the same food—hunter's rations—and two waterskins. There was a firestone, and a small pot of ointment for wounds. Packs of herbs for chewing, strips of cloth with which to bind feet for travel.

In addition to a few other odds and ends, there was a small prayer talisman. These were made from stones chosen for their unusual beauty, then polished until they glimmered wetly against the dry sharpness of the desert. Each was carved with Sazer marks, often for blessings and petitions. This one bore a mark which Talit knew to mean *the homecoming of a dearly beloved.*

There was also a stone-bladed worker's knife with a bone handle, whetted sharp enough to cut a breath, meant for long hours harvesting in the sacred gardens. Talit touched it with reverence. Its closeness brought her a little nearer to the future, a little nearer to the salvation of all the Burdened.

Ziek's voice interrupted her thoughts. "Where are we going?" he said.

She had not told him the plan as they fled: partially out of fear, partially because she was not sure she had one. She walked with a burning desire to see the Lord put things to rights. That was all. Even as she closed her fist over the knife's handle, she would not let herself think any further.

"We're following the river," she told him. "We're going west, to look for a cure. To look for Lanon."

Ziek did not answer for a moment. He was looking at the dust between his feet, stirring it with a stick. "Why else are we going west?" he said.

She watched the patterns he traced. Over and over he was drawing the Mark of the Sazers, a little cluster of them looking up at him. She did not know how to answer him. Tell him what? That they were hunting after a hopeless children's tale? That even if they found who they were looking for, Talit's intention was to threaten him—to hurt him—until they got what they wanted?

"I should have stayed," Ziek said, his voice soft.

"Why? To turn into—" She could not voice it aloud.

"It was my duty to suffer. Instead, I ran." The scratches in the ground were getting deeper.

Talit's face heated. "I don't want you to end up like that."

"It is the law," Ziek said. "The only way to atone. My—"

"Haven't we atoned enough?" Talit said, and found that she had surged to her feet, and was standing over him now, shouting down into his surprised face. In the wake of her loudness, the desert was abnormally quiet, listening, even the sound of the animals stilled.

Ziek stared at her, his drawings forgotten. She looked back at him dumbly, tears pressing hard at her eyes.

"I am a coward," Ziek said, finally. "What if they are suffering because of me? What if I have brought a curse down on them?"

Talit didn't answer.

"Maybe we should go back. You were right. Now I dragged you into this. They might forgive us."

"No," Talit said, her voice too sharp, panicked. "It won't work." Already she saw that he was staring to make up his mind. Already she saw it: her asleep, fitfully dreaming of his salvation; him, creeping back to the city, alone, accepting his fate.

"What?" said Ziek.

"Prophet hasn't taken your soul yet. You're still here. Talking to me." She was clutching for something, for anything, making things up as she went. "I asked him to spare you—as long as he could. I promised we would go to the Lord, and beg at his feet."

Ziek said nothing, his eyes dark, doubtful. Despite herself, she found her eyes drifting downwards, to where the growth pressed against his tunic, bulging out like a second, deformed ribcage. At the discoloration that was already beginning to creep up his neck, mottling his skin.

"We have to go, Ziek. I know I sound crazy, but I swear it's true. Prophet said he would pray for us—he'll protect us. The Lord is waiting."

"Waiting," he repeated.

"Yes. West. Prophet said that if we find the Lord and bring him back to see the Burdened, then he will finally see how much we suffer faithfully. He might forgive us. Be merciful. Lift the curse." The lies were coming faster and faster. Talit tried to keep the surprise from her face.

Ziek's face had smoothed, unreadable in the gathering darkness. He must believe her, then. He had gone back to drawing in the sand, avoiding her gaze.

Talit let him think, turning her gaze up to the sky.

Prophet will spare you for as long as he can, she had told him, because she did not know what would happen. What if tomorrow he no longer could speak; what if in ten minutes he was gone? What then?

She waited, her skin prickling.

"Why us?" Ziek said, slowly. "Why now?" And she saw then that he was suspicious, that he wanted her to tell him that it was not just because she loved him that she was saying these things. More than anything, he wanted it to be true.

"I don't know why it was me that Prophet spoke to. But I think it must be because we were—we're bellringers. We are going to become Consecrated."

Ziek had hunched over now, pulling into himself.

"We have to try," she said. "If we go back now—then what?"

Neither of them had an answer for that. No Sazer had fled the city before. In Saze, there was safety and justice. Nobody knew the consequences of leaving. But Talit knew at least this much: if they returned, then Ziek would die.

And there was more to it even than that. There was a strange hope stirring in her chest, now that she had woken it with her own lies. She could not understand it, but there it lay, a small thing that would not dislodge itself.

What if this little hope meant something? What if the Lord truly did wait? What if for years he had been sitting alone, and the voice of only one grieving pilgrim would crack his will of stone?

The conviction would not leave her. They must go. They must try. And if it was all for nothing, then they must end it all.

"Please," she said into the emptiness.

Ziek stood up slowly. "Is it real?" he said.

"Yes." Did it have to be?

He smiled suddenly then, his face so full of excitement that she had to look away, her heart like shards in her throat. "Let's go," he said.

What if he was right, and they had condemned their city to the Burdening forever?

She knew the answer to this question already. They would die in the desert, picked apart by birds to become clean white bones, criminals, buried by the changing sands. And their city would die with them.

But Ziek had somehow grown lighter, his movements quick and fast as he helped to pack up camp with shaking hands. He had shed his doubt like a child. They could not look back now.

Talit kept her mother's knife with her, pressed close to her body, its weight comforting her

They walked again, keeping the river to their left, and the sands to their right. Ziek trailed a little behind her, perhaps thinking.

Talit could not stop thinking about their conversation. *Why else are we going west?* he had said. And the same selfish thought kept coming back to her: it had not been enough for him to go with her into the wilderness, to save his own life. Not enough that she had tied her fate to his.

But after a while he lengthened his stride and caught up with her, sliding his hand into hers, and she thought maybe he had not believed her lie as much as she had thought.

In the days, they slept. Talit learned quickly that they had to spare enough energy each evening to make camp. They would venture into the forest, and Ziek would fill their oiled waterskins while Talit kept watch. If they were lucky, there would be a place for them to sleep with an overhang and barriers on three sides. If they were not, they slept huddled in the shadows of a rock, too afraid almost to breathe.

Talit had never been trained as a hunter; as a Consecrated, she had not been expected to carry out the smaller, more menial tasks of the city. It had been an honor, as well as a concession for their long hours of study.

Now she regretted her lack of skill. Her hunting was clumsy; what meat she brought down was out of sheer luck. More often than not, they forged through the foliage around the river. One evening, they blistered their fingers tying a reed net, and from then on, they sometimes had fish.

Often they talked, to keep Ziek's mind from his pain, though he would never take the arm she offered him.

They spoke mostly of silly, inconsequential things, but sometimes their talk turned to the mysteries of the ancients, the chants and stories which they had been tasked to understand.

Ziek had always been the more enthusiastic scholar of the two. It was he who had been trusted to study the ancient Relic alone, sequestered in the Archive until the last drop of candle wax had been burned.

He had not just studied, though, he told Talit. He had begun to create his own songs, as well. He scratched them into stone slabs, taking his best guess at the notation of the ancients to record the tones and rhythms. And he had begun to try and create notations for words as well, to capture the stories that had been passed down for generations.

Sometimes they passed the time by retelling those stories, learned from long hours at the feet of Storyteller.

Neither of them could recreate Storyteller's masterful inflections or turn of phrase—these were generations old, and learned from a lifetime's worth of training.

Still, even told in broken and dry breaths as they marched, the stories took on new meaning. Many were fantastical and meaningless, little silly tales for children. But there were also many that were stories from the time before the Yellow Year, and many which spoke of the Lord and the first Sazers, those who had come a hundred generations before.

Maybe there would be something that would give them a clue as to where the Lord had gone. Something that hinted as to how the ancients had lived; if there had been some way of finding the Lord more easily, some hidden knowledge that would change everything.

But even stories could not preserve them. Ziek grew steadily worse. He walked more slowly, and breathed shallowly, his storytelling coming in spurts.

One day as the sun was rising he reached out and took Talit's arm, and even with her carrying his weight, they walked only another half hour before she wordlessly drew to a halt and began to set up camp.

Neither of them spoke of it, but instead of helping her, Ziek curled up onto the ground, and pulled up his shirt to look at the Burdening which spread across his torso in long, irregular ridges. Other parts of him had begun to purple and twist strangely, as if his flesh were bruising from the inside and pushing its way out. His skin had taken on a white-green tone.

As they slept huddled together in the animal skin, she could feel the alien, diseased curves of his body against hers; despite his pallor, he radiated a feverish warmth.

She would never admit it, but the thought of his Burdening somehow spreading to her was just as terrifying to her as it was to see it grow on him. Even so, the loathing she felt for herself, for being afraid to be close to Ziek and his suffering, was worse.

One evening at low dusk, Ziek went to the river to wash, and Talit sat alone, cooking their meager evening's catch over a little fire. She hunched with her knees drawn to her chest, alone with her thoughts and her disgust, the growing weight of her lie to Ziek like stones in her stomach.

Something moved at the edge of the fire's little circle of light, and Talit's bowels turned to water as a creature emerged from the bracken.

It was the first large living thing they had encountered since leaving the city. Its outline, deeply shadowed, glistened red and purple; the light had caught translucent lumps and veins which did not belong to any beast Talit knew at all. It moved swiftly towards her, long-limbed and spindly, with an uneven loping gait.

Talit screamed as it reached toward her, scrambling for the knife at her waist. It was only as it came closer, stooping, that the fire illuminated its face, and she recognized Ziek, shirtless and flush-faced and dripping from the river.

That night it did not matter how much she comforted him, apologized, held him, mumbled excuses. He cried bitterly, and would not sleep in the blankets with her.

I am cursed and I am a curse, he sobbed, over and over. Take it away. Let it all be over. Let me die.

It was only after he had exhausted himself that she could creep close and fold them both into the bedroll, her heart sick with shame.

Ziek was sicker, and delirious with fever the next day. If he remembered what had happened the night before—and if he was a little more careful returning to their camp, shyer about letting her take his hand— neither of them mentioned it.

"Do you think we are going the right way?" he asked her, once. They were scrambling up a dune, clinging uselessly to desert vegetation that gave way as soon as they touched it.

Before them lay the wilds, unchanging sand and rock. In the distance, carrion birds circled a kill; a heat-haze rose and twisted the horizon. But there was still the river, and on the ground in front of them, their shadows stretched forward. They still traveled West; they still followed the path Mother had given them.

"Yes," Talit told him. "Prophet tells me so, when I pray."

He did not ask again.

Now when they looked back, even at the crests of hills, the city's long plumes of cookfire smoke were not visible. There were no more signs of Sazers in the desert, no quiet hunting outposts, no marks of the Sazers etched into stones as waypoints. They had passed beyond the radius of that which was known.

Ziek insisted that they pray as they traveled. Each day they performed the chants of lamentation and petition. Ziek begged for understanding, for patience, for mercy. Talit asked for food, for water, for safety. Mostly, she asked for nothing at all.

One day all the rolling hills fell suddenly away, and they found themselves standing on a plain. There was little vegetation but for what clung desperately to life at the edge of the river, which was thin and weak, little more than a trickle. In all directions the air was heavy with dust and sand kicked up by rowling winds.

The same desperation of that little dying river crept into Talit's heart, too. There would be no settlements here, no chance of discovering a city.

Maybe it would be easier to lie down and sleep, to let the wind blow hot thick sand over her until she could not feel the eyes of the wild always needling her, always the sense of someone curled in hiding, waiting to strike.

"I feel it now," Ziek said, as he looked across the nothingness. "We are going the right way. Prophet is guiding us. Do you feel it, Talit?"

"Yes," she said, and they went forward.

And as the nights ground on, Ziek's fever worsened; as his fever worsened, the fervor of his chanting grew strangely stronger. His eyes were bright and glassy, and he seemed to grow even more excited as his body failed.

It frightened Talit. But by then, she didn't think he was in any condition to see her fear.

The monotony of the plains passed, and on the other side were more dunes. And then the dusty rise and fall of the sand became more irregular, more broken, with rocky ridges and cratered expanses that sheltered them from the eternal land.

As the days passed, it warmed, and the winds felt like tongues of flame against Talit's skin, which became red and chapped, and burned as if she had held it against hot coals.

And with the change of the land and the turn of the weather came the dustwalker.

CHAPTER 9

Jacob did not mention his encounter with Aitor again, and Aitor began to think that perhaps he had imagined it.

The Travelers' settlement looked more like a town now. They had worked to clear away the rubble from the old buildings, and to remake them into stronger, sturdier constructions. This was where they slept now, rather than in tents pitched under the remnants of roofs. They had constructed rough tools, and dug a channel to divert river water into a cistern that they had lined with rocks, and baked with clay. The walls surrounding the compound had been rebuilt and reinforced.

The priests had their own small building, apart from the other homes. Noah had built Aitor a covered porch so that he could sleep outside. But even in the shelter of the low walls, he felt himself enclosed as if he were in a box again, and he could not breathe. Noah helped him to build a ladder, and more nights than most, Aitor climbed laboriously to the rooftop, where he slept with his face upturned to the sky.

The Travelers survived, though not in luxury. The animals they brought back from their hunting were strange, sometimes with too many limbs or eyes, sometimes familiar, but with growths that no one could look at for too long.

But the meat tasted as meat should, and they could not be picky.

As they had settled in, some of the Travelers had become content to work at gathering and building and creating, turning their camp into a village. Others, though, set out into the wilderness, going further and further on expeditions to scavenge for supplies, to search for other survivors. Each exploration returned the same result: as far as they knew it, there was nothing and no one left.

They had left *La Trascendencia* a diverse group, people from one hundred different walks of life, different countries, different heritages.

And though war had made them all thin and worried, they had all been young, energetic, full of grim hope.

Life in the desert had changed them. They were hard now, lean and sunburnt. Though they had guns, they did not dare to waste their small supply of bullets, and so they had fashioned primitive tools and weapons that made them look like a tribe displaced from ancient history. English was the communal language, but even now it was blurring into a hodge-podge which borrowed from twenty different tongues.

Of the Travelers, Aitor and Jacob alone remained apart.

Aitor remained close with Noah. The soldier went out often on the hunting expeditions, spending more time afield than he did in the settlement. It did not take the others long to take note of how often he went separate from the rest of the group and came back hours after their return, always carrying something useful with him.

It was Noah who became Aitor's provider. He brought water from the cistern and carried away waste; there was always a portion of his catches cooked and waiting for Aitor. They ate together in the rectory, often in silence. When Aitor read from his tattered Bible or went about his own small tasks, Noah sat propped against the wall with his eyes closed, dozing. On the occasion that he was gone for longer than a day, he left provisions stacked in a neat pile, and Aitor learned to judge from this how long until his friend returned.

"Where do you go?" Aitor asked him once. Noah had just slipped into the rectory with a parcel of smoked meat, his pack over his shoulder. It was deep night; the rest of the Travelers were readying themselves for sleep. "What are you looking for?"

Noah shrugged. "Anything."

"Have you found it?"

Another shrug.

"I will pray that you do," Aitor said, and he meant it.

Noah never participated in the Masses. When he was around, he sometimes stood in the back of the chapel, motionless, his arms folded over his chest. He always left early, and when Aitor returned to the rectory, there was a small fire waiting for him, ready to boil the bitter tea that Aitor had found to ease the soreness of his joints.

Of all the Travelers, he was the only one who did not answer to Jacob in any way. Aitor thought of him almost as a son.

It was not that the others viewed them with hostility, but the camaraderie of the early days had worn off. While they were always respectful, and greeted them politely, it seemed as if they did not know how to incorporate these two odd spokes into the smooth-rolling wheel of the society they had built.

Aitor's and Noah's separation was a natural thing. Yet where the solitude seemed to have followed them like a living thing, Jacob chose his own seclusion.

It was stranger, even, because he did not remain separate in any way from the rest of the community. It was the opposite, in truth. Nearly every waking moment was spent with the Travelers. Jacob observed the building of looms and the beginnings of gardens which had been turned and planted on the riverbanks. He was consulted for the development of a town hall, and lent his own strength to its construction. Often, it was he who was the leader on hunting or scouting parties.

But for all that he was there, he was not present in the same way as the rest of them. Where the rest of them had abandoned the clothes of the old world for the new, loose tunics that they had begun to weave, Jacob wore his cassock, now gray-brown from wear, patched and ragged. He carried himself starkly upright, as if drawn up by a string leading straight to heaven.

There was something otherworldly about him. He rarely ate, rarely slept. He delivered his homilies in a resounding voice, addressing the people as God's chosen, the survivors, the new sons of Judah. His every word was poetry. In comparison, Aitor's sermons seemed dull and small.

The Travelers left room for Jacob as he walked, and fell silent when he was among them, hanging on his every word. Jacob did not seem to notice. The hardship which had worn down those around him had only sharpened his beauty. His thinness gave him an ascetic look, of a saint of old who had gone into the desert to fast. The shadows under his eyes gave him the torment of mystical revelation.

Sometimes in the evenings after Mass, they would sing and pray around the fire in what was now the town square. Even those who had not been Catholic before the day of departure joined in these days, except for Noah.

After, Jacob would often speak to them from a platform they had built for him.

Rejoice! he told them, again and again. Have faith, for we have been saved, just as God's covenant proclaimed. We will build Him a mighty city with what He has left for us.

To the people, Jacob walked so closely to God that to be close to him was to be close to God, too.

Aitor wrestled with jealousy, and with something that was darker, something he did not want to give a name. It was worse now than ever. He did not speak of it, not to Noah, not to God.

He was being stupid and selfish, he told himself. This is why God does not hear you, because envy breeds in your heart, because you will not let truth grow in your empty and bitter heart.

But he could not shake the thought from his mind that something was wrong.

That Jacob was lying.

Preposterous. No one would lie with as much passion as Jacob had. What kind of man could unite a people with the driving fire of a single faith, if he was a liar?

Still he replayed all his conversations with Jacob again and again. Jacob, screaming in the cryostasis box, huddled, sobbing. Jacob—all those years ago—reaching out to him on the mist-soaked cliffs at the End of the World, taking his hand, saying, "Then we will be priests: servants of God," with something quiet and lost in his eyes.

Looking now at the vast wasteland of the earth with those same eyes, even deader yet, asking Aitor where mercy was, if it could not be with them 1,600 years ago.

Jacob, saying, "Will you pray for me?"

Aitor invoked all the angels and the saints. Let it mean nothing, he prayed. Take my doubt from me.

For a while, he could let the anger go. He began instead to write scattered fragments of poetry in his small precious journal of dreams. He helped the Travelers tend to the gardens, which they had planted with seed from storage. He coaxed his arthritic fingers to try and weave. There was always something to be done, and he pushed himself at mindless tasks until he could sink immediately into dreamless sleep.

He continued to say Mass every other evening. Often he spoke on the importance of tradition, and remembering the world they had left behind. We must never forget the sacrifices which others have made for us to be here, he said.

The people went away very quickly after Mass; the smiles they gave him in passing were kindly, but vague.

You're doing well, Jacob told him gently, after a homily where he had had a coughing attack and had been unable to finish.

But Aitor still could not look at him.

He spent much of his free time haunting the chapel. At times he and Noah ate there, looking out at the curling plumes of smoke from dinner fires. From listening to the conversations of the people, he learned that Jacob took his meals with all the people, moving from dwelling to dwelling, never staying too long.

When Jacob came back to the rectory each night, Aitor was already wrapped in his bedroll outside, nestled in his niche in the rooftop. He would listen to the sounds of Jacob within, preparing for sleep. For long hours afterwards, he would remain awake.

Every night, without fail, he prayed for faith, for trust. He prayed for an end to the blackness that was eating him from within.

He prayed also for Jacob, but more often, he prayed to somehow forget him.

The summer had begun to wane, the afternoons becoming more tolerable. The trees visible from the edges of their settlement turned violent shades of vermilion and gold. Aitor imagined that sometime in that period, his seventy-seventh birthday came and went.

For the first time since they had arrived, Jacob announced that they would have confession.

The Travelers lined up in the little town square, Catholics and non-Catholics alike. It was as if, Aitor thought, the months of their survival had blurred boundaries. As if having an alien faith was better than no faith at all.

Aitor heard confessions as well, sitting across the square from Jacob, sheltered from the sun by a small makeshift pavilion.

The last person he had confessed had been the nameless priest who kept vigil before him. All these years later, the sight of that priest's eyes as he was sucked into the empty arms of space haunted him, even as he listened to the sins of those before him.

There were more people who wished to be confessed by Jacob, and so eventually Aitor was left sitting in the buttery sunlight, watching how it glittered as it caught the sands stirring in the breeze. It was very still in the settlement, stiller than it had been in many days. Without the sounds of work, the world felt suddenly a thousand times bigger.

He strained instead to hear the voices which had kept him company during his vigil. The voices of his parents, siblings, people known and unknown. Lost, now. He wondered if he should mourn their loss, or if they had ever truly been there.

A movement startled him. He looked up from his feet in their faded sandals to see Jacob sitting across from him, face grave.

"Bless me, Aitor, for I have sinned," he said.

In all their short time as priests together, Jacob and Aitor had never confessed one another. They had never agreed that it would be so. But there had been an implicit understanding that to tell one another one's deepest shames would be too much—that it would be reveal a part of their souls they had quietly put away.

Aitor made the sign of the Cross. "How long has it been since your last confession?" he said.

"Sixteen hundred years." Jacob's voice was soft. Neutral.

"All right, then."

Jacob paused. He looked beyond Aitor, over his shoulder at something Aitor could not see. It was difficult to resist the urge to look, too.

"I have been angry," he said.

Aitor said nothing.

"Everyone has been angry," Jacob said. "But I have been angry my whole life. I have said it a hundred times in confession and I expect I will say it a hundred more before I die. Everything I have ever loved has been taken away. What is there not to be angry about?"

"And your anger—are you sorry for it?" Aitor's voice came out brittle, cold.

Jacob was still not looking at him, his eyes searching nothing. "I want to love God." His voice was very low. "I want back what I had before. When everything was falling apart, when the world was dying . . . I thought, good, let it die. If I serve and love God in the final days, then I will go to heaven."

There were times in those last days of ministering to the sick, the wounded, the dying, that Jacob and Aitor had gone to their place at the cliffs, and there Aitor would weep bitterly in Jacob's arms. And Aitor remembered it, how Jacob would never cry—how he would hold Aitor and stroke his hair, and whisper that they would be saved, after all—how he would look, expectantly, across the sea, as if he waited for a ship to come and take them home.

"But we are here instead," Jacob said. "And I am left to lead them. And you are old. And I—" He stopped. He had been talking in that detached voice, as if he were far away. Now he looked Aitor in the eye.

Aitor looked away first.

"No," Jacob said. "I do not believe that God is merciful."

"You lie," Aitor whispered, then. He could not swallow down the bitterness and dread at knowing at last that he had been right. And there were other feelings there, too, that warred and fought and which he could not give voice or understanding. "To everyone. You live a lie."

"Yes," Jacob said, and his fists were wrapped in the fabric of his cassock, now. "But I cannot stop, can I?" He inclined his head towards the Travelers, who moved reverently around them, giving them a wide space. "They must have something to believe. It sustains them. We survive; we have peace. It is all they have."

"And what do you have?"

"Does it matter?"

"Yes, it matters. It matters very much."

"Tell me I'm not right." Jacob leaned forward, his elbows driving hard into his knees. "Tell me that there is something left. Tell me why I should have faith. I married the Church and its people. I am true to my vows. I will protect them from the truth because I love them. And what reward is there for me?"

Aitor's thoughts were full of darkness. "This is not a confession."

"You have not despaired?" Jacob was getting angry, now, his shoulders thrown back. "You do not wonder why God has damned us?"

Aitor's breath was coming too short and shallow, like a hummingbird's wings drumming at his lungs. "I wonder," he said, and he felt the beginnings of tears. "I am in the dark, searching for the sun. But at least I will not make-believe with candles."

"You think you are better than me?" There was something of seminary-Jacob in his tone, a remnant of the ardent and dedicated scholar. His pride was wounded.

"No." Aitor thought of that man. How intimidatingly beautiful he had been in his brilliant passion for the divine.

"God would understand," Jacob said. His voice was no longer raised. Again he was looking away. "Or, it seems, He does not."

Aitor did not answer.

"Did you sleep, during your time in the box?" Jacob said.

The question took Aitor off guard; he stumbled over an answer.

"Did you dream? Did you feel as if when you woke no time at all had passed, and suddenly nearly every one of our order was dead and gone?"

"I—yes."

Jacob leaned forward, swift as a snake, seizing Aitor's wrist. "I was awake." Suddenly there was no composure left in him. His eyes were wide and they burned with a fever that Aitor saw now not as zeal, but as fury, as burning, vengeful hysteria.

"I was awake the whole time. Something went wrong, maybe. I thought it was God's punishment. I was trapped in my own mind. Begging for escape. Praying. At first I knew what had happened. And then I went mad. You were alone for fifty years, Aitor. I was alone for sixteen hundred."

Aitor's blood felt frozen. He did not feel the pain in his wrist, of fingernails digging cruelly into his skin.

"I thought I had died. I thought I was in hell. I hallucinated. Lived a hundred other lives that were not mine. When I was lucid, I asked God to save me, and He did nothing. I knew then that I had been truly abandoned. And when I realized that, I realized God had not just left me, but that He had left everyone. Look at how everything ended. The evil, the suffering, the death. Where was the Judgment, the Last Coming? We were all expecting it. I never thought we would have to live here in our own mass grave. If there was mercy, Aitor, where was it? If there was God at all, then where has He gone? Why has He done this to us? I was so faithful, Aitor."

Aitor opened his mouth; closed it.

Jacob let him go, and sat back. Calm again. As if he had flicked a switch. "The days of the Bible, when He walked the land and spoke from burning bushes are gone. Maybe He was here. But He saw us, and spat on us, and gave up."

Aitor said at last, "You have given up all hope, then."

"And you have not?"

"No." The word felt like a bitter promise.

"How?" And with that word, the last of seminary-Jacob, the fiery intellectual who had railed against heresy and seen angels at each consecration, was extinguished. Aitor saw him as he was, and he tried not to despair.

His insides were made of stone. His throat had closed; his head pounded. He felt a strong revulsion, but he could not say against what, or whom.

"Will you absolve me?" said Jacob.

Aitor only shook his head.

Jacob said, "I thought you knew something I did not. I thought you could help. You have always helped me, Aitor." His hands lay open in his lap now, facing upwards. "Do you hate me now?"

"I will never hate you," said Aitor. A half lie. He did hate Jacob in this moment, and yet he understood him, and loved him, just as he always had. In that same way, and for that same reason, he hated himself as well.

A smile touched Jacob's lips, only a little bitter. He stood, brushing sand from his cassock with long and spindly hands. "I pray for my own salvation," he said. "Do you?"

Aitor did not answer him.

Jacob left.

CHAPTER 10

Talit saw the dustwalker near midnight, when the moon was highest, and their shadows were hidden beneath their feet as they trudged ever onwards.

That was how she spotted it waiting for them atop a far dune—a tiny patch of indigo that was slightly darker than the rest of the world around them, outlined in a splash of varicolored starlight. If it had been any darker, had she not happened to glance in that direction, she never would have seen it.

Talit knew of dustwalkers. Young hunters bragged of sightings when they began their apprenticeships and made their first excursions; adults spoke of them in tones of dread. The criminals of Saze were bound hand and foot and left overnight as food for dustwalkers, their remains strung from the City walls as a warning. They were a result of the Yellow Year, one of the first and oldest abominations that the ancient ones had created. Of the creatures that roamed the lands, the dustwalkers had always been the most feared.

Talit's mother had encountered a few in her lifetime, during her ventures from Saze when hunting was lean. But whatever those encounters had been, she had not liked to speak of them.

Talit had no doubt now what it was that locked eyes with her.

It hunched on the ridge, surveying them. She could not make out much of it. A monolith of flesh, a spray of fur or spines. Limbs that were unnaturally long, bulging in odd places. A flash of red, of too many glinting eyes. Even from this far away, she could see that it was enormous.

Even as she saw it, it moved blindingly fast, and was gone.

"Ziek," she whispered. "Did you see that?"

"See what?" He had been struggling to walk, his gaze fixed on his feet. There was no more argument about leaning on her.

85

"There. On the hill." She pointed.

They stopped and looked, but nothing moved again. The night around them seemed to wait, too.

"A mirage." Ziek's words were slurred, half-awake.

Talit wished that she believed him.

For the better part of two hours they pressed forward, sweat standing out on their foreheads despite the chill of night.

Ziek mumbled to himself, as he did now. He still told stories to pass the time—to keep himself walking—but she could no longer understand what he said.

Near the end of the second hour, though, he leaned so heavily on Talit that she could barely pick up her own feet, and his head hung low to his chest. His breaths were sharp, irregular gasps.

It was yet several hours until dawn, Talit thought, and despaired. But all the same she directed their struggling steps towards the trees near the water, and they collapsed once they were in the shelter of the forest.

Talit hunched over her knees, and watched him. He lay where she had clumsily set him, with his head propped against a gnarled tree root. He made no effort to move, nor speak.

She wondered, What is happening to his spirit right now?

What have I done?

She thought of going hunting, of going to the river to collect water. But her limbs, her head, her heart, they all felt as heavy as if they were weighed with rocks. If they lay there forever, then perhaps they would slip from the world quietly and peacefully, with no one to mark their passing.

This was foolish, Talit thought. I am a fool.

It was then that she realized that the sounds of the wilderness around them had stopped.

The hair on the back of her neck rose. The silence swelled. It was so oppressive, so deafening, that she couldn't believe she hadn't felt it. How long? How long had they been caught in the moment before the predator strikes?

The dustwalker must be watching them.

She rolled onto her feet, and swayed. The world, painted in dark and fuzzy hues, heeled and rolled around her. Her bones screamed in pain, but she forced herself to walk to where she had left Ziek.

"Get up." She put her hands on his shoulders, and he did not move. "Get up," she said, again, louder, and this time she dared to shake him.

His eyes fluttered open, and he sat up. For a long and breathless moment she thought that he did not recognize her, that his soul had left him. But then he took her arm, and labored to stand.

She waited for him to ask why they were getting up again, why she was pushing to continue long after he had given all he had to give.

Instead he only stood, rocking slightly on his feet. His eyes fixed blankly on her face. He waited for her to lead.

The empty docility was so much like that of a Burdened—shuffling where the crowd went, standing aimlessly, staring into the empty sky— that Talit's eyes welled with sudden angry tears. She took his wrist and said, "The dustwalker is real. We have to go."

It was a futile effort. They were dead already.

But until the moment she died, she would not let them suffer the death of a criminal. Ziek could not die because she had brought them here.

She reached to her belt and touched her mother's hunting knife with fingers that were too numb with fear to feel it.

Still the dustwalker did not attack.

Talit felt as if her eyes would dry and fall from her face as they walked back out from the shelter of the trees into the open. She strained them anyways, trying to see that dark, odd-shaped shadow again, could not stop turning her head this way and that until her neck ached and her toes were numb from tripping and ramming them into rocks.

But nothing happened.

The dustwalkers take their time to stalk their prey, Talit heard Storyteller's voice say. They wear them down until they are too exhausted to move an inch. They exude fear as their smell. If you ever come close enough to touch a dustwalker, then you are dead.

There was another thing Talit, remembered, too.

They will not hunt in the day. In sunlight, they cannot see.

She dragged Ziek to a halt, and obediently he waited beside her, his head drooping, his eyes sagging shut.

Quick, quick, quick, she told herself, and fumbled blindly until her fingers found what she sought: firestones, a little clay jar of animal fat they had collected in their meager hunting, a bundle of green sticks.

With shaking hands she ripped a swath from her tunic and knotted it around the sticks; she unstopped the jar and spilled what fat there was over the bundle. This, and the firestones, she clutched tightly to her.

She could not light the torch now; it would last for an hour, at best. They must save it for those last and most desperate moments.

The land was changing faster. The trees crept closer and closer, and she had to adjust their course to keep them free from any surprises from the lurking dark. And the ground was less sand, now, and more a fine dirt; they were struggling uphill, over rocks that grew increasingly larger.

Everything was agony. Talit felt as if her body was being torn to shreds as she strained forward, as she half-supported, half-dragged Ziek. He was trying—through the fog of the Burdening he must have sensed her urgency—but his body failed him over and over again.

Talit wanted to cry, but could not summon the energy. At last came the point where she could not feel her own limbs at all. Her mind felt like it was floating away from her body; there was a hazy orange tint over everything. The presence of the dustwalker never seemed to leave her—it was around every corner, behind every rock.

Time and time again, Ziek tried to stop.

"Come on," she told him. Her voice didn't sound like hers to her own ears—scratchy, raw, full of sand, like she had aged twenty years.

"I can't." Ziek could barely hold on to her; his arms were wrapped around his side as if he were trying to squeeze it shut. He was piteous, shivering and slicked in sweat at the same time.

"We're going to find the Lord," Talit said, desperate. She would have said anything, now. "We can't give up now. He is waiting."

And Ziek would raise his head and move forward again.

When she could no longer stand the claustrophobic confines of the dark—the sense of eyes near, the nakedness of walking across open ground—Talit lit the torch.

It took five tries to get the firestones to produce sparks, her hands shaking more with each failure. But at last the torch blazed up in her hand.

In the wideness of the wilds, the light was no more than a puddle. But it was light, and even Ziek huddled in closer to it, turning his face often to look at the flame, as if entranced.

Somewhere near the end of the hour, he began to sing.

At first she thought he was crying. She had no energy to stop him. What difference did it make?

But then the words distinguished themselves. The singing coming from his battered and worn body was eerie and tremulous, his voice cracking and warping with each step.

He was singing the Night-Song, the chant which Leader performed in the early hours between midnight and morning, which was attended only by those who grieved.

Talit had heard the Night-Song for many months in the wake of Lanon's passing. Mother and Father had gone long after the usual mourning period. She remembered waking in the silent hours of the night to walk to Church of Prophet, when her mouth felt full of cloth, and the giant pictures of people on the walls of the Church were stark and forbidding and grim.

Ziek must have learned it from Leader, Talit thought. He sang it softly as they walked, but not well; it was a deformed and unpleasant mantra. His singing went on and on until at last his voice died in his throat, and he shuffled as the Burdened do, his head down.

As he fell quiet, another voice lifted, from very far away—a mix between a howl and a screech. It was joined by another, and another; and then there was another cry, too close. The night was awake with the sound of dustwalkers.

They were mocking their prey, Talit realized.

And the torch sputtered and gasped in her hand, every moment bringing them closer to darkness.

They had come now to rolling hills of dirt and soft shale that spread in a long field, and nearby, the river and the forest cut a winding path between them.

Talit lurched to a halt, catching her breath on a sob. If they were to go into the woods, it would be easier to be stalked. To go over the hills, though, was impossible.

There was death on all sides.

She turned just in time to see a dustwalker leap towards her, to hear Ziek cry out.

Her body went flying and hit the ground, and bounced several times; she felt her head smack the earth, and then she came to rest. She did not even scream. She felt the torch roll from her fingers.

In a flash of regret, she thought: May the Lord and the Prophet forgive me.

The dustwalker was screeching, an inhuman sound that might have caused her pain, had she been able to feel anything.

Ziek, she thought, and she felt a very faraway regret.

The dustwalker had not yet sunk its fangs into her, had not stripped her flesh from her bones. But she felt certain that it would not be long.

Would she meet Prophet, now? Or would she wake in the next life to see the wrathful face of the Lord, seeking his revenge on the girl who had meant to kill him?

Her vision was blotchy and filled with spangles of light. Flame, she thought. Everything was on fire, all around her.

She felt within her a crazy urge to laugh. Dawn was so close. They had almost made it.

She closed her eyes.

CHAPTER 11

SUMMER FADED INTO FALL, AND fall sloped toward winter. The game became scarcer, and the hunting parties had to range farther and farther to find food.

Yet the Travelers had been thriving. Under Jacob's guidance, the community had been confident, peaceful, happy. The settlement was a steady and well-oiled machine.

This is God's blessing upon us, Jacob told them. With Him, what shall we fear?

And when he said these things, Aitor watched him, and thought of how terrible it was that he could not find a trace of deception in Jacob's clear and ascetic face. Only that terrible light in his eyes as he stared into a world no one else saw.

But they did not speak of it again.

Aitor had begun to draw up plans for his cathedral. He scratched them into one of his journals, using sticks of charcoal gleaned from the fires.

In this, his lack of architectural knowledge became both a hindrance and a benefit. He spent many hours sketching churches in his journal, as small as he could scale them, to save precious paper. He imagined soaring structures, stretching unbelievably far into the distant heavens, layers on layers of halls filled with moody chiaroscuro, bathed in all the grandeur which the barren landscape of the wilds could evoke.

When he was not doing what he could to help the Travelers, he began to go on small scouting excursions of his own, hunting for a place where one day the foundations for this church might be laid.

It was a stupid, fruitless thing. With what would they build this church? Who could do it?

But the need to go searching would not leave him; it was compulsive, a consuming thought that covered up all the other thoughts he did not want to think. And Noah accompanied him wordlessly, holding his arm, asking no questions.

One afternoon as Aitor sat in the sun, bent painfully over his sketches, Jacob came to him. He wore his cassock, as he always did. While the rest of the people clothed themselves now in light garments, an attempt to hide from the baking sun, only Jacob and Aitor remained stubbornly in black.

They had not spoken since the day that Aitor had refused him absolution.

"Can I see?" The request was simple, blunt, unburdened with the words they had spoken before. Aitor moved wordlessly so that Jacob could sit beside him.

Jacob examined the drawings closely. There were new creases in his brow, crows'-feet heavily marking his eyes. He no longer looked only thirty-one.

Aitor said, "Maybe if there were something left over, it would be easier—for us."

In Jacob's hands lay many weeks' dreams and wishful thinking, smudged and stark. There must have been more than a hundred sketches, poorly-drawn, the lines marked and re-marked with a shaking hand. Aitor saw the drawings as Jacob must: the crazed and obsessive scribblings of an old man, clinging to something that would never be.

"We are what is left over," Jacob said.

They sat like that for a while, saying nothing. Jacob continued to look through the book, his gaze lingering on each page.

"Are you happy?" Aitor said.

"What?" Jacob's hands paused in turning the pages.

"Are you happy, pretending?"

Jacob let out a soft breath; closed the book. "Are you happy, waiting?"

"You were always the happy one," Aitor said.

Jacob stood, then. "Don't go away on one of your trips tonight," he said. "There will be a wedding. Please come." He handed the journal back to Aitor, and walked away.

Aitor looked again at his drawings. He willed the beautiful images from his mind to burn themselves onto the pages, without the clumsiness of his old, crippled fingers. Towering pillars. Solemn saints and angels watching over hosts of adoring people, bearing witness to an Ineffable

Presence which no living mortal could look upon without being consumed by holy flame.

But with a striking sense of loss, he saw that all of the churches he had drawn were empty.

He went to the wedding that evening, and there was dancing, and feasting despite the shortage of food. There he saw the people happy—contented—alive, laughing beneath a careless blaze of bonfires—and for a while, that memory kept him. And though he could not forgive Jacob, he understood him.

But as the cold came, it brought a stiffness and agony to Aitor's joints that had, in the climate-controlled belly of the ship, never bothered him before. With the cold, he could no longer go out and explore the land around him, and he was confined within the boundaries of the city. Restless and in pain, he began to have nightmares, and with the nightmares came the screaming.

In his nightmares, Aitor was once again aboard *La Trascendencia*. He lay on his back in cold storage on a hard bed, and above him the lid was sealed. In the dream, he again awaited waking to take up his vigil.

This time, though, his eyes were not sealed shut. Instead they were propped wide and staring, so that the darkness was not a cushion around him, but a stifling presence which leered back at him. And instead of seeing the lid drawn back so that he saw the face of the priest who went before him—instead of the painful flush of blood sweeping through his veins again, he remained frozen.

He could neither move nor breathe. He simply existed, sealed in a box, and in the dream he had the sense of a thousand years passing as he lay there, his eyes frozen wide. He gaped into darkness as time folded in on itself in an endless madman's kaleidoscope.

All around him he could hear the shrieks of the dying. His brain replayed, endlessly, the last hours of his life before he was rushed aboard the ship, pressed into the bed, and frozen.

There were the sounds of bombs detonating, of buildings collapsing; gunfire and wailing. His nose was filled with the acrid tang of fire, the strange combination of death and cleanliness that was napalm, the charred scent of roasted meat that was burning bodies.

Wake. Wake. Wake. O God, O Jesus. Let me wake.

But in his dream he knew that it would be centuries before he would be able to pry himself from the dream, his body rigid and paralyzed, unable to sweat because he was frozen away in a cryogenic tomb.

The first night the dreams came, he woke to find Noah's face inches from his, hands pressing him to the ground. Someone—it sounded like Jacob—was swearing loudly from near his head.

"Hold him—damn it—get him awake. Don't let this go on. Slap him. For Christ's sake—"

Aitor's body was trembling, but he had no control of his limbs for the next few minutes. He managed, barely, to tilt his head, and to see that there were people crouched on the rectory roof beside him, holding flashlights that blocked out the stars.

They stayed with him, talking in low tones.

"What's wrong with him?"

"I think he's having a nightmare."

"He's just old."

"He could have fallen."

"He can't sleep up here. He'll break his neck and kill himself, if the cold doesn't kill him first."

"God knows how he's still alive anyway."

Aitor's gaze found Jacob, crouched just behind Noah's shoulder. His expression was full of pity, but beyond that there was also horror. Jacob knew what Aitor had dreamed. He had lived it.

They lifted Aitor down and carried him gently into the rectory, where they made up his bedroll in the rectory. But even hours later, with a candle burning at his bedside, it wasn't until the first light of dawn that he managed to doze off, vaguely aware that a presence kept watch at his bedside.

Some time early in the morning, Aitor found himself awake, with a touch on his collarbone, just above his heart. He did not open his eyes; long instinct from his youth made him pretend that he slept, with long, even breaths.

"And so He has left us to dwell in the dark, like those long dead," someone whispered over him.

Aitor knew the voice well, without having to look. Jacob.

In the morning when he rose, his bones aching and laden with cold, Jacob was no longer there.

After that, Aitor avoided sleeping, enough that he felt constantly drunk, and shadows leapt at him from every corner. He went for walks instead, roaming from fireside to fireside like a ghost.

When he did sleep, he chose a rocky outcropping that overlooked the Travelers' camp, far enough that his cries might not wake the people.

No one mentioned it when Noah abandoned the little dwelling he had built, and set up a small camp of his own at the base of the hill. Nor would anyone in the city admit to leaving him a few heavy-woven blankets at his chosen site.

More and more frequently, Aitor built a fire in the chapel, where he would not be near Jacob at the rectory. There he sat and prayed for a release to his nightly torture.

He had long one-sided conversations with the ugly crucifix, fighting sleep. Sitting alone, he fed the flames slowly, and told stories of his childhood. He said the things he had never said to anyone, not even to Jacob—how his father had been a part of the mafia, and how he had kept it hidden from his sons until one day he came home in a sports car without explanation, how the following day he came home in a bag.

He whispered of the people he had met and confessed. It was strange, but he remembered them all. It was so easy to fall in love with so many people—even in spite of knowing their most intimate sins and flaws and failures—perhaps because of it. Aitor had loved so many people.

All long dead and gone, now.

In the darkest parts of the night, he would sometimes speak of his time in the seminary. For so long he had tried to be like Jacob, to become him.

To the darkness he confessed his feelings—how at first, in the days after their return to earth, there had been crawling shame and anger each time that same brilliant, magnetic seminarian looked at him and saw a broken old man, whose life had been already spent.

Now there was nothing left but grief and anger for the death of them both: Jacob and his ghost, unmoored, despairing.

Once, when it was very silent indeed, he whispered of a night beneath a moody and coruscant midnight sky, sitting with Jacob atop the sacred stained-wine stones of Fisterra. A night where, their sides pressed against each other, they had looked out over the End of the World, and let themselves dare to imagine what it would be like to forget their duty as priests, eternally sealed to Christ.

When, for just a little while, they hid away from the death which came upon the world, and the terrible obligation which rested on their shoulders.

And they had confessed that they were afraid, and everything had been so close to perfect.

At last, when all of Aitor's stories were told, he sat in weary silence.

He had thought that Noah would deem him safe each night, and return to sleeping in his home. But every time he would turn to leave the sanctuary and find the soldier's long form dozing against the wall in the far corner.

There was nothing left for Aitor to do in the town. His fragility was his curse. Word had spread of his attacks; they all saw his stiff movement, the dark circles under his eyes.

The Travelers were graceful about it, of course. He had offered to help? He didn't need to—this work wasn't suitable for him. They had it taken care of. Please, sit and rest.

And Aitor nodded, and sat, or wandered away, while inwardly he screamed, raged, begged for anything to do.

He no longer was a part of the gardening, the building, or the cooking. All he had left were his unfinished dreams of a beautiful church, and the Mass.

One evening, he slipped and fell moving from the raised platform to distribute Communion to the people.

Aitor lay breathing through his mouth while people gasped and rushed to his side. They turned him over, exclaimed again, prodded him, cushioned his head. He knew already that he was not badly injured, but there was dread, lingering, and not because a broken bone would have been a death sentence.

They helped him to his feet. "I am fine," he said, "I am well; let me continue."

"You should rest," Jacob said. "Perhaps it is too much to ask of you."

There was murmuring of agreement around him. A forest of hands herded him gently away from the altar to sit, and as Jacob returned to the altar to continue where he had left off, Aitor knew that what life he had in the community was truly over.

After all, what need was there for an old man when there were a hundred able bodies? What use for a surly priest who was haunted by nightmares and woke the village with his cries? Who mumbled to himself, answering questions no one else heard?

They did not mistreat him. Far from it. They provided him food; made sure to care for him. But he knew that they spoke of him with worry, and when they were not solicitously turning their attention on him, he was one more mouth to feed, an inconvenient decoration for their town.

The world of the Travelers turned smoothly without him. He said one Mass a week, after that. Then the Communion bread and wine ran out, and then there were no Masses at all.

Aitor came to the chapel the next evening anyways, only to find that there was no one there but Gisele. She knelt on the floor, taking down the crucifix, affixing it to a tall tent pole with rope and nails.

"What are you doing?" he shouted, and ran to her, crumpling to his knees ungracefully to batter at her hands, to fight for the mallet she held.

She fended him off easily, pulling the crucifix away from his scrabbling reach. There was no offense in her gaze. Of course there was not.

"Forgive me, Padre," she said. "We are moving it from the chapel so that we can see it more easily. The chapel is so far from us. We will worship in the square. The people asked Father Masalis and he gave his approval. You understand, don't you?"

Aitor understood, a little. And what could be wrong with moving a symbol of God to a place where it might watch over them? How could he argue? But he felt tears come to his eyes as he watched Gisele bear the crucifix out of the humble little chapel. Its place over the altar was starkly empty.

They put the crucifix by the large firepit, where it loomed up forbiddingly over the Travelers, its shape distorted by the flames.

That first night Aitor was there, standing alone with his back against a wall. The service began as it always did: a hymn, the readings from the waterproofed lectionary. The Travelers sat at rapt attention, their eyes fixed on Jacob.

In place of the homily, though, Jacob did not give forth words of wisdom or admonition. Instead he coaxed and cajoled them; he spoke of signs he had seen in their daily work.

And then he prophesied. God had spoken to him, he told them, telling him that their labor was good, and like the tribes of Israel they would now build God's holy nation. His voice was rich with laughter and joy. Let no one stand in their way. They walked with the favor of angels.

Aitor watched as Jacob transformed then from more than a man, more than a leader. Before his eyes, lit by the towering flames behind him, Jacob became to the Travelers a mouthpiece of God.

The chapel was forgotten, and from then on the city square became their place of worship, where Jacob prophesied for them every night.

Over time many of the Travelers were married, and several announced that they bore children. The anticipation of new life, even in a hard world, breathed new energy into the town.

The gardens were producing crops, enough that the excess could be dried and saved. The people built snares and lay them in the nearby trees and by the river, and so they had enough meat to cure and store as well. The fat was made into tallow; the candles into soap.

They had even captured a few animals that seemed domestic enough, happy to stand in the crude pens which were constructed for them, in exchange for shelter and what food could be scrounged. Now that they had livestock, some of the Travelers took it upon themselves to begin to train the animals to help in their labor.

With these and other advancements, the Travelers had settled comfortably into their new home. Life was returning to familiar old patterns, an echo of what they used to know.

And they were happy. Even Aitor saw it. They sang old songs, and began to make new. They were at peace, and grateful for every lie Jacob told them in his thunderous prophet's voice.

Only Aitor, it seemed, was not content. And he, alone and frightened of the darkness which grew within him, remained apart from the rest, hiding in the abandoned chapel. There he curled around his sketchbook, and planned a beautiful church for his God, praying that even if it were realized only in his dreams, he might find that God had been waiting for him there all along.

Then one morning they awoke to find the animals missing.

Uneasily, they dismissed it as a fluke, and sent out a party to seek and capture more. It was Noah who pointed out that the gate had been closed behind the missing beasts.

Weeks later, they were woken by a shout.

Aitor descended from his sleeping place and entered the town to shouting and chaos. Some of the guards pushed past him, racing to the perimeter to look for signs of entry. Others stood and wept dumbly out of shock. Still others shouted accusations at one another. Who was on watch last night? How could they have let this happen?

The storehouse doors had not been locked; there had been no need for locks. But now they stood wide open, and as Aitor pressed forward, he saw that the smoked meat and dried vegetables they had so carefully stockpiled were gone, leaving only a few scattered leftovers trampled in the sand.

The ground was too soft to read prints, but it was churned and pocked heavily, as if by many silent feet.

Jacob lost no time in doubling the watch, and sent a hunting party into the forest, more heavily armed this time. Usually only five or six would go, but this time they sent a full two dozen.

"You are going to find food," Jacob told them, as they left. "Food only. You are not hunting the thieves."

The air stunk of fear and rage as the remaining Travelers surveyed the bare storehouse, the scavenged gardens. Winter was coming, and the food that they had saved in preparation was gone.

Worse, though, was the idea of having been watched. Aitor felt the eyes on them as sharply as if they cut his skin. Once more, the Travelers walked pursued by a cloying paranoia that they had not felt for many days of safety.

It seemed that it had not occurred to any of them that after everything, there might be someone left.

For the first time since the cold had come, Aitor went into the desert. He took with him nothing and told no one.

In the growing cold, the wasteland seemed even more foreign; what life and warmth there had been which reminded them of Earth now sapped and gone. The dunes lay unruffled, the sky purple-orange and cloudless.

Aitor walked for a long time away from the city of the Travelers, up out of the dust bowl until he saw only long expanses of dirt and stunted vegetation, and the bare bones of fallen cities, visible as ghostly fingers, miles away.

There he knelt down, facing the unknown, and he prayed.

He prayed until night came, and the stars arrived in their cold glory above him. Undisturbed now by pollution and manmade light, the arm of the galaxy sprawled out across the sky, an impossibly beautiful purple wing.

Why are you angry, Aitor?

The small voice which asked the question could have come from himself or from anyone. He was too distressed to know. All around him there was a turbulent silence which seemed to strong to penetrate, a silence which whipped his soul into a lathered frenzy, a maddened and desperate thing.

I am angry because if there are Others, the Mission of our Order has been a waste. Fifty years of my life, for nothing.

But Aitor knew that was not why he was angry, selfish, bitter, lost. It could not have been a waste. Their mission had not been simply to exist as the last humans alive. It had not even been to preserve the human race. No. Their mission had been to pray for as long as time lasted, to bring Christ where there was none.

The mission had not been a waste.

Why are you angry?

In the violent silence of the desert, Aitor turned his head up to the sky and screamed until his throat was raw.

Nothing answered. The voice of God and the voices of those on *La Trascendencia* had nothing to say to him.

As he lowered his face into his hands, he did not at first see the hunched shapes gathered on the horizon.

It was only when Noah came to find him—shaking and sweat-drenched, despite the cold—that he noticed them, restless and shifting shadowy sentinels lined in neat rows.

They were so far away that they were tiny, dots barely larger than the tip of his finger. But even from that distance he felt their eyes on him, steady and unblinking.

As Noah picked him up and carried him back to the Travelers' camp they turned, one by one, and disappeared into the waste.

CHAPTER 12

PERHAPS TALIT WAS DEAD.

Her aching, battered body no longer felt any pain; her mouth and throat, which had been parched until they felt as if they were on fire, had the faint taste of sweet weedwine.

She lay atop a dune, and the wind blowing from the south was fragrant, and as familiar as a kiss. It stirred the sand around her into playful eddies that lapped at her as she rested.

It was full night, and even so, the world was warm, as it never could be when the sun was hidden. The moon hung incredibly close to her, as big as a shield she could reach up and touch, the sky a mass of stars so brilliant that they lit the world as bright as day.

The fact that she might be dead did not frighten her. The world, at this transcendent and eternal moment, was too beautiful to allow fear.

It seemed to her that the moon had drawn near, that the light of the stars wove together to create one greater, more unified light. Joy overtook her as she contemplated being engulfed by the sea of brilliance.

It seemed to her that the moon came closer, that the light of the stars wove together to create one greater, more unified light. A gentle joy overtook her as she contemplated being engulfed by the sea of brilliance.

It expanded, blooming closer and closer. Beyond—

With a peal as loud as a shout, a bell rang with a familiar voice: her bell, which hung in the tower of the Church of Prophet.

The sound of it was so close that she might have once again stood in her tower observing Morning Chant, looking down on the solemn faces of the pictures which guarded the Sazers in prayer. With it, the moon, the stars, the warm sea of sand—all were flung away, splintering into shards. She woke.

Her eyes were closed now, and she lay flat on her back, but this time there was pain. It infused her from the crown of her head to the tip of her toes, pulsing like a living thing.

Memory returned in waves as she lay there, trying to sip her air so it did not disturb her bones

Surely the dustwalker had killed her. How was she alive?

Or had it nearly done the job? Did she lie mangled and ruined in the sand, like the corpses of the criminals hung outside the City, with only hours left to her?

But even as she lay there, waiting again for the end, she realized that she could not be dead if she felt the blazing sun beating down upon her, and the discomfort of rocks against her back. And very close, there was the sound of running water, and the birds were calling again.

The memory of the dustwalker appeared, unbidden. She played it again and again in her mind. Her and Ziek, coming to the end of the desert, both slow and weak, shambling to a halt like broken dolls on strings.

The dustwalker, gliding from nowhere at an uncanny speed, savagely graceful, striking her so that she flew away from Ziek, limp prey, a crumpled heap. Looming over her, prepared to tear her flesh to shreds.

The dustwalker's grotesque body splayed out, so close to her that its heat burned her skin, its stench enveloped her. Spinning away from her suddenly, leaving her gasping for air—

She should not have lived. Perhaps she had, indeed, not lived. Maybe her bell had called her back, and now she was alive, in defiance of every one of the Sazers' stories.

Perhaps Prophet really had chosen to protect them.

And if she were truly alive, then, she thought, then perhaps Ziek could be too.

Every part of her wanted to get up, to look for him. But she was too hurt and worn to move, and the world swam around her. Even in her delirious half-paralysis, she felt tears of frustration burning her cheeks.

Drifting in this state for some time, she forced her mind away from thoughts of the dustwalker, hoping she could find the place with many stars again.

Instead, she dreamed of the Church of Prophet. In the dream she climbed the tower to ask the bell why it had woken her. Why it had bothered with a heretic who planned to kill a divinity? But she climbed for a hundred thousand years, and never reached the top.

At some point she was able to open her eyes, swimming up into half consciousness.

She lay on the ground beneath the harsh wildland sky, her head propped on something very hard. It was late afternoon.

It took every ounce of will she had to turn her head. Several excruciating moments later, she could see that she lay where she had fallen, on a broken pile of rock and dirt. The torch lay, extinguished, not too far from her.

"Ziek," she croaked. The fire had saved them, somehow. And then the sun had come, and driven the dustwalker away, after all; the stories were true. She thought of offering a prayer of thanksgiving—to whom, she did not know.

"Ziek," she said instead, louder.

Slowly, slowly, she took stock of her aches and pains. She tried to think as Mother would, as a hunter, always aware of danger first. Her shoulder and ribs were all heavily bruised; the back of her head throbbed as well. Her left arm, when she began to stir, felt as if it did not sit right in her shoulder. It had perhaps been twisted roughly by the pack on which she lay, skewed uncomfortably, as she fell.

The worst pain came from her side, and flared whenever she breathed. Broken ribs? She had broken her ribs before, falling from a low section of the belltower on one of her first runs, and had had to ask one of the older bellringers to take her duties.

This pain was similar, yet worse. Slowly she lifted her hand and brushed against it. It was wet to the touch.

But it did not matter, because now she saw Ziek.

He lay crumpled behind her, unmoving, as if dead. His chin had tipped back toward the sun to expose the purple, creeping veins of his neck.

Talit went to him, panic and pain making her clumsy and awkward as she half-scuttled, half-limped to his side.

His heartbeat was slow, almost too faint to detect, and his breathing was equally small and thin. Scrapes and deep bruises marked his side, starting at his cheek and vanishing down all of his arm and what she could see of his leg. But despite that, he was peaceful, his mouth turned in a smile.

Talit stopped and listened. They were near the forest, and it sung with the calls and howls of its birds, flitting from branch to branch. The sky had brightened to a brilliant pale green. Near them, the branches and foliage stirred as animals sought shelter from the heat.

Just Ziek and her, now. No dustwalkers hiding in every shadow, no dread prickling her skin or icing her bones until they froze solid inside her.

And somehow they were both safe and alive—some miracle of fire, of daylight—and at last, she thought, they could rest for a moment.

First things first. She ripped the hem of her tunic free and hesitantly lifted her shirt to see her wound.

The dustwalker's claws had torn two long, thin furrows in her, leaving ragged edges of flesh curling away in wet red smiles. She gagged as she saw it. The stench of dustwalker, of blood and hurt and death, filled her nose like a curse. She had made the injuries worse by moving, and now they seeped, staining her shirt even more.

It was agony to untangle the pack from where it had twisted around her shoulder. Her head was filled with ringing as she took the bone needle and the longthorn thread from the pack, and her hands shook so badly it took her five minutes to put the thread through the needle's eye.

Clean the wound, Mother would have told her, but she had nothing to clean it with; she did not trust the river water they had been drinking.

She set to work.

It was terrible. She thought, at times, that she would have preferred to die. But she remembered when the same had been done to Mother once, when she had been gored by a beast while hunting, and how though Talit had refused to watch, Mother had borne it bravely, and smiled afterwards, to show Talit that she was all right.

When it was finished she lay panting for long minutes, panting, her face wet with tears. But there was too much to be done to rest for long, and when she closed her eyes, she saw the dustwalker leaping toward her again, its mouth stretched wide, its blackened and twisted fangs slicing—

They could not travel by night any longer. When she closed her eyes she saw it again—the dustwalker's maw bearing down on her, the feeling of eternal loneliness as Ziek was ripped away from her, and then it was just her, falling, falling even as her body hit the ground.

Whatever had caused the dustwalker to leave them—whatever might have saved them—it might not happen again.

This peace could not last.

They had to go. They could eat as they went. She didn't want to spend any more time here than she had to. They would suffer the heat of the day as they traveled, and at night they would hide, more voiceless and motionless than the most humble of prey.

Ziek, though, remained asleep, as unchanged as the moment she had first woken and seen him.

Perhaps they could wait just a little longer. She had no idea how he had managed to survive. Would Prophet still take his soul willingly when the time came? Again, fear seized her. Let him rest as long as he could.

She wondered if he saw the place with stars when he slept. His body was betraying him, turning him into a hideous and wretched thing. And yet he smiled a child's smile.

Talit knelt down, let the packs slide to the ground, and took his hand in hers, and with her eyes closed, felt his pulse fluttering warm in her palm.

Did he really believe her lie? she wondered. Was that all that kept him going?

But she could never ask.

She opened her eyes. The sun glittered high and white, and she blessed the light with all her heart. If the night never fell again, she would not miss it.

Squeezing Ziek's hand, she said, "We have to go." The cruelty of her words was enough to make her heart wrench.

His eyes opened, but they did not focus on her. His bruised, vein-torqued face was squeezed strangely, as if he were trying very hard to remember something.

"Fire," he said. "Everything was on fire."

Talit remembered, but only vaguely. "Yes," she said, uncertain, looking again at the spent torch on the ground.

"The stone burned," Ziek said, his voice coming from him slowly, as if his tongue struggled to shape the words. He pointed.

Talit's heart squeezed inside her then, for she looked further now, and saw what she had not noticed before.

All around them in a perfect ring the ground was blackened and charred—as if a fire had exploded outwards from where they had been thrown to the ground.

Impossible, Talit thought; the ground here and all around was only stone and sand.

But there it was, undeniable; in places the sand had fused and become hard, glinting like stone through the layer of soot which covered it.

A set of bloody and blackened prints tracked away into the wilds, where a dustwalker had sought the comfort of shadows.

Awe passed over Ziek's face. He said, "It is like Storyteller says. It is a miracle. Prophet blesses our journey. The Lord will receive us."

It was the longest and most coherent thing he had said in days.

Talit did not answer him. The idea that the Lord waited for them—wanted them—was her lie and her shame. But there was a small hope blossoming in her now. What if it had been—somehow, gloriously, wonderfully—true? What if Prophet did guide their steps?

What if he, who had suffered in his alien form for thousands of years, his spirit prostrate at the foot of the throne of the Lord, grew tired of tyranny and suffering just as she did?

She put her hand to her belt for the first time. Her mother's knife waited there, warmed by sunlight.

"We are safe, but only for now," she said. "Come on."

His eyes flickered, and focused on her. "You are injured," he said.

And you are dying. "It doesn't matter. We have someone to meet, and it can't wait."

She helped him stand. He didn't argue, only took up his share of their load, but she saw now that there was a strange look on his face, a look she couldn't read.

They left the clearing, keeping the river again to their left as they began again on their destinationless, hopeless journey. Ziek moved slowly, but without her help, finding himself a strong stick to lean upon.

As they followed the water, it grew narrower and faster, and Talit realized that the ground was sloping steadily upwards. The trees became sparser, and she saw that the long expanses of brush-stippled hills flanking them were foothills leading to something grander, something even higher.

They walked until a few hours before nightfall, where Talit found them a small cave in an overhang of large gray rocks near the river inhabited only by a few insects and tiny scaled beasts that flickered their tongues and ran from her when she tried to catch them. She was too injured and tired to hunt, and so their dinner was a small fish that wandered into their nets, and that was all.

They curled under the animal skins by the smoking remains of their fire as darkness grew, beaten into a fatigued haze. Talit's stomach pulsed with a continuous ache that seemed to wash her further into unconsciousness with every beat. When Ziek finally spoke, she was only barely awake.

"Did you see it, too?" he said, his breath ruffling her hair.

Talit floated back to wakefulness. "See—?"

"The fire," Ziek said, and even with her eyes closed, she could hear the smile in it. "It was so beautiful, Talit."

"No—I didn't get a good look—did you see what happened?" Talit whispered. Hoping, maybe, that he would reveal that he had seen a miracle. That Prophet himself had descended from the sky to save them—

But Ziek did not respond, at least not in a way that she could understand. His voice had trickled into fervent mumbles that made no sense, into gibberish. She felt his body rack with a spasm of pain. He raved of flames, and climbing towards the sky on an endless ladder. Of a freezing face that was forever, of burning, too, always burning. It did not matter how many times she asked him what he had seen. It was as if he had forgotten it entirely.

Talit squeezed her eyes shut against tears, but she felt them pop out anyway. They huddled under the same blanket, only inches away, her face tucked into the hollow of his bruised, melting neck. Yet as he tried to tell her what he thought he had seen—in a delusion she had given life, and in words that could not come to his faltering tongue—he felt so very far away.

Much later, as she was half-drifting off, he spoke again, his words clear once more.

"You should have seen it, Talit," he said. "If you looked too long, you might die of happiness."

CHAPTER 13

A s the day wore on, the Travelers' settlement seethed with unease.
Ahead of them lay starvation; they imagined the unknown thieves
around every corner, lurking just out of view.

There was blame to be laid everywhere. It was Jacob's fault that no
one had thought to secure the storehouse. It was the fault of the guards
on watch, who had not seen their visitors. No—the people who had constructed the storehouse in the first house were to blame.

There was murmuring of discontent, but there was also shouting.

Jacob prayed with them and consoled them. From his lookout above
the little town, Aitor could hear him as he called out to them from the
square. God will see fit to provide, he told them. All day he apologized,
reassured, ministered, mediated.

No one required anything of Aitor. He was free to sit in the abandoned chapel, letting their clamor fade into the background.

He contemplated the empty spot where the crucifix had been.

Ad maiorem Dei gloriam, he told himself. *God is pleased with my
sacrifice. Will not my reward be great?*

He could not have eaten even if there was food to be had.

The hunting party Jacob had sent returned later in the evening. Aitor saw at once, even from a distance, that they were covered in blood,
and bore large sacks.

As they came into the town, the Travelers flooded from their homes
to crowd around, shouting questions. What had happened? Who had
done this to them? Did they bring back food?

The story was told by all the hunters at once, boisterous and angry.
It took several tries before it was clear what had happened.

The hunting party had set off in an eastern direction, following
the river, and their usual hunting grounds. They had found evidence

of passing—vague tracks, scattered vegetables half-buried in the sand, trampled plants.

They had come upon a rudimentary camp—just a pit that had been scrabbled into the sand, and some rough-made walls, a few stones piled together to keep out wind. Within the camp there had been a dozen creatures, and their stolen food, bundled into the rough-made sacks the Travelers had made.

At the mention of creatures, the Travelers' rejoicing grew subdued. Creatures, they said. Creatures?

The hunting party fell all over themselves answering. Creatures—more like monsters. No, they had been human-shaped. No, someone else argued, they had had extra limbs, skewed faces; they walked hunched and their skins were tough and hard and not the color of flesh at all. No, not tough skins—they were covered in open wounds; they shrieked like demons—no, they didn't speak at all—

At this a cry went up from the Travelers, a hundred voices talking at once. Bad enough that their food had been stolen. Now it had been stolen by grotesque creatures out of a child's nightmare.

Did they see you?

They will hurt us.

What are they? Are they animals?

Humans?

—Both?

Oh God, said one of the Travelers, close to Aitor. How could this happen?

The shouting grew, and then the hunters were shouting back. It doesn't matter, they cried. The beasts are dead. We shot them.

Jacob pushed his way to the front of the crowd, and like magic, a hush fell. The words of the last hunter to speak hung heavy in the air.

"They are dead?" Jacob repeated, voice neutral.

One of the men stepped forward to speak for them. Amir, who was a tall and handsome man who had once worked a comfortable desk job as a civil engineer. His face was streaked with sweat and mud, and his shirt had been rent apart to expose a wound opening the front of his chest which was caked with grime and blood, and yet seeped openly.

His words earlier had been boastfully reassuring. Now he sounded strained.

When they had entered the camp, the creatures had woken from their sleep and confronted them, howling and charging them in an attack.

The Travelers had been threatened by their hellish faces and open jaws, the long claws and the grasping hands, and had opened fire.

But they had been outnumbered, two to one, and they fell just as any prey would when it was pumped full of bullets.

They would not trouble the Travelers again, Amir promised, but the promise had no bravado this time.

There was a murmur. The hunting party drew together, some with far-off stares.

"And it was they who attacked first," said Jacob.

"Yes," said Amir, and the others nodded, shuffling closer together.

"Did they carry weapons?" Jacob said.

"No."

There was a long pause. Then Jacob said, "Perhaps they will leave us now. We are strong in number and have our guns. If they had no weapons then they will fear us greatly. We will set a watch over the storehouse tonight, and God will watch over us."

After the people had returned to their cookfires to make their dinners of the spoils which the hunters had retrieved, Jacob remained in the square. His expression was flat and grim.

Aitor stayed, too. He knew what Jacob was thinking. For a moment, even his turbulent resentment towards Jacob was numbed, overwhelmed by the fear that yawned in his belly.

"Fools," Jacob said.

"Yes."

"He was lying."

"Yes." Amir and the hunters had attacked first—out of fear, desperation, vengeance. Their eyes had spoken the truth.

Jacob put a hand on his forehead, rubbing back his hair.

"You said nothing to them," Aitor said, and almost, almost regretted his sharp tone.

"Would it have done any good?" Jacob's gaze snapped to him unerringly, even in the gathering dark. "They know what they have done. And now there will be war. We will have to strike first, while we might have an advantage."

"Must there be war?" Aitor said. "Could we not seek peace?" Even saying it, though, Aitor felt his stomach twisting to imagine what it was the hunters had seen. Whatever had happened at the camp, their visceral terror and disgust at the sight of the creatures had been real.

Surely they must be abominations, the accursed left over from a disease-riddled world long ago. Whatever they were would no longer have any semblance of humanity.

"Peace," said Jacob, tasting the word slowly. "When will we ever find peace?"

"We should leave them alone. Maybe they will not retaliate. Maybe they will do nothing."

"Do nothing?" Jacob laughed, and there was something too bright, too sharp, in his laughter. "Even after everything we have seen, you still believe that what will happen is *nothing*?"

"What if they are human? How could we do this to them?"

"You have seen what humans can do," Jacob said. "If I did not think they could be human, I would not think they would retaliate. And if they are, then how can you argue that God has not abandoned us?"

Aitor turned away from him wordlessly. He would go to his sleeping place on the ridge, and there he knew he would think of what Jacob had asked him. He would think about it until he wished he could die.

As he brushed past Jacob, a hand on his arm stopped him.

"Aitor."

And the feel of physical contact once again brought Aitor to a trembling halt, wanting more, clinging to the memory of it, a starved man.

"Tell me you understand," Jacob said. "Tell me the truth."

Aitor could not meet his eyes. He stood, his head downturned. "I understand."

That frightening energy surged in Jacob again. Aitor did not have to see it to feel it—tipping the world around him in that strange way, leaving just them, their souls very close together. "Why does He not just come?" Jacob demanded, his voice very low. "How could he not forgive one who despairs, when He does not even dare to show His face to bring hope? I dare Him to come. I dare Him to stop this. For your sake, Aitor, I dare Him. If only so you can finally see that He will not."

This time Aitor had no answer. This was what they had always been taught: the sin of despair, the unforgiveable offense, the turning of man's back to God.

Have I turned? Aitor thought. How can I turn my back upon someone if I do not know where they stand to begin with?

Jacob stared at him in the twilight, his eyes full, hands twisting into the cassock at his side. It was Aitor who turned away first, his steps slow.

Behind him, Jacob said, "You should sleep in the town tonight. To be safe."

Aitor walked faster. He did not want to listen. He could not be near Jacob, not right now. He could not look at him. In Jacob there was a tragedy they shared; a desperation which shamed him to consider.

"Please," Jacob said. "Aitor."

Without looking at him, Aitor turned his course for the rectory. Jacob did not follow.

Noah was waiting for him there, his expression grave. He, too, knew what the Travelers' hunting party might have done. And he seemed to understand, too, that Aitor could not stay at the rectory, not tonight. In silence he put his arm out for Aitor.

Noah's home was spartanly vacant—only small stacks of his belongings, neatly arranged. He had constructed himself an elevated bed; there he had already placed Aitor's bedroll, while his own sat on the floor by the near wall, tucked into a heavily-laden pack.

But Noah did not immediately move to help Aitor to roll out his blankets, to climb onto the bed and pull the covers around him. He stood poised by the door, his hand at his belt, where his gun sat loaded at his hip. The hard square edges of his jaw and shoulder seemed harder and tighter, tonight.

Aitor, remembering the war in which Noah had deserted his honor to escape, whispered without thinking, "I am sorry."

Noah shook his head then, and when he turned to look at Aitor there was a wry sadness to his expression. "Let's go, Father," he said. "We can leave, tonight."

For a moment Aitor imagined the two of them, swallowed by the vast expanses of the waste, seeking the old world. In his imagination, the two of them were haloed by amber light, a sign of God's promise, that something good would be waiting. As the soldier carried the old man over the final hill, they would cross into a beautiful new Eden, and at the base of a verdant valley there would be a church waiting for them, a church with open doors—

But: "I am old," he whispered. "Noah, I am too old." A pause. "And I cannot leave Jacob."

Noah said nothing, but his eyes held neither judgment nor anger. His hands were gentle as always as he helped to lay Aitor down and to pull the blankets tight around him.

Even long after, Aitor could hear him, pacing quietly in the small room, and he could not speak past the lump in his throat to thank him.

In the morning, the Travelers emerged from their homes to harsh cawing, and a chill gray dawn. Aitor stepped out behind Noah into the cold, his arms wrapped around himself.

The sky around the square was filled with circling birds, screeching displeasure at having been interrupted. They made a dark cloud; occasionally one of them would stoop, only to think better of it, and rejoin its fellows in the sky.

As what they were circling over came into view, Aitor felt his blood run cold. Beside him, Noah let out a stifled blasphemy.

Two Travelers had been staked to the doors of the storehouse, spreadeagle. Their tunics were bloodied and strained over swollen flesh, which abuse and decay had marbled hues of purple, gray, and blue. Aitor recognized them, if only barely: the leaders of the expedition who went to reclaim their food. Simon. Amir.

Amir had been one of those who had married. Now his widow's voice lifted in a wail above the others' shocked silence.

Someone else's voice joined hers, shrill and panicked. "Who was on watch last night? Who has let this happen?"

The question was answered minutes later. The Travelers who had been on watch had been knocked unconscious and lay, cold and sick, at their posts.

They were woken and asked how many had come. There had been more than three dozen of them, the guards told them. A flood of the creatures.

What did they look like? the Travelers demanded, eager for another garish painting of the Enemy they faced, half in hope that it might be better, that the images the hunting party had carried had been exaggerated in the heat of battle, half in morbid fear that it would be worse.

They were beasts from hell, the guards told them. Part-animal, pocked and tumored and twisted. Some had extra limbs, many had skewed faces, as if a sadist had created a parody of humanity. They wore tattered rags sewn with teeth and bones, the clothing making a mockery of their deformities.

Just outside the compound, the sand had been trampled by far more than three dozen feet. And within the storehouse, their food had been taken, and replaced with heaps of rotting offal.

Jacob took down the bodies, and buried them just behind the chapel. Amir's wife's low keening set them all on edge. Those who had gone on the hunting expeditions watched with ashen faces.

Aitor spent the day in the chapel, when everyone else had left. Various people shadowed in and out to kneel behind him. He barely noticed their passing.

He prayed for peace, over and over, a simple prayer in his own language. He prayed also for the souls of the departed, wherever they might be.

Later, he dozed, and dreamed of war. Fiction and memory blurred together in a hellish nightmare he could never escape. Even with his eyes half open, he could see the final day on earth so clearly.

Aitor had never seen fighting up close; the Front had never reached close enough. But he had seen enough war for ten lifetimes. After the tumult of the instruments of war, what came home was almost always silent. Broken people without shelter; injured shells of people whose spirit had left them alive and empty.

He and Jacob and Mateusz had worked tirelessly, ministering to the dead and dying. He remembered how it had felt as if the blood would never leave his hands, no matter how he washed.

Was this how that last war had begun? he thought. One small act of violence—one unforgiveness—one shot in the night that started it all?

What had it felt like? A soldier, lifting his gun, squeezing the trigger—had his thoughts been scattered, terrified, only for his own defense? Or had it been calculated and angry, fueled with hatred for his foe?

That night, the Travelers' prayer gathering began early, before dark had set in, and Aitor was still in the chapel when he heard the singing begin.

The sound of it was discordant and melancholy tonight. The odd thought struck him that he wished that there had been music, aboard *La Trascendencia*. The sound of it these days brought him always to the edge of tears.

Noah lay asleep in the shadows by the chapel door, where he had been keeping watch. Tonight his pose was oddly childish; he curled his legs to him, his cheek pressed against the palm of his long and callused hand. A rush of tenderness came over Aitor; he raised one hand to bless the sleeping soldier, and then stepped quietly over his sleeping frame, and walked alone to the square.

All of the Travelers were congregated there, save for the dozen who stood atop the city walls, backs stiff. They carried their guns loaded. They would not risk playing with spears and clubs tonight.

Jacob stood atop a platform—altar, Aitor thought, before he could stop himself—with his back to the firepit, which burnt low and steady behind him. A full six feet above the people, he loomed above them all, with only the crucifix on its stake higher than he.

He sang with them, head thrown back. He was a picture of holy beauty. The fire beneath him hollowed his cheekbones, cast his eyes into pits of shadow, outlined him with a sacred glow. The Travelers lifted their hands.

Aitor lingered near the edge of the crowd, transfixed, his stomach churning. It was beautiful and false, he thought, built on a lie. Or did that matter?

The song swelled, and came to an end. There was a hush as the people waited.

A voice raised suddenly. "Prophesy!"

"Prophesy," someone else called. A handful of the people took up the cry.

Jacob turned his head upwards, as if he bent an attentive ear to a God who stood just behind him, waiting to deliver counsel.

There was a brief lull, in which the wind blowing over the desert hushed, and the world was silent.

When at last he spoke, his voice was deep and seemed to carry with it the power of the fire which rose and fell around him, the age and weight of another world. His eyes had rolled back in his head, and he had thrown his arms wide. The muscles of his neck and shoulders seemed to strain like wire beneath his skin.

There was a berserk light in Jacob's eyes as he threw back his head and shouted a long string of words in Greek; it seemed as if the glow of the fire were a pool of radiance that had gathered around his feet to touch him, the beautiful apostate.

How Aitor loved him in that moment. It was a fierce and sardonic love that closed round his heart like claws. One might look upon him and never see him as a liar. An unbeliever might stand beneath his shadow and look up into his eyes and believe in God.

Only Aitor knew that this was Jacob maddened, daring God to strike him down. That he waited for the divine hand to stop the oncoming slaughter, or if not that, then at the least, to stop Jacob himself.

It was, Aitor thought, the cruelest irony.

The people swayed beneath him, transfixed.

Once again Jacob affirmed them as the people of the Divine. He told them that God had found favor in His people, that the souls of Simon and Amir had been found pleasing to him in their sacrifice for the Travelers.

Humanity had tried to end the world, long ago, but these holy few, the Travelers, God had preserved—and the world, now, was left to them.

The Beast, the Deceiver, Jacob shouted, had sent his creatures to destroy them. If they were man at all, they were the descendants of those who had wrecked the world, those who had not been chosen to bring restoration, twisted beyond repair.

There was a roar of approval. Aitor saw the relief of the people as the threat was simplified into something they understood without guilt, giving it a face, giving them a purpose.

They waited as Jacob wove on his feet before them, his arms stretched out. He cried out again in Greek, one long rapturous breath— then waited, his head tilted a little, as if he listened.

They waited breathlessly, enraptured, for him to calm, to return from whatever sacrosanct place he had gone.

God urged them to wait, Jacob said. To plan and to grow, to defend carefully while their strength was small. To give the beasts no indication of retaliation, to hide and to build a strong nation of God's chosen, the humans who had come to cover the face of the Earth in His image.

Murmuring, then; a mix of consternation and agreement at once.

Jacob was not finished.

When the time came, he said, God had promised to stand with them. To see them through a holy war. They would avenge the death of their brothers: eye for an eye, tooth for a tooth. Let the hounds of hell fall to the wrath of God and His people. The enemy would come under their heel, and they would be trampled down like the mire of the streets.

And Aitor watched as the people gave their assent—at first under their breaths, hushed and low, and then swelling into a shout of galvanized pride.

Jacob did not let the cheer grow. He pointed up to the crucifix which jutted over him, its arms outspread to encompass them all.

"This is the God of nations," he told them. "So long as He is with us, all will be well."

And the people answered him: *AMEN*.

Then a Traveler pushed through the crowd leading an animal from the pens.

Sacrifice, he called. Let us assure the favor of God.

The rest of them took up the chant, worked into a frenzy, unified by their fear, by the savage heretic beauty of Jacob on his altar, by the vicious fire which licked at the sky and filled them all with bloodlust.

And so there on the altar, they tied it down and Jacob slit its throat, declaring it pleasing to the Lord.

With the animal dead and its blood sprayed across the altar, its body consumed in the fire, the Travelers concluded their ceremony with a song, and they returned to their homes for the night. They walked more upright, and their faces glowed; the fear they had felt upon finding Simon and Amir was defiance, now.

They were the people of God.

It was Gisele whom Aitor caught leaving the square, Gisele who had been kind to him in the early days, who had been one of the first to help with the construction of the chapel. She had become, in this time, as close to Jacob's right hand as she could be when there was no real official leader of the people. It was her whom Jacob consulted about many things, to whom he delegated many of the important tasks of his leadership. And so, despite her kindness to him, Aitor had not been able to bring himself to speak with her in the weeks since their arrival.

Hard work and sun had weathered her face; she was so tan now that her skin seemed as if it were made of leather. In contrast, her pale eyes stood out sharply, keen, and colder than they had been.

"Please," he said to her, reaching out to catch her arm. She came to a stop beside him. "Will you answer a question?"

Her expression held the same gentle pity to which Aitor had slowly accustomed himself. She looked at him almost fondly, as a mother would a child. "Yes, padre, of course."

"Do you believe him?" Aitor said. "Do you believe he truly is a prophet?"

Gisele was silent for a long moment. "You know I did not believe in God, before."

"No. Many of you did not. But now you all worship and sing and now you sacrifice. You have attended the Masses. Do you believe now?"

"Do you not?"

Aitor flared with the bitter white heat of anger. "I do not believe in Jacob, because he does not believe," he said. Saying it aloud felt wrong, terrifying. As if Jacob's secret might unbalance the world from its axis. But he plunged forward. "He makes it up. He wishes to control and placate you, and that is all."

Gisele laughed, then. It sounded surprised. "Padre," she said. "Even if we know he does not hear God, we wish to be placated."

And then she pulled open the front of her tunic and exposed her torso to him. Even in the half-dark, Aitor saw plainly what she showed him. A few inches below her collarbone there was a discolored lump. It stuck out like a strange knuckle from her skin. Around it, her veins radiated from it as if they had been drawn to the surface with suction, bruised and dark and malicious. The skin around it had peeled and was ghastly pale and riddled with burst blood vessels; it was beginning to slough, chunks of it clinging to the fabric of her tunic.

Aitor's words caught in his throat. Gisele's face tightened, and she jerked the front of her tunic together again, but her eyes remained fixed on his, in a kind of forced defiance.

"How many?" Aitor breathed.

"I do not know." Her smile was bitter as she waited for Aitor to say something, anything. But when he did not, and she spoke again, her voice was gentle. "I know this is not how it always was," she said. "But if there was a God—so what, if He is gone? Jacob makes Him real for us, and as long as we hold to that, we hold to ourselves. Otherwise, we are lost."

Crippling sorrow swept through Aitor. He could not take this away from them, nor could he accept it. If he could blindly accept Jacob's words—if he could wish away what he knew—life would be sweeter. Even to know, and to choose ignorance anyway, as Gisele had, might be easier.

But he had been cursed with the knowledge of something more, perhaps even before Jacob confessed his secret. Perhaps it had started earlier, when he was a young boy tugging on the cassock of Padre Aguilera, begging to know who or where the Watcher in stars might be.

It was not enough.

"And," Gisele said, her gaze seeking his, begging understanding, "those creatures are what have made us sick—then to be rid of them— maybe there is some hope for us, at least."

Aitor said, "You know that it is not them."

She snorted softly. "You're a good man," she said. "But you are old enough to accept that we will die. Most of us are not." And she put her hand on his arm, briefly, before she left him standing in the street.

Aitor went to the altar where Jacob had prophesied. There, he climbed the rough stone stairs, and he stood directly beneath the hideous crucifix. He felt himself trembling, full of too much to express.

I will not yield, he shouted in Spanish at the crucifix, at its suffering face, its gaping mouth, its huge tortured eyes staring back at him.

From the edge of the square, Jacob stood and watched him, a silent black figure.

Aitor did not notice him or care. The air around him seemed to have compressed, to have grown small and hot and full. It held him as if he were a fly pinned to a board. It battered him. It was movement within stillness; it was a presence nowhere. It pushed him to shattering; it cradled him.

He was at once filled with boundless joy and an immeasurable wrath. Again he cried out: *You will not break me! I will not yield! I will believe!*

He stood there listening to the silence roaring back at him. For a long time he listened.

At last he wiped at the fouled stone altar with his cassock. If it were to be a place of worship, let it at least be clean.

But the cassock did not help; the blood merely smeared, and dried, black and forbidding. When he looked up at the crucifix once more, he saw that it had spattered across the feet of the wooden Christ. Clutching his soiled cassock to him, he made no effort to clean it.

Aitor descended the platform, hugging the tattered remains of his cassock to him, and returned to the chapel. He passed Jacob, who stood wordless, and watched him go.

It shamed him that he could not stop thinking about Gisele's hand on his arm, thinking of how perhaps the disease now crawled in him as well—that even as he lay there now, humanity was being eaten away from him.

Sucked away, bit by bit, until he could not build the Church for which the Superior General had asked, until he was nothing more than a forgotten worm in the dirt. Then he would look in shame upon his ruined form, and he would die because not even the left-over image God was left to him.

CHAPTER 14

TALIT AND ZIEK HAD COME to the end of the hills. The trees turned into stiff, short scrub that carried a sharp, tangy scent, and the ground grew rocky and sharp. Then on the third day of this, the scrub grew sparse, leaving only rock, which seemed to ascend forever.

Talit looked back often. On clear days, she imagined she could see the city of Saze glinting up at her from the distance, where the desert was only the width of her hand outstretched, when she squinted with one eye. She had never been so high in her life, never seen such a steep or enormous hill.

Now that the river was narrower and the terrain steeper, its banks made now of pale orange rock instead of soft sandy soil, their travels had slowed even further. They kept close to the water, for the sun beating down on them as they walked in the day made their thirst too great for what they could carry in their skins.

Game had become even scarcer, only small and frightened creatures. Soon they were forced to start in on the hunters' rations in their packs. Once in a while they caught tiny fish, but they never lasted more than a mouthful. Talit found that some of the shrubs bore small, alien fruit, and after a careful examination and tasting, they ate those, too.

Occasionally, Talit saw bigger animals in the distance, watching them—large, tough-looking creatures with many-pronged horns. They were fleet, though, and bounded away when she came too close.

They would sleep for as long as they dared—four hours, maybe five—always with Talit sitting up an extra hour to keep silent watch. Then they would go on.

Ziek was not always lucid. There were times he woke from his sleeping without recognizing her at all. Sometimes it lasted for minutes; other times for hours. He moved with his mouth hung slack and drooling, his chin slumped to his chest. With simple obedience he plodded after Talit, leaning on his walking stick.

The first time he had gone silent and unresponsive, she had wept. For a whole morning she listened to his feet shuffle-drag across the rocks, tried to catch him as he stumbled forward, heedless of any obstacles.

When she had had no more tears, they went on. And when the sun reached its highest point, she stopped, and thought that maybe she could not go on any more, not in the deafening silence.

And then a hand had touched her face. Ziek turned her chin so that he could see her face.

"Don't worry, Talit," he said, his voice dry and cracked. "We'll be there soon."

The vacancy in his eyes came again, later that afternoon, and again in the evening. She could not get used to it, could not help but to think that every time his eyes went slack, it was the last time.

The feeling of being watched had returned. Talit chose a smooth, flat stone from the river and when Ziek was asleep, she sat a short distance away and sharpened her mother's knife. When she walked, its handle in her palm comforted her.

It would do her no good if the dustwalker struck again—they had no kindling for fire, and no more grew—but it allowed her to pretend that it might.

And she looked to the future. They could not go back, and so they moved forward. The knife she held was both a promise and a wish.

She dreamed, both waking and sleeping, of the day that they would find the Lord's house.

It would be a tall and beautiful dwelling, twenty times the size of any Sazer home. The floors would be covered in the tanned skins of rich and exotic beasts; its yellow stone walls would be buffed until they glimmered, and painted in the finest artisans' work. The entryway would be long, longer than any entry she had ever seen before.

She would come at night, when all was dark. And yet the Lord would be expecting her; all the torches on the walls would be lit.

She would enter, in the guise of a supplicant, her head lowered as she came into his house.

He would be sitting in his dwelling. Perhaps he would have been eating, or sleeping, or however he entertained himself, and yet when he heard of her coming, he would have put aside everything, and he would be waiting for her.

"This is how I will do it," she told Ziek, once, as he slept. She kept watch atop a rock a short distance away, looking out across the world from above. "I will come close . . . I will get on my knees. I will beg for him to return. I will kiss his feet. I will promise to do anything for you."

Ziek's face had grown swollen and distorted. The veiny disfiguration which had crawled up his neck had pressed outward from his jaw, and it stood out from his face like a ridge.

To her surprise, he turned his head slightly, and opened his eyes to smile at her. The smile, for those few moments, was so perfectly radiant that she could forget the Burdening.

When Ziek closed his eyes again, even long minutes after, she did not dare finish her thought aloud.

And holding the knife, secret in my hand, I will reach to embrace him, and—

But even that moment was somehow too much to contemplate. Instead she looked out across the land spread out below them.

The world was bigger than she had ever imagined before. It curved out away from her like the stories of the ocean which the Storyteller told, of a body of water so wide that you could not swim it, that was a hundred spans wide, and so deep that the bottom had never been found.

It made it seem impossible that in such a huge world, she would be able to find the one person who could put things right. But she had, now, a growing conviction that she would.

How else could they have survived so long? All odds spoke against it. It must be Prophet.

A part of her had begun to believe the lie they had told. She clung to the part of her that whispered this, that gave her hope as they climbed.

And climbed. Their skin peeled and blistered, and their bodies begged for rest, but still they climbed.

On their second day of climbing, the river came to an end.

It was midday, and Talit had been planning on walking for a few more hours, at least as long as Ziek could. They had followed the ever-narrowing stream on a narrow and winding path, staying carefully close to its meandering curves. At times they had followed it by ear, when the path grew too treacherous.

Now it was gone.

What had been the river ended in a tiny spring which rose from a small crack between rocks, little more than a puddle.

Talit stopped dead as she saw it. She tried not to let panic sweep her away, but she could not ignore the angry buzzing that began in the back of her skull and grew until it seemed to rattle her bones.

Follow the river, Mother said. Follow the river.

There was a seemingly endless ascent ahead; there was a sharp blue sky. They had reached a small plateau, and around them the walls of rock were striated with many layers of color. There were remnants of trees, dried and gnarled and sun-drained to white.

And there was no one, not even a trace that someone else might have passed this way.

Talit felt her thoughts scattering. They would die here, on this hill; they would die in the desert; it did not matter.

"Talit," said Ziek. It was the first thing he had said in days. He was already ahead of her, moving past the spring, further up and further in. He now hunched over his stick, waiting for her. He looked almost as he did when he prepared to race her up the belltower, eager and impatient. Alive. Awake.

She stared at him. "Where are you going?" she said.

Ziek turned, and began to walk without her.

The buzzing of her thoughts had increased. She caught up with him easily. "Ziek," she said, and she caught at him, tried to see what he was seeing. "Where are you going?"

He tried to shake her off. "This way," he told her.

"Ziek, we don't know what's there. This is the end of the water. We can't keep going." She pulled back at him, and he was too weak to fight her.

"This way," Ziek said again, insisting, and he pointed upwards. It wasn't the same way they had been climbing earlier; his finger tracked to the top of a towering, dusty ridge, a huge shelf of rock jutting into space high above them. "Do you see?"

Talit did not see. "We could go back," she said. "We could ask them to forgive us."

But even as she spoke, she knew that they could not go back. Ziek would not live that long. To go back now was death.

"We are so close," Ziek said. "I know we are."

"How?" she said, even though she knew that she would not understand his answer.

But he did not give her any answer at all, only cocked his head and listened to something that only he heard. Then he pulled away from her with a startling burst of strength, and walked on without her.

Talit followed him with feet that felt as if they were made of stone. Their waterskins were full, but that would not last. They could chase Ziek's delusion, but how could they be sure they were going the right way?

But it no longer mattered, she realized.

They ascended beyond the plateau, and the sun began to drop in the sky. The ground became even more tenuous; the rocks were too small and fine for their feet to find purchase. They scrabbled and slid and fell until their legs were shredded and bleeding.

Talit felt the pain as a faint sting. What clarity she had had as she walked earlier seemed to have left her. A part of her had expected to come across Lanon standing by the river, waiting for her, just as Mother had said. He would look just as she remembered him from all those seasons ago. He would make the mark of the Sazers in greeting, and then they would embrace one another.

She had always expected this, even if she had not admitted it to herself.

In the late afternoon, Ziek's mind slipped away again. She knew it by the way his limping walk suddenly turned into an aimless stagger. This time he did not stop, as he usually did, and stare at nothing until she coaxed him or dragged him. Instead he blundered slowly forward, his glazed eyes fixed on something above him, and though his eyes were blank, his course remained straight.

Before Talit could catch him, he sprawled forward like a bag of bones, striking his chin and cheek against the ground.

She walked to him. It was a dull sort of dread she felt, resigned, tormented by the knowledge that there would come the time when he would not get up again.

But when she pulled him to his feet again, he began to move forward again, and she could not stop him, not by tugging at him, nor pleading, nor crying.

He walked on, and she held on to his arm as he went. All she could do, she thought, was follow him wherever his madness took him, until it finally consumed him, and he moved no more.

They walked for hours, and for those hours Talit was terrified to stop, terrified that if she let go, he would just shamble onwards and upwards, until he made a misstep, or came to a cliff's edge he did not see, and go plummeting to his death. She forced herself onward with a parched throat and a stomach bloating with emptiness and pain. The world seemed to narrow down to a sliver around her. If she had ever imagined that the world was too big, she could not imagine it now.

She began to see things as she walked. For a while the world seemed as if it were peeling apart, the ground before them ripped up at the seams to curl around them. Chunks of ice hurled from the sky and pelted them, and she felt not a thing. The rocks sprouted flowers that climbed with them as they ascended, egg-yolk yellow and searing orange, and the blue of shallow stream water at noon. When she reached to pick them, they turned into white birds, and fled from her hand.

It was growing dark when Ziek finally collapsed. Talit could no longer hold him up. The two of them fell together, and they slid in the gravel for a short way before coming to a halt, tangled.

As she pulled herself away from him, cursing softly to herself, she saw that his mouth was moving silently, and life was coming back to his face.

"What?" she whispered, her voice a hoarse creak.

Ziek was repeating the same thing, again and again, but it wasn't until he had repeated himself the tenth time that she understood what he was trying to tell her.

"The Lord is waiting for us," he was saying. "He was here—he is waiting—"

Delirium, Talit thought. She pulled her sweat-soaked pack from her shoulders and found the waterskin with shaking hands. They had to ration it, she told herself, but she couldn't stop herself from taking a deep draught, even though her stomach, aching and unaccustomed, cramped painfully.

She gave Ziek a drink, holding the waterskin for him as he lay where he had fallen, and then half a ration of jerky and sun-dried fruits. He ate automatically, his eyes far away, while Talit devoured hers faster than she had known she could eat. Even the smoky, dull taste of the food had become rich and incomprehensibly good.

When she had licked the ration packet and her fingers clean, she at last looked up and was able to take stock of their surroundings.

They had come to the top of the ridge Ziek had indicated. They were higher, now, than ever; it felt as if they were climbing into the belly of the sky itself. Even the emerging moon and the stars felt like they were leaning down, a fragment of her dream.

They were surrounded by fingers of stone and large rock formations which rose around them like watchers of a solemn ritual. Looking back, they were now too high to see the land which they had crossed what seemed like ages ago. Now there was only the hill behind them.

Talit looked ahead, then, and caught her breath.

Ahead, the forever-hill no longer loomed to encompass everything. Instead, it fell away on both sides of the shelf on which they rested, coming to a gentle peak not too far away.

They had reached the end, and yet it was not the end.

The sky blossomed all around them, a riot of pink of gold and deepening blue; the sun was nearly gone. And jutting into this joyous explosion of color were more hills.

They were bigger than hills, though, Talit thought; and she wished she knew a name for them. They were the great-great-grandfathers of the hills she had crossed before, stretching out in a long row as far as she could see, until they clouded with distance and became only faint upward streaks of shadow.

It looked like the uneven spine of a huge beast, perhaps like the giant lizards of which Storytellers spoke. Once, it was said, they had roamed the world and wreaked destruction in order to survive, and when the world was broken at last, they had all gone to their peaceful sleep beneath the surface of the earth, their only wish in life granted to them.

A feeling stretched wide inside of Talit's heart, so big he could not comprehend it, as big as the hills themselves.

Ziek was half asleep when she finally turned back to him, curled on the hard ground and heedless of the animal skin which remained attached to his pack.

Talit folded the blanket around them both, the heat of his feverish skin filling the trapped space quickly. She helped him gently to sit up, propping him against her so that he nestled in the crook of her arm.

"Look," she told him, and she wrapped her arms around him.

Ziek looked at the sky with its furor of color, at the river of hills drenched in a thousand different lights.

He drew in a long, deep breath, and let it out. That was all, but in that breath, she heard his smile.

Up here it was quiet, and colder. The wind, caught in the fingers of rocks around them, made a hollow whistling that was the only real sound.

"Ziek," Talit said.

"Mm."

"We can stop. We don't have to keep going. We can find somewhere safe and rest. Maybe we can wait until you feel better."

Ziek didn't answer her for so long that at first she thought that her empty promise had disgusted him, and then she thought he had fallen asleep.

Wait, she thought, for the end.

At least everything here was beautiful.

If they closed their eyes, then maybe they would go peacefully, in a deep sleep.

She felt him stir, settling his arms around her, his scraped and swollen hand finding hers. They had never held hands, at home, but it was normal, now.

"I'm happy," he whispered. He looked out across the hills.

Ziek would have told such lovely stories about them, if he had been able to see them healthy, if he had returned to the city of Saze with the pictures of these wondrous things stored away in his mind.

She squeezed his hand as tight as she dared. "Then will we stay?" she said, keeping her voice steady, gentle.

He didn't hesitate. "No," he said. "We have to go on."

And she did not answer him, for the terror that rose in her throat like a living thing.

But it was as if she had spoken aloud.

"Do not be afraid," he told her.

It wasn't until the next morning that Talit saw the heap of animal carcasses just outside their makeshift camp—stripped of their skins and covered in flies and carrion-birds, exposed bones cracked to splinters.

These hills were the home of the dustwalkers, she realized, and with that realization came a great despair, for they could not stay after all.

She could have begged Ziek, cajoled, whined, fought him, tied him down. Anything for a rest—to give up, to rest for just an hour more, to go quietly into sleep.

But she would not let them die like dogs.

And so once again, Talit and Ziek turned their faces to the hills, and walked.

CHAPTER 15

FOR TWO LONG WEEKS, THE Travelers went hungry.

Jacob called a halt to the hunting parties going into the forest, where they had the most chance of encountering the beasts. No one spoke out against him; they were all afraid to enter anyways.

The hunters, instead, returned in shifts to the city where they had first landed, hoping to find something amid the ruins. Each party left before dawn to make the long trip, and returned, worn and exhausted and empty-handed, long after the sun had set.

They came with only stories of the sad and grim things they had seen. Remnants of a past they had hoped to forget. Faces grew grayer, tempers shorter.

The cold had set in for good, but Aitor's restlessness and the heavy anxiety of the town made it so that he could no longer stay confined. The sky seemed too far away when the bonfires blocked out the stars; the buildings and walls leaned in around him.

In the hushed pearlescent gray of the dawn when Noah had at last fallen asleep—for even his wakeful vigils could not last forever—Aitor crept from the town, carrying a flask of water, his rosary, and his sketchbook.

He did not go far. It was the sky and the air he needed, the empty vacuum of the plains which mirrored the long solitudes he had hated so much aboard the ship.

But alone and free beneath the sky he walked, his mind empty, reaching out and hunting, always hunting, for the Watcher who might lie in wait.

When he had walked to his limit he stopped, and found a hill on which to sit; there he remained for hours.

There were stretches in which he sketched feverishly, his pencil bringing to life once more all the cathedrals he had visited, and those of which he had only seen pictures.

Stephanskirche, il Duomo di Milan; la Sagrada Familia as it had stood lovely and raw and full of heaven's billion colors. Cathédrale Notre-Dame de Chartres and Hagia Sophia, and Knesiyat ha-Kever in Jerusalem, where the world had shattered as the dead Savior stretched His arms out to embrace the universe.

All of these places he tried to draw as he remembered them. They were poor imitations, but it was enough. Drawing them he dreamed beautiful dreams: of a midnight when he knelt in peace before an incense-clouded altar covered in fragrant roses, bent down before an exultant host and its God.

And at last when his pen and shaking hand failed him, he sat motionless, the page empty as he dreamed instead of the church he would build—his offering, his duty to the Superior General.

He did not need to draw it to see it as it stood magnificent in his mind. White-gold and laden with scarlet silk, towering, filled with a monolithic grandeur.

A monument to God. Tall enough that He might see it, beautiful enough that He would remember that humans were still good—beautiful enough that He might come down once more to indwell it, and bring Aitor home. A place which spoke of Mercy in a merciless world.

It was foolish to go out alone. It invited death, or more.

He did not want to admit it—even to himself—but he knew why he had done it.

As long as he could, he waited alone in the desert, but the strange creatures did not appear again.

On Aitor's return back to the community, he met Noah waiting at the gate for him. Neither of them spoke of the excursion. But the next morning he rose from sleep as soon as Aitor stirred, and accompanied him in silence, his gun and his knife on his hip.

It was thus for the next morning, and the morning after that. But because Noah said nothing, it became companionable and good to have someone else walking alongside him, perhaps searching also.

He walked as far as he dared, most mornings, always looking for some sign of change in the landscape, for some sign of a place where one day he could build his church. He looked, too, for the silhouettes he had seen on the horizon once, distant and watchful.

Each day he ranged in a different direction, and found nothing but sand and plains.

Then one day a Traveler went missing from a hunting party that had gone out along the river; none of the others had seen him taken. Conor, a thirty-year-old with the face of a teenage hooligan, who joked so loudly and inanely that it was hard to believe that he was a talented doctor who had been acclaimed for his steady hand in surgery.

They sent out search parties with rapidly dwindling hope for his return; they were timid, and did not go far, clinging to their guns.

On the third day Conor had not returned, the Travelers congregated in the square, and this time held not a prophecy, but a funeral.

Jacob presided, his voice grave. He followed the ritual as a priest should, with grieving and empty eyes, and Aitor thought that this, at least, was genuine.

After the funeral, though, the people did not disperse. They stood and mourned loudly, singing, their voices going from sorrow to outraged frenzy.

Beneath the altar they clamored at Jacob, working themselves into a lather as they called for the deaths of the creatures which had surely claimed the boy. Let the Devil's hellbeasts be exterminated by means of slow and merciless torture.

No, Jacob told them. No, we cannot act now; we are too weak. It is God's will that we wait, and pray, and prepare.

Night fell. Aitor burrowed into his blankets at his little lookout post, and from there he could hear the sound of hooting and cheering as the people sacrificed, the stamping of their feet as they cavorted and summoned strength for vengeance.

Some time later Aitor awoke from a troubled dream to see Noah nearby, crouching with his gun in his hand, trained on something distant. The sound of the town was the deadened peace of slumber, but there were footsteps coming down the hill towards the town, heavy and labored.

Slowly Aitor pushed himself up so that he could more clearly see the dark figure which approached them.

Jacob stopped there, holding a limp shape in his arms which was wrapped in a tarp, and left a wet dripping trail behind him. His face was drawn. Aitor saw in it the same look he had worn on the day of his waking, the same hopeless horror.

He stopped without any sign of surprise, and did not move as Noah approached him and pulled aside the tarp to expose what he carried.

In his arms lay Conor, eyes fixed in a gaping stare. His skin was ghastly blue in the moonlight. Half of its surface was congealed with the same hideous discolored growths which Aitor had seen only in their beginnings on Gisele. The poisoning had spread up to his neck, where it might have finally peeked over a collar; it swelled his stomach into a gnarled lump.

What Conor had done to himself was clear enough.

They took him to the chapel and buried him, where the guards atop the town walls would not see.

When they had finished, Aitor whispered the prayers for the dead over the gravesite.

Eternal rest grant unto him, O Lord; and let perpetual light shine upon him.

May he rest in peace.

Jacob let out a soft sob, once, more of a compulsive spasm. His face did not move from its stone expression, but his dark eyes spoke.

Almost, almost, Aitor reached to take his hand—to give comfort, and to take it—but in the end, he did not.

They dispersed into the darkness with no farewell. Jacob left first.

There was no word spoken of what had really happened, and if anyone else knew, they did not tell.

The Travelers walked lightly, jumping at shadows. Every noise could be a beast, waiting to catch them, to steal food, to torture them and stake them in the dark.

Hunger made them paranoid. There were fights in the city, more than usual. Smaller groups among them began to emerge, and cookfires became private, closed things. Hunters still contributed to the whole community, but choice morsels were saved, squirreled away for inner circles and trusted friends.

While they had all been lean before, they were now stringy and defensive, kicked street curs slinking along the edges of walls and buildings, afraid of entering the open.

The only times they came together in peace were the sacrifices.

Each night when the hunting parties returned, Jacob called for one tenth to be offered to God, and they burnt it. Some nights it was no more than a handful of bitter plants they had scavenged from distant hillsides, and on richer nights, perhaps the flank of a thin animal.

Always Jacob presided with a voice harshened and hollowed by hunger, the shadows on his face sharp valleys where once there was flesh.

The creatures did not return, but their extended absence made it somehow worse.

Aitor felt the anxiety as a persistent ache that made it difficult to move. The chill of descending winter only exacerbated it, so that his morning walks with Noah were short and laborious, and left him gasping with shooting pains and a faint heart.

Even so, he would not give up his search. To give up his freedom to look for the unknowable was to die twice. Noah seemed to understand that he would not be stopped, and accompanied Aitor with endless reserves of patience, bearing him up when he needed it, often carrying him home. Though he, too, grew gaunt, he never complained.

He slept so little and so shallowly that he saw moving figures at the edges of his vision where there were none. Paralysis would come from time to time, leaving him drained and trembling.

There was some comfort, though. Since he had begun to make his journeys—he sometimes thought of them as pilgrimages, even—his dreams had taken a turn.

No longer did he walk in cratered, apocalyptic hellscapes swept with burning, acidic sand. Instead, his sleep took him back to the sweltering streets of his childhood, following the distant singing of Padre Aguilera Alejo in the dusty little church by the sea. Again he ghosted the littered beaches full of sunbathers and children at play.

Often, he found himself sitting on the cliffs of Fisterra on the night of his ordination, and looked out over the black waters at midnight, the moon a pearl on the horizon. In this dream, Jacob sat beside him in companionable silence, and they both were yet young, and strong, and soft-hearted.

Some small peace at last; some small blessing to his nights. In the morning, Aitor found that his eyes were wet with tears of joy.

Yet the fear and hunger in the city of the Travelers grew. It was as if the creatures had been swallowed back into the desert, invisible. There were no more tracks and no more encounters. But though they had vanished, every Traveler seemed to claim that they had seen one just yesterday.

The creatures had become almost a mythical thing, metaphysical demons that hunted them through the night.

Jacob was making a plan. Though no one spoke of it to Aitor, some of the Travelers walked regularly to the rectory, in which Jacob now slept and ate alone. Each from a separate cookfire, they wore purposeful faces, and greeted each other with grim and furtive smiles. Among them was Gisele, and the rest of them wore her same easy manner of quiet authority.

They had begun to create more weapons. Crudely made swords and bows joined hunters' spears and clubs. Soon every Traveler carried at least one weapon aside from their guns.

Then Aitor saw the creatures again.

He and Noah had walked west that day, up the slope of the basin opposite the city, leaving before the break of dawn, so that as they walked, the sun behind them burnt away the heavy smoke-gray mist in sheaves.

Something compelled Aitor to push himself farther than he would go, normally, and they walked long enough so that thick sands, broken rock, and tough vegetation gave way to tufts of unfamiliar grass, and gently rolling plains.

Perhaps it was only restlessness, and a desire to prove himself young again; perhaps it was something more than that. Either way, Aitor found himself at a large outcropping of stone long worried away by hundreds of years of wind, a lone new landmark in a strange world. There he stopped and could go no further, and Noah helped him sit.

They rested. Aitor watched the pallid blue of the cold sky, strangely contented. Today, he felt, was a day of little drawing, and many dreams.

It was the abrupt click of the safety on Noah's gun releasing that startled him to wakefulness.

The things stood atop one of the slopes near them, poised. Even having never seen them before, Aitor knew immediately what he looked upon, and yet nothing could have prepared him to see it.

They were hideous: their limbs were twisted, elongated, and scabbed over with gruesome imitations of flesh-color. Their faces might have seemed human, had they not been twisted and melted grotesquely. Their entire bodies were stippled in raised lumps which the light suffused sickly yellow and pale, and as they breathed, their skins did not seem to move right over joints that were not shaped as joints should be.

They wore tattered clothing which seemed to be sewn from the same type of rough-woven cloth the Travelers had begun to make. Crouching on their haunches, balanced with one forelimb splayed before them, they stared back with bright glazed eyes at the humans before them.

Neither Aitor nor Noah moved, and they did not move even as the creatures advanced.

Aitor's breath had stopped.

Kyrie eleison. He looked unblinking upon the faces of those whom hell had touched, on the kin of those who had tortured and killed his brothers in unspeakable violence.

He felt the urge to weep.

The creatures carried something, he saw, then, hidden close to them. Weapons? Yet they inched towards Noah and Aitor not like those who wished to provoke, but in cringing fear.

They had seen the guns, Aitor thought; they knew what could happen to them, but they drew close anyways.

The world was very quiet.

Then they were only scant yards away, clutching their bundles to their chests.

Abruptly Noah pointed his gun straight into the air and fired. The report was a deafening crack, even in the open air.

Startled, the creatures turned on their heels, spraying sand, and fled, scattering the contents of their bundles. In the space of a breath there was nothing left of them; their long limbs carried them away at a shocking speed.

In the next breath Aitor was moving forward to see what they had dropped, his curiosity overwhelming fear.

They had left behind a small handful of gemstones: polished flat until they were all roughly the same shape and size, veined with vibrant and living color. They fit easily inside Noah's palm.

The stones had been carved with patterns—each one different, but all perfectly symmetrical.

Noah's eyes were troubled as he gave one to Aitor, and tucked the rest into a corner of his faded pack.

They returned to the town by unspoken agreement, Aitor leaning on Noah's arm. The little stone in his palm frightened him and he could not say why. He clutched to it until it was slick with his sweat.

When they returned to the town late in the evening, Aitor saw it with new eyes. The Travelers had abandoned their chores. The cookfires lay in unkempt heaps of ash; looms stood abandoned, the gardens untended.

The people were gathered in the square, putting together a map of the surrounding land. They were making, cleaning, sharpening weapons; they were busy constructing fortifications for the town walls. Their talk was of planning raids, hunting for hiding places, and setting up fighting squadrons.

Aitor meant to speak with Jacob that night. He would say something to them all. He would show them the stones, that maybe the threat was not as great as they had thought. He would tell them that he had seen the Others, and had escaped unscathed.

But full dark fell early that night, announcing the heart of winter; the chanting for the nightly sacrifice began early.

Aitor chose to sleep in the rectory that night. He would catch Jacob when there was no one else around. Then the mask would come away, and Jacob would listen; he would have to understand.

But in undressing to change for sleep, Aitor discovered a small purple blotch on his ribs—the size of a thumb laid across his side—and he did not tell Jacob, after all.

The days passed without event. Aitor was cold and aching and troubled, and did not go out into the wilderness again.

Noah went without him, disappearing at length into the wilds. He returned always with some small food that the two of them could share, or something for the dwelling that had become theirs, but he did not talk about where he had gone.

In his absence Aitor found himself painfully lonely, although it was rare that they ever spoke.

Near the middle of the week, he realized that he had lost his sketch-book on the last excursion. Noah went out to look for it without complaining; he returned empty-handed.

Aitor mourned then for his church, which seemed to slip even further from him each day as the nights grew mor bitter and his feet more weary. He could not cling now even to pictures of a dwelling-place for his God; and without the sketchbook to hold, his hope was a small and wingless thing, dying and dead.

At the end of the second week, a Traveler hunting party returned bearing the bodies of two creatures.

Aitor recognized the hunters immediately. They were the people whom Jacob had gathered in his rectory daily, the leaders of each cook-fire. Gisele was one of them; she stood straight and tall, her shoulders thrown back.

They dragged the creatures through the entrance of the city, and the activity around them came to a halt. Slowly at first, and then rapidly, the Travelers came from their homes and their work to see what had been caught.

The Others had been braced together with a makeshift rope harness, and were caked in sand and clumped blood where they had been dragged through the desert. If they were conscious, it was impossible to tell.

One was large, more repugnant than the others; there was a third arm that protruded from its ribcage and hung at an eerie angle. The other was small and lanky, jaw protruding crookedly; its head seemed listed permanently to one side.

The Travelers gathered to stare in silence. Even after all their vitriol—after all these days planning revenge, planning violence—it seemed that none of them knew what to do now.

"Christ," said someone, softly, an oath and a prayer at once.

Someone else picked up a rock and bounced it off one of the monsters' foreheads. It didn't move.

Jacob stepped forward. His face was expressionless and composed in the gravity of the Prophet the people had come to know.

"Behold, the spawn of Satan," he said.

Gisele stepped forward then, and spoke for the hunting party. For the first time, Aitor learned of the plans the Travelers had laid.

For weeks now they had been scouting for tracks, and hunting for the homeplace of the creatures, baiting them, pretending to be injured, setting ambushes. But there had been no luck; the creatures were clever, and practically invisible, Gisele said.

These two, though, had been alone, and traveling in full broad daylight towards the Travelers' town. The hunting party had given chase, and tried to capture them; there had been a brief fight which the creatures would have had no chance of winning.

They had been loners, carrying no weapons. There had been no sign of others with them.

This was the plan, Jacob announced then, and the triumph in his voice carried and spread throughout the people so that they picked their heads up and put their shoulders back, and looked again like one people, unified.

They would leave the creatures' bodies a short distance from the city. They would be allowed to recover, to escape, and return to the rest of their kind.

And then the Travelers would follow them, and lay a trap of the worst kind. They would set fire to the home of the beasts, and they would destroy every last one living.

The creatures were dragged to the ridge not too far from where Aitor had slept, and were left untied. They lay unmoving even when the Travelers retreated, hasty despite themselves.

A watch was set. Occasionally even those who were off duty climbed the walls to stare in morbid curiosity. But even as the day waxed and waned, the huddled shapes far in the distance did not move.

Aitor went to watch, for a little while, and the longer he watched the creatures on the ridge, the heavier he felt his own cruelty, and he went away to the chapel to pray.

But more than anything, the weight of Gisele's secret bore down on him, heavier than all else. Embedded in her flesh lay what might be the same terrible, unknowable suffering these creatures had lived. He let himself entertain the unforgivable thought that perhaps this was the end towards which all of them were destined, after all.

Evening came, and he could not bear it any longer. He went to find Jacob.

The people seemed surprised to see him moving about, but they pointed him in the direction of 'the Father' without trouble. Around him, they moved with antlike efficiency, each one of their faces renewed with purpose. At some point without his noticing, they had reinforced the walls of the town and elevated the watchtowers. Now they were working to fasten sharpened spikes around the perimeter of their territory.

Jacob stood atop a watchtower closest to the rectory, on the far side of the little town. There was no wind that evening, and motionless, in a rare moment of rest, he looked like a statue, his face cold and empty of humanity.

"What is wrong?" he said, as Aitor approached him.

Side by side now, the two of them looked across the wilds into the twilight. It was blue-purple, muted and pastel. The daytime sky was rarely like this, delicate and sweet.

Often they had stood like this during their time in the House at the End of the World, always in the evenings, when the work of the day was done, and their simple meal lay warm and pleasant in their bellies.

Aitor reached out and offered Jacob the small scratched stone the creatures had left for them.

Jacob looked at it blankly.

"It belonged to them, the creatures."

"You saw them?" A flash of anger, then, in Jacob's eyes.

"This is decorated. There are more stones like them, each different. The creatures are intelligent."

"Maybe," said Jacob. "Maybe not. Does it matter, if they kill us and torture us?"

"They have not attacked again."

"There was Conor."

"We both know they did not kill Conor."

Jacob turned to look back out at the desert. The little dark shapes on the ridge could be so easily mistaken for uneven bits of landscape, had fading sunlight not illuminated the edges of their tangled limbs. "Perhaps they will not attack again. But there are more of them than there are of us. We do not have a way to communicate with them, whatever they are. In the course of history, it is inevitable. We fear them and they fear us. Sooner or later we will be conquered or killed. If we act first, we have a chance at saving ourselves."

"It is not certain."

"Is it not?"

Aitor said, "We are sick, like them." He touched his side, nausea sweeping him in waves.

For the first time, Jacob faced him fully. His chin was up, nostrils flared, his eyes black holes. "Maybe."

"But you will burn and kill the creatures. You will fight a hopeless war."

"We do not know if it is the same sickness."

"And if it is? If they are what all of us will be in a week? A month? A year? Then we burn too?"

"Would you want to live as a monster?"

"That is not a reason to kill them." But Aitor was thinking of the twisted fingers, the diseased, scabrous flesh, the extra limb. He felt his own skin prickle.

Jacob laughed. "Don't you think I know we are lost?" he said. "Don't you think I know that we are all going to become crawling and pus-leaking horrors?" He swept an arm wildly, gesturing at nothing, his voice rising a fraction. "Aitor, what would you have? Would you let us bow and scrape to the monsters, and go hungry in fear that we are murdered in our sleep? Or should we wander forever, preyed upon by everything, homeless? Worse yet, should we live constantly staring upon our own accursed fate? Do you want to look at them, and hear God laughing at us as we go to our miserable, forsaken graves?"

He gripped the railing of the watchtower so tightly that it creaked in his hands. Looking at them, Aitor saw that his skin was split and peeled and bleeding.

"No," Jacob said, soft again. "We go out with hope, fighting our foolish crusade. I will tell them to have faith, and when they die, perhaps some of them will have a chance to enter Heaven, if there is one. And if there is not, then at least they will die believing that there is a future for man, on earth and in death. They will be at peace. It is the best way."

Aitor was silent.

"I envy you." When Aitor looked up again to meet Jacob's gaze, he saw that Jacob's jaw was clenched. "Caged up in a ship all your life. Yes. You were alone, but you were safe.

"I thought that God would come back to lead me when I took the people into the world again. I thought it would be easy, if I trusted. I was happy, when they chose my name to be the last to wake. So selfishly happy."

Standing beneath the filigreed baldachin of the cathedral, cloaked in heavy incense, shrouded by night. Aitor remembered again the rush of hatred he had felt as he realized that he had been sentenced to a life of solitude and creeping death.

"And then I realized it would be worse. No one believed there would be anything left, after, if the world didn't end first. It was a stupid thing. We all knew it as soon as we entered the ship, and it was too late, by then. All I could do was pray that God would end things, save me."

What color Jacob had left had drained from his face, leaving him the sallow color of a corpse. "I have lived twenty miserable and empty lives in a box, and all that remains to me now before the final death is yet more suffering and misery. I wish that I were you, Aitor. If only I had been condemned to just live in a box with no one depending on me. An old man, praying endless Rosaries, ready to die."

"Jacob," Aitor whispered, the cruelty choking him. He remembered Jacob's face, as he had sunk back towards the box that would hold him. Jacob, restrained by the Superior General, clawing his way towards Aitor, face contorted.

Please, no, he had said. *No!*—

Aitor had thought of this moment many times. He had thought that Jacob had clawed toward him out of love, out of fear for him. Wishing to exchange places, allowing Aitor to be the one who would stay young.

But he understood now that perhaps Jacob had only been afraid of the fate he had seen so clearly before him: tasked to restore humanity to a dead world, to bear hope for all, when he had already lost it.

Jacob's mouth was a hard line. "You were too weak to do what was necessary," he said. "It would have been so easy."

Aitor did not know what he meant. He hunched in on himself against the bleakness in Jacob's voice.

"I could have ended it." Jacob's voice was hushed, almost reverent. "All at once. It would have been a quick and peaceful death for all of them. And then me, just as you said. The airlock." He let out a gentle sigh, as if he imagined an unimaginable peace, as if he had sipped at honey, warmed at a roaring fire at a brick hearth. "So easy."

"You would not have done it." Aitor could not look at him, could not bear to see Jacob's expression. "You were different then."

"Maybe," Jacob said. "But I was never as strong as the rest of you."

Aitor did not want to hear him say that. He stood struck dumb, thinking of what it meant, if Jacob, the heart of the men at the Fisterra seminary, Jacob of the unflagging faith, was not as strong as the rest of them.

At last he said, "I thought of doing that." His own voice was low, too. "Every day for years, I thought of it."

"And you did not. Tell me, why?"

Aitor found himself touching the tattoo of the passcode to cold storage, which was now faded and smeared on the inside of his wrist. "I do not know," he said. The words felt like a betrayal. "I wanted to understand why we had suffered so much already. I thought that when we lived, I would find an answer."

Jacob smiled, a sad and bitter little smile. "Do you have it, then?"

"No," Aitor said. "Maybe I never will."

There was a lull. Jacob turned to look up at the creatures on the ridge again. His eyes still burned with that beautiful and frenetic light. "I always loved you because you would not give up," he said.

"And I you."

A long pause. "I will burn them," Jacob said. "Aitor, we will die, but we will have some hope, too. Do you understand?"

Aitor straightened as much as his stiffened and arthritic frame allowed. Words meant nothing to Jacob now, and he was weary, and old, and wanted nothing more than to be far away from him. He needed solitude, where he could wrestle to understand how he could both love and hate someone so much, and how that someone could be dead and alive at the same time.

Jacob's voice followed him.

"Go to the creatures, Aitor," he said. "Look at them. Look in the face of God's curse, and tell me that you can believe that He is merciful."

CHAPTER 16

T HE SPELL OF SAFETY HAD been broken.

The pile of bones was long behind them, but Talit felt as if she could still smell the stench of rotting flesh plugging her nose, souring her insides until she herself rotted, too. There had been over a dozen creatures piled there, the spoils of a predator who marked its territory and feared nothing.

The cold had woken Talit just before dawn, and she watched again, sleepy and aching with the beauty of it, as the sun climbed the horizon and lit the hills. The light was gold and white, and under it, everything glittered with the strange warm magic of the night before, as everything were coated in rain-slicked crystal.

They packed up their meager camp, and Talit watched as Ziek moved forward, once again following an invisible thread that only he could see.

They had walked only five minutes before they came to another heap of carcasses.

She had thought that perhaps their long ascent had put off the dust-walker, that it might have stayed among the rolling dunes far below. For a while, her night terrors had faded into a low and seething anxiety about simpler things—water, food, shelter.

Now every time she blinked, she saw its face.

Her hands shook as she walked. Where her mind had found peace in empty, thoughtless suffering before, she could no longer stop thinking about it.

It had already found them. She knew this the way a Sazer knows that one day, sooner than you think, you will die, whether from old age or from violence—it was there, watching them, waiting for an amusing moment to end them.

What would happen if it chose to kill them for sport? What if it decided suddenly that these small worthless beings were not worth the torment, and that it would be easier to kill them in a few moments' fun?

She had not liked to look at the corpses of the criminals hanging from the city's walls, but the glimpses she had stolen lingered with her nonetheless: stripped and sun-seared flesh, stark bone where the sun had scoured it white, gaping holes where there had once been eyes. And always the buzzing of flies and the shrieks of circling carrion.

It had become harder to breathe. They walked along the top of the forever-hill, a steep slope to either side. A single misstep, and they would meet a certain end. The world spread like a wrinkled cloth around them.

Ziek had not seemed to understand what the piles of carcasses meant. Nor did he seem to hear that the air had gone perfectly motionless, nor realize that the animals, even the birds, had vanished.

He did not even hear Talit.

The clarity of the night before had faded. He walked a step ahead of her with a dogged, manic energy that did not waver, even when their path dropped steeply out of view of the city, and the path became treacherous and narrow.

He is waiting, Ziek told her, and it was the only thing he said to her. He did not stop. The sun turned his thinning skin translucent, until he looked like a misshapen spirit guide, ghosting before her.

At least she did not have to drag him. They stumbled on. Their sandals had long ago worn themselves to shreds. At first, accustomed to hard-packed dust streets or soft-shifting desert sands, their feet had bled and blistered as they climbed over unforgiving, sunbaked rock.

Now Talit's feet were hardened and numb. They were someone else's purple and swollen feet, hinged to the body of a stranger. She could no longer feel them as they carried her deeper through the hills, dusty, caked in blood.

Doom stalked her, a constant presence just behind her.

As the day moved on, illusions crept in at the edges of her vision again. This time, she thought that her fear must surely color them. Once she looked down and saw a lake of fire. Dark shadow-creatures snapped at her from only inches away, their slavering jaws closing on her, and leaving no marks. Lining their way were towering black figures which bowed their heads to stare balefully as they passed. They moved only when Talit was not looking directly at them, but the weight of their gazes never left her.

She prayed as they walked, a gibbering mantra of fear and exhaustion and desperation.

O Prophet. Let us not die. Let us not die. Let us not die.

Help my friend.

But as she prayed, she felt the distance between her and home stretch into vastness. She could not imagine that Prophet heard her, from all this distance. Far away, where he could no longer see them, he stood, shiny and coal-colored, beside his Church. In his gravelly voice, undisturbed and untroubled, he announced the call to prayer.

Her own prayers, though, unconfined by any ceiling, drifted into an unknown, and the unknown did not say anything back. She had the feeling of a great ending approaching, something vast and definitive. If it was her own end, then perhaps it was better than this fool's errand.

Evening was coming quickly. She had tracked the descent of the sun with dread turning her belly to ice. Though it could not possibly be true, it felt as if they had climbed and descended, climbed and descended a hundred times.

They climbed their hundred and first hill, the steep slope shortening their breath. Her body cried out with every step, which seemed to Talit to be an impossible feat, for she felt dead already. The city she had glimpsed was no longer in sight, hidden on the other side of the hill.

Ziek, a skinny and deformed puppet ahead of her, staggered drunkenly. His head tucked down, he no longer looked at whatever delusions galled him on. His clothes clung to the Burdens which now grew from him in profusion, from his chest, neck, sides, back. He did not smile or sing.

The cold wind set in then, with nothing to shelter them. Talit knew that if they were to stop moving, they would slow, and then stop, and they would never move again.

Her mind filled with thoughts of the dustwalker—leaping toward them, its long and twisted claws reaching—scoring across her side—its gaping mouth smiling triumphantly, its eyes filled with bloody light—

In that moment of weakness, she turned, and saw it.

She knew immediately that it must be the same dustwalker that had attacked them in the desert. She could not have said how she knew—whether it was the curve of its hulking shoulders, as it watched them from the crest of the hill they had just descended—or if it was the way it moved, one moment there, the next gone, without so much as a blur—but she sensed it unceasingly, a malevolent hatred that gnawed at her edges with poisoned teeth.

Perhaps it was only the flickering of shadows or her imagination, but she thought that it shimmered, like a heat-mirage of a real thing, only half in this world. It opened its mouth in a lazy yawn, exposing its rows of dripping, crooked teeth, a show of power. It could kill her at any moment it chose. It would take its time.

They walked now in the bowl between two hills. To either side of her, uneven rock dropped sharply away into stairstepping ledges that a giant might have struggled to climb, quickly lost in rising fog and growing night.

Ahead of her, Ziek sprayed up loud showers of pebbles with his dragging steps. The great-hill which reared its head before her was higher and steeper than any they had yet scaled, smooth and forbidding.

"Ziek," she whispered, and she tugged at his sleeve once, twice, then tried to bring him to a full stop by seizing a fistful of his tunic.

She wasn't sure what he might do. Some part of her wanted him to tell her that it would be all right, that she was imagining things, that they would wake up and be home.

Maybe she wanted to tell him that it would all be over soon, that they could give up, that they had tried their best.

At least let him acknowledge that it was there. Let her not face this alone.

He fought her, feet scuffling against the ground uselessly, whimpering like an animal tethered just out of reach of food and drink. And Talit saw in his eyes that he did not see her.

His whimpering took on words. "He is waiting!" he cried out, again and again, and his voice took on strength, until he was bellowing, and his voice rang out incredibly loudly, bouncing back again and again until it filled her ears like the clanging of a tower full of bells.

I WILL GO!

It enraged Talit suddenly, this blind passion, this hope he carried. She was angry with Ziek—with the Lord, and Prophet—with herself. She grabbed Ziek by the other shoulder, and brought his face close to hers until she could see the last light of day wetly glimmering on his reddened eyes.

"I lied to you!" she shouted, her voice cutting through his cries. He quieted, as if she had sliced through invisible threads she had not known were there.

"I lied to you," she repeated. "I don't know if the Lord is alive. I don't know. I lied. I just wanted to save you. I thought I could do it on my own. I lied, it was wrong; I am sorry."

Ziek's face changed, then, but it was not what she expected. He did not seem angry, or betrayed, or hurt. "No," he said.

"I'm sorry," Talit said, tear-choked. "I'm so sorry."

Ziek frowned in confusion, then, and she thought—did he know what she had said? Had he understood?

"He's not alive," Talit said again, urgently, her voice lowered. She did not know why it was important to her that he understood her, that he realized that she was trying to crush his hopes, and yet she could not stop herself. "And even if he is, I came to kill him."

He pushed her away. It was a surprisingly strong movement; it startled her, and she stumbled backwards. His face was unreadable, but his eyes were locked on hers, his focus sharp and unwavering. "No," he said again.

And then he turned away from her and walked, his feet finding the invisible track that he somehow, impossibly, still followed. As if he did not see the dustwalker at all—as if it were not closing on full dark—as if there was nothing more important than the moment immediately before him, and then the next, and the next, and the next.

Talit knew then that Ziek would not stop. She could beg him, attack him, scream at him, tie him—he would only keep moving his feet, step by step until his body fell apart. And though he loved her, whatever it was that moved him—whoever she had managed to convince him waited ahead—he loved it far more.

Talit had an urge to laugh wildly, to laugh until she split.

Let him go, then. Let him find whatever it was he saw. She would believe in it, too. She would do anything for her friend so that he got there.

Talit stopped and faced the dustwalker, her throat seizing too much to speak. Now she stood between Ziek and the enemy, and her muscles spasmed as the wind beat against her trembling body.

The dustwalker had not moved from its position, watching them almost with a morbid amusement. She could see that its sides were swollen from its kills. It did not need to feed, but it would devour them anyways, simply for the enjoyment of an easy death. Now as Ziek lurched away from them, it began to move, its movements blurring with the shadows of the hill, its eyes smoldering, hellish pits.

She was small; she was tired; she was no warrior. Even as she looked at it, it shape seemed to divide into six, blurring—or had it merged? Was it one, or did they come from all sides?

Talit's pack slid from her shoulder, almost of its own accord, and spilled open at her battered, bloodied feet. She knelt down, fumbling blindly, until her fingers found what she sought: the firestones, her mother's hunting knife, the small clay jar of animal fat which they had collected in their meager hunting.

There were no green sticks, there was nothing for kindling left. Nothing—

No time.

With shaking hands, she unstopped the jar and spilled the fat over the bundle; got the firestones out and held them very close.

She struck the firestones hard, praying for sparks.

Strike. Strike.

The enemy made no noise as it approached, its feet as silent and creeping as despair. As she looked up, the divergent shadows merged to become a beast whose flesh was seared in red-black scars, the skin puckered and scorched. She could smell the stink of its hot, pungent breath, ripe with blood and death and hopeless things.

Strike. Strike.

The dustwalker grinned down at her from an arm's length away.

There was fire.

She leaped toward the dustwalker with her arms outstretched, clutching her mother's knife in one fist. Her hand was ablaze. Her tunic was ablaze. She was ablaze, a pillar of flame in a sea of night. The dustwalker flinched, more out surprise than anything, but the sight of it hesitating, jaws frozen agape—at the sight of her, a tiny piece of sun—gave her courage.

The dustwalker backed away, its eyes swollen, luminous orbs from where it stood crouched. Its face, close to hers, seemed to her almost to be that of a man—a flat, broad nose, its expression intelligent and wary. But its mouth was too wide, and its jaw distended and monstrous; it pulled back its lips now to expose its teeth, and she sensed that it no longer smiled.

The wind fanned her flames dangerously thin. She could not even feel them; they had consumed her tunic entirely and she did not know what it was that fed the fire now, nor did she care.

And she felt herself, giggling now, compelled to step forward, and then forward again, until she was running at it. And she saw that her light had blossomed and fragmented into a thousand lights, brighter than any sun.

She ran within a chariot wheel of fire. And in her laughing madness she knew that the fire was a person, and that it ran with her, to deliver her to her destiny, even as it devoured her whole.

The dustwalker stood braced for her approach, and she saw that it could not see her, that its eyes wept blind tears at the inferno which she carried with her like a great storm.

At the last moment, it turned and rose up to meet her, its mouth gaping wide, and she plunged her knife deep into its jaws and up, up, driving the blade into the back of its throat and the roof of its mouth.

She was not Talit, the Sazer. She was Talit, the Chosen, the Shining, the Ascended, a bearer of Holy Flame. She had arisen from sleep, and here was her salvation. She saw it all so clearly now.

The dustwalker bellowed for eternities. If her own screams were loud, then the dustwalker's broke the world.

So close, it shattered something in her ears with a resounding explosion, a thunderclap of noise. She heard nothing, then, but she felt the air tattered, all realms above and below shaken with its force.

Her arm was deep within its mouth when it snapped its jaw shut. Its head jerked in an involuntary convulsion; it flailed, as if it tried to rip itself apart. In the time it took her to blink, she thought she saw that its head burned, that its eye sockets put forth gouts of white flame, and that the flame multiplied on itself again and again.

In that moment, despite her ruined hearing, Talit heard the singing of a grand choir, of voices reaching impossible heights, voices which were so deep they felt as if the heavy bones of the world ground together.

Then the dustwalker struck her with its shoulder as it spasmed and died.

There was no pain, only a sharp change in her momentum. Her feet lost track of the ground; her mind forgot the world.

She flew.

Chapter 17

Night fell, and when Aitor climbed the ridge, no one stopped him.

By then they were used to his wanderings, for which Aitor realized now that Jacob must have quietly given permission. But the fact that the night guard turned a blind eye to his leaving told him that he truly no longer had a home amongst the Travelers.

Perhaps they were tired of his nightmares, or his silent judgment of the nightly sacrifices. Perhaps they were only tired of feeding an extra mouth who could not do any work at all.

Or perhaps they meant it as a small kindness to him, but in any case Aitor felt it as disinterested cruelty that they would let an old man wander into the desert at night, alone.

Go to them, Jacob had said. He had drifted away to his bedroll then, and Aitor as well, but sleep had not come.

Go to them.

He carried only a small, dull knife he had taken from Noah's home, and a canteen of water. He had not dared to ask anyone for more.

Fasting had made him weak, and after all, he was old. The walk up the ridge made his heart spasm, and his lungs were aflame. Alone and without Noah's hand to support him, he walked plagued by the vertigo that comes just before the fall, and by the thought that in their selective ignorance, the guards atop the city walls would not see him if he slipped.

The figures lay nestled together atop the ridge. Aitor's solar flash-light illuminated them in stark relief, caked in grit and sand.

Aitor found himself holding his breath, his fingers white-knuckled on the hilt of the little stone knife.

Jacob's words had goaded him, but there was something else that drew him closer—a need to be near to these things, to face them as they were, to understand them.

Even as he approached, his awkward feet scattering small rocks, his breathing a low whine, the creatures did not move. Their bonds had been cut and lay to one side, blackened, grimy bits of rope. The rock was stained with blood where they had attempted, at some point, to drag themselves away.

He was close enough to touch them.

The bigger creature turned its head then slightly, and looked at him. It made no other move. But in its eyes Aitor thought he saw a glimmer of—recognition? Hatred? Despair?

There were no words to describe how revolting the things were— worse yet because of their untreated wounds, which glistened wetly, dis- figuring what was already ruined.

Swallowing his bile, he sank slowly to his knees beside them.

The larger creature's gaze dropped to the knife clutched in Aitor's knotted, trembling hand. But even as he brought the flashlight closer to them, it did not react.

Beneath its ragged attempt at clothing, the smaller creature's side barely moved at all. What skin was visible was beaten and bruised black and blue. Its eyes were wide and glassy; its tongue curled from patchy, flaking lips. Its ears and nose seeped a too-dark liquid.

Aitor had seen the same vacant expression on the faces of men who were struck down in the street where they stood, trampled and defeated, looking up in unseeing wonder at the world drenched in the blue-red lights of emergency vehicles. This creature was dying.

The larger one shifted so that its back was to Aitor, cradling the smaller one to its chest. It let out a soft, whuffing sigh, and closed its eyes. Despite the cold, it did not tremble.

Aitor understood suddenly that it was not too injured to leave. It waited here with its companion. It mourned.

His little knife seemed silly, a mockery. He tucked it into the belt of his cassock. Instead he found himself unscrewing the lid of the canteen, thinking to offer it.

Unsure how to get its attention, or if he should, he waited so long with the canteen clutched to his chest that his flashlight blinked out, the power exhausted. For long minutes he knelt, his joints stiffening, in complete darkness, until his eyes adjusted to the stars and the moon, and he could see everything again in a pale silvery wash.

The smaller creature began to cry in soft, piteous whimpers that were so small and quick that they could have been a child's. The large creature curled around it, its bruised body wracked beneath swathes of dirty cloth. Though it trembled, it made no noise.

Aitor did not move. He recognized this moment. To witness the instant of death is to never forget it.

As quickly as it had begun, the small creature's crying stopped. There was a long hush.

Then from the larger creature came a low keening. It was so quiet that from ten feet away, no one might have heard it. But Aitor, nearly shoulder-to-shoulder with the strange other, heard profound torture in the gentle cry.

Above all else, that cry was human.

Aitor found himself praying in a desperate whisper: half to block out the nightmarish noise, and half to give it voice, words, meaning—*De profundis clamavi ad te, Domine—Domine, exaudi vocem meam*—

The whine went on for what could have been years. And when it was ended at last, the—person-thing—remained curled around the body. It shivered, but Aitor did not think that it was from cold.

When it lifted its head and looked at Aitor, he saw a person looking back at him.

He slowly reached out and proffered his canteen.

The person—the other—stared at it with red-rimmed eyes. It did not take the water. Instead it looked down and past Aitor, to the watch-tower far below them, at the small dark figures which stood waiting. It rose, and gently scooped up the body of its friend.

Aitor struggled to get up, too, scrabbling on the hard, uneven stone.

They were roughly of a height. The bulk of the creature came from its huge, bunched shoulders, and the presence of flesh where there should be none. But looking more closely, Aitor saw that the rags hung from those shoulders limply; the wind knocked the cloth against emaciated ribs. Still, though, it carried the body as if it weighed nothing.

Below, a shout rose from the town. The hunting party was gathering, preparing to follow the creature.

It had been staring at Aitor. Now it put out a free hand to him, its blistered, scabbed palm upturned.

Aitor did not know what it wanted. They stood like that—the Other waiting, Aitor suspended before a choice or a request that he could not possibly have any means to understand.

Slowly, he put his hand into his cassock pocket and drew out the little engraved stone. He placed it the Other's palm.

"I am very sorry," he told it.

The Other's face changed, then. It took Aitor a moment to realize that the grimace, exposing gnarled, twisted teeth, was a half-smile, a look of near-surprise. It reached out and took his wrist, gently pulling him towards the open desert.

"No," Aitor cried out. His wonder turned into panic—panic that it did not understand his age, that he would die lost in the sands; panic that it would lead Jacob and the Travelers straight to the heart of its home. "No!" He fought away violently, staggering back.

It released his wrist, suddenly tense. They stared at each other in the darkness. It still made no sound.

Then the person-thing lifted its hand once more, slowly. Before Aitor it made the Sign of the Cross, as priests do, three twisted fingers extended in solemn blessing.

It was an unmistakable gesture. Aitor's blood chilled.

The Other waited, but Aitor did not know how to respond. Finally, it turned to go once more, bearing the body of its friend, trailing its bloodied rags behind it.

Something spurred Aitor to step forward, to grab for its sleeve. "No," he said, "you can't. They will follow you. They will destroy you. Or themselves. There will be blood. Please."

The creature did not pause. Perhaps this was what it wanted, for him to follow it into the wilds, wherever it was trying to take him.

A surge of strength caught Aitor, and he seized it by the shoulder, felt the hard lumps and whorls of massed skin under his fingers. He pulled at it until it faced him.

"No," he said, and he tried to infuse his voice with all the urgency he could. "You will die." He pointed back to the city.

At that, the creature looked. It saw the little dark figures huddled in the entrance of the Travelers' town, just slight slips of wavering shadow.

Understanding grew in the creature's eyes. In its hesitation, there was despair.

"Go away," Aitor said, and pointed away from the town, away from the direction the Other had originally been headed. He stabbed his finger randomly, hoping that he would be somehow understood. "Hide, there, or there, anywhere but home."

But the Other did not go. Instead, it seemed to have come to a decision. It lay its friend down gently at its feet. On its deformed and beaten face, Aitor saw resignation; he saw it making a choice. It would not go into the wilderness, exiled from its people to protect them, a sacrifice to the desert. Perhaps for someone of its kind, that fate was worse than death.

It ran: straight down towards the town of the Travelers, towards the hunters that waited for it, all armed, hoping to follow it home. It charged with reckless abandon across the uneven descent, seeming to shed all injury. It remained mute even as it ran.

The hunters far outnumbered it, and they were terrifying and efficient in their wrath. Aitor watched as they struck the creature down. He watched as it did not make any effort to fight back.

More and more people spilled from the gates of the town, crying an alarm. They brandished weapons and called for reinforcements, although the body of the Other already lay broken.

Someone fired a gun.

Aitor watched in numb horror as God's chosen people, the survivors of the Last Days, struck a spear through the creature's ribs, just to make sure that it was truly dead. A mockery. Even before, its body was torn to pieces and almost unrecognizable. Only its face remained intact.

He could not stop watching. He could not stop seeing it.

He could not stop seeing it and its human, human eyes, even after Noah came to find him, and took him away to a quiet place where no one could hear him cry.

CHAPTER 18

W HEN TALIT OPENED HER EYES, she was alone.
There was no comforting water full of stars overhead, no expanse of amber sand. Consciousness came to her all at once, and she was cold, her body contained more pain than she had ever thought possible, and she was so very alone.

A cradle of stones surrounded her, a tower of stone rising dizzyingly high around her on one side. On the other, not too far away, the ground dropped away again, disappearing steeply into mist.

At first looking at it, she was confused; it was curiously flat, and seemed almost like a picture. And then she realized that she saw it with only one eye. The vision in the other was gone.

It was close to morning, but there was no way to tell if she had slept for hours, or for days.

Get up, Talit, she told herself. There seemed to be nothing else to do. She could get by.

And then she realized that she was missing an arm, too.

The realization came with a skipped heartbeat, a shock that felt as if she had plunged off the edge of that cliff, and could not stop falling.

A lost arm. She would no longer climb the belltower of the Church of Prophet. She would no longer be the most acclaimed bellringer, but rather a fool who had received justice for her heresy, who, if she lived at all, would live sorting foods into baskets, with the children and the elderly.

They would look upon her, but only with small pity.

Talit's breathing came faster and faster as she stared at it, the missing place where her arm had been.

She must be calm.

She must hold herself together.

Ziek. She made herself think about her friend: stumbling up the side of an endless hill, following some star she did not see. He had looked at her so strangely. As if he were sorry for her, in that last moment she had seen him.

The dustwalker was gone now too. Dead, maybe. Had she killed it, or had the fire? Had she wielded the fire, or had it wielded her?

She forced herself again to look at the stump of arm that had carried the knife, her vision swimming with nausea.

The fire had saved her life. The flesh around the wound had melted and sealed around her shoulder and halfway down her side, leaving it a wet and scabrous mess. A tentative exploration of the side of her face and neck with her remaining hand told her that her face was the same.

She did not want to know what she looked like, could not bear to see the rest of her body, melted into itself, destroyed. Perhaps if she returned home, defeated and broken, they would not even recognize her. Perhaps there would be relief in that.

Her pack had fallen with her, tattered and scorched. She fumbled for it, a sudden desperate hope lifting in her. If she lived now, then maybe she would live further—maybe she would not die here, after all.

As she opened it, though, she saw that most of its contents had been spilled. All that remained now was a half-empty waterskin.

She struggled to open the skin with one hand, feeling her face burn with shame though there was no one to see her. Her muscles spasmed and her mouth did not seem to function right; the water splashed everywhere as she drank. There was enough for several deep mouthfuls—her throat burned with pain as she swallowed—and then it was gone. With her ruined ears, she heard nothing, not even her own noisy gulping.

For long minutes she sat on the ledge with the empty waterskin in her hand, her brain oddly empty of thought. She only existed, contemplating nothing. The silence was deafening.

She had been so close, she felt, to understanding, but that understanding had slipped away now until it was a hairsbreadth out of reach. It was as if the world wore a mask which, for a little while, had become translucent. And yet now that she had glimpsed it, it lay hidden to her once more.

All was lost. Lanon, her brother, who had not been waiting for her by the river. Her parents surely must be grieving two children now. Her life as a Chosen of Prophet, a holy bellringer, a guardian of the sacred.

And Ziek.

She looked up to the ridge above her. That was where she must have felled the dustwalker, where Ziek had left her, walking towards that wonderful delusion which she had made him.

No, he had told her, in an incredulous voice, as if she were a child, as if she were insane. No.

It would be foolishness to imagine that he was alive. He had walked blindly, a shell of himself, broken, his body a deformed mockery of itself, along the spine of the world.

She had killed him. She, who had brought him up into the hills to go hungry, to be stalked by dustwalkers, to suffer fruitlessly. She had lied to him, given him false hope. All for nothing.

But perhaps he really had seen something, Talit thought, and she clung to the thought. That thing which she was forgetting already, whose name was on the tip of her tongue. He had reached for it—he had believed in it—wasn't it better, then, that he had died happy, instead of frightened, submissive, beneath Leader's hand?

The Burdening was usually completed in the space of the ceremony, all the Sazer's soul offered to Prophet in a single moment. But there were stories Talit had heard, of the very first Burdening, the very first woman to be struck down by the change. It had taken days before she was gone from her flesh, her body walking stupid and empty and grotesque amongst her horrified people.

How much longer had Ziek lived than that? Talit had lost track of the days.

Something had propelled him, pulling him ever upwards along the rocky slopes, falling and cutting open his flesh like ripe fruit without even realizing.

She stood.

She had come to a decision, she knew, without really thinking about it. It was not something to be thought about. It merely was: the only option left to her, the only thing which made sense to her tired heart.

Every movement caused her agony, and yet there was no choice. She walked.

First she climbed to the place from which she had fallen. It took her the better part of an hour; her body would not do as she ordered it, and she fell many times, hunting for a good footing, for a place which was not as steep as a wall.

But she began to understand, now, what had moved Ziek so inexorably to the top of the forever-hills, despite his failing body, his clouding mind.

She must find the Lord; she must climb until she stood before him, or died trying. She must look upon his face and demand an answer.

That was all.

At last she clawed to the place where she had fallen, and she lay there, bleeding and blistered, for a long time, before she could pick herself up to look at it clearly.

The dustwalker's body lay crumpled in the path where it had been left. In the bald light of day, its grotesque killer's shape seemed worse somehow, something out of a bad dream that had been realized and left here to rot, charred and bloodied.

She saw that once again the body lay in the exact center of a perfect circle of soot and ash, as if an explosion had flattened the landscape around it. Her steps slowed as she approached it. Even in death it was fearsome. Its eyes had been picked clean by carrion birds already, but even so, the sockets laughed at her.

Her mother's knife lay buried in its throat, piercing up through its tough skin and leathery, blackened tongue.

This was what she had come back for, the reason she had made the effort to climb to this terrible place again. For if she did not have this, then how could she finish what she had come to do?

She pulled the blade free from the jaw of the dustwalker. The blade miraculously did not seem to be damaged, nor was the polished white of the bone handle blackened at all. She held it in a shaking, blistering hand, gripped it until she felt real.

Prophet guides me, she told herself deliriously, and then said it out loud, tasting the words on her scorched tongue: "I am not alone."

The path seemed to appear to her as she moved forward, her steps slow and deliberate and heavy. With the sun at her back, she followed her shadow, and she discovered that she was following a small and narrow path, a thin ledge which wound down the side of the great hill.

She thought at first that it was natural; it was uneven, and sometimes she walked freely, other times pressed fearfully against the cliff wall, picking her way over scattered rock debris. But as she pressed forward, she began to see small markers—small piles of stones stacked in tiny towers, or arranged in undulating patterns bordering the edge of the path.

Morning wore into the afternoon, but the sun's heat was carried away by the constant wind whistling through the crests of the hills. As the path ascended, she left behind the crags of the lower rocks and found herself walking along the tops of the hills again. It seemed that there was no end to their peaks; she would crest one, only to see that the path descended again, and there was another, higher than before.

Below, the desert and the trees and the river were far gone, hazy and one-dimensional through her single eye. The sun washed the land out until it was featureless, and she saw only the endless cascading of rock and rock, and more rock.

When she looked back, she saw that somehow there were two suns watching over her, unwavering eyes of fire. When again she went forward, she saw that her shadows had diverged, and she was flanked by two—no, three—no, four of herself as she walked.

When the sun had reached its highest point, the bells of the Church of Prophet sounded, as loud and clarion as if she crouched on the walkway high above the congregation, gathered for prayer. They tolled in exultant voices, and as they did, she heard the chanting of the faithful rise around her.

Though the words were meaningless, the sound was familiar, comforting, carrying her forward. The Sazers stood at the sides of her pathway, the wind catching at their veils and tunics, their hands folded to their chests. As she passed them, she felt that they sighed; that they mourned her, and for that, she was glad.

The pathway had broadened even wider now, and the stacks of stones became towers which grew more frequent, and gained shape. First she thought she saw a shoulder emerging from one of the pillars, and then she saw the slope of a neck.

The towers became the figures of people, and they loomed over her with chipped and crumbling stone eyes. They were not Sazers, but bore the alien smoothness of the beings depicted in the Church of Prophet—symmetrical, lean, strangely beautiful. As she passed between them, they, too, opened their mouths and joined the chanting, their stone throats giving unearthly voice.

Talit pressed on, and the road—for it was a road now, not just a pathway—bore her and up and up, and at last she crested the rise.

She found herself looking at the highest hill—not a hill. She had not really been walking up hills for a long time, she knew, but this final summit of rock could not be imagined as a hill in any way. She had no words for it. It towered over the rest of them, its shadow vast.

And just below it, nestled in a hollow between that massive hill and the one upon which she stood, highlighted by a flush of pink early-evening sunlight, she saw a city.

It was ancient and strange, far older than the city of the Sazers, which had stood for many hundreds of years. The sun's light seemed closer and heavier, somehow, painting the city a brilliant gold. Among its columns and shadows, the stone glowed amber, the color of a fire's last smoldering embers.

Its walls were unlike anything Talit had seen before. They rose smooth and impossibly high, each stone aligned too perfectly to be natural. At each end, peaked watchtowers stood even higher. Within, buildings seemed to flow into one another, layers and layers of unthinkably old halls stacked atop one another.

The road, lined with singing creatures, led directly to its gate.

Looking at it, Talit knew that this was where Ziek had been going all this time, that his trajectory had led him ever upward to find this ancient place, this city of unspeakable beauty; that something waited for her there, and she must go.

Starving, wounded, dreaming, dying: she began to run.

CHAPTER 19

NO ONE MOURNED FOR THE Others but for Aitor and Noah.
For the better part of an hour, Aitor grieved in Noah's home.
The soldier left him there quietly, and went to stand silent at the door,
keeping guard, his gaze tracking up and out as if he could see through
the walls to the home of the Others, where perhaps someone awaited the
homecoming of a brother, or a parent, or a child.

Look what we have done, Aitor prayed, and if he had prayed aloud,
his agony would have been a shout that could have been heard for miles.
Again and again: O God, have mercy on us. If there are but ten good souls
left here, have mercy. If there are but five. If only there is one. Have mercy.

When he was spent, Aitor went back out into the town. He would
give the creatures a burial, if nothing else. If God and all the world had
abandoned them, poor monsters, he would not.

The rest of the town had woken from their sleep, and stood talking
quietly in the streets by torchlight. As he passed them, they looked on his
grief-stricken face with cold and dispassionate eyes.

A great opportunity has been lost, they whispered as he passed, and
he pretended not to hear them, or to see the looks they exchanged. The
old priest gave them warning. He has ruined this for us, somehow.

Jacob met him at the gate, his face streaked and dusty from long
hours of standing at the watchtowers, swept by wandering desert winds.

When Aitor looked at him, he saw that this was not seminary-Jacob,
nor was it the Jacob of the apocalypse, he whom Aitor both loved and
hated. Tonight he was no one, a dead face and dead eyes, looking at a
stranger.

"Why have you done this?" he said, his voice low.

The Traveler guards—those who had been on watch, those who had murdered the Others—began to gather around, now, pushing Noah, speaking out, clamoring to be heard.

He must have warned it, Father, they told Jacob. He told it that we would follow them. We saw him pointing. It is his fault.

It attacked so fast, Father—

It might have killed us if we didn't defend ourselves—

We were afraid—

He has betrayed us—

Jacob lifted his hand, and the explanations sputtered into nothing. "He is only an old man," he said, his voice the color of a stone. "He does not know what he has done."

"Let me bury them." Aitor's own voice was raised; he heard it as Jacob must, old, feeble, shaken, hoarse. "Jacob, let me pray over them."

Jacob turned away. "He is no longer fit to be out and about by himself. You have all seen how he can no longer think clearly. Do not let him disturb the others."

Then he was gone.

Aitor cried out as they pushed Noah back, fought him as he struggled, one against twenty. There was something terrible and broken in Noah's eyes as at last he gave into the futility and stood watching, surrounded, as they led Aitor away.

They took him to the chapel, the only building now which was unused, and well-fortified. Once inside, they left two armed men at the entrance, and the rest of them dispersed.

Now long-emptied of its meager decorations and its only setpiece, the chapel was a bare room with a single stone slab, and many mats strewn over the grimy floor. It was no longer a holy place, only a hollow shell.

Aitor tried to imagine what might happen next. Would he be sacrificed? Would he live out the rest of his life here, forever watched, but in truth forgotten?

But it did not matter. If the creatures were not human, then neither were they, and they did not deserve to live, either.

He gathered up the mats on the floor, his back aching, and shuffled to the slab which had served as an altar. The men at the doorway glanced inside, but made no effort to help him.

Aitor piled the mats on the altar, forming a rough bed, and climbed atop it. He lay on his back at first, as he always did, and found his eyes searching for stars where there was only dark, cobwebbed ceiling. The walls of the chapel closed in around him and he felt the old claustrophobia closing in. Again he felt the walls of a box holding him imprisoned, tight, waiting for a future which, when it only came, would be wracked with uncertainty.

Outside he heard singing: the Travelers, mourning. Jacob's voice, indistinct, rang out as he spoke, reassured the people, condemned Aitor. The gathering lasted for well over an hour before sleep fell again on the town. At some point, the guard standing at Aitor's door changed.

Aitor paid neither the ceremony nor the guard any mind. He wept tearlessly on his crude bed, his body too dry and too ill-used to produce water. He wept for the Others and for the look on Noah's face as Aitor was taken away; he wept also for Jacob, and for the people of God who had inherited this cruel and soulless world.

Long into the night he pled for God to come, that He might explain why this great suffering was necessary. Let God justify why He would turn his back as His disciples slipped into darkness; why He gave no consolation as they died slowly, crying out in the tongue of pagans as they were consumed.

At last Aitor turned onto his side and curled into a ball, trying to empty his mind. But he saw instead the image of the Other on the ridge lifting its hand, crossing him with the same sign which he had made a hundred thousand times, the same sign with which he had been sent into his priesthood. Over and over the moment played—

He opened his eyes to see firelight playing off the walls of a building which had not seen true light in many weeks. Jacob stood over him, empty-handed, his torch settled into a sconce on the wall. He stared down at Aitor.

"Tell me," he said. "What did you see?"

Jacob's anger made him strong, wild. Aitor saw it building him, holding him together, fleshing him as ore fleshes plain rock. His beauty had been changed by it, until it was a feral, primitive thing.

Aitor was frightened, but not of Jacob, nor of death. Rather, he feared the bitterness which he felt lining his own veins, pulsing as a living being. If he died now, he would die with it in him, that part of Jacob which had taken root in his soul.

He closed his eyes so he did not have to look at Jacob's face. "I saw them," he said. "I saw that we are them."

"Yes," said Jacob. "We are them. We are God's forgotten ones. The exiles from the Promised Land. Do you see it now?"

I see it. Aitor would not say the words, would not believe it. No.

"Humanity," Jacob said. "Honor. A good death. That is the only salvation that is left to us. I know that you understand me. I know that you see as I do. You are just too proud to admit it. This is the only way. We have been abandoned. At last God has shown His true face, and we at the end of the world look upon it."

Aitor curled tighter. Very softly, he began to pray:

Blessed be God.

Blessed be His Holy Name.

Blessed be Jesus Christ, true God and true Man.

Once, aboard the ship, he had heard—had he imagined?—other voices praying with him. His voice alone now was frail and small. A dying man's voice.

"Will you praise God, then?" Jacob demanded, raising his voice now so that he spoke over Aitor. "Will you praise God when you are covered in sickness and your flesh is left to rot on this Christ-forsaken place? Will you praise God when you have spent your whole life in sacrifice for Him only to find that He shut the doors of Heaven and walked away from us? When you have lived and died for Him, and have nothing to show for it but misery and death? Aitor, will you praise him? Will you say that you love Him?"

And they were shouting at each other, then, Aitor, desperate, weeping again, his voice cracked and raw, their voices thunderous in the tiny chapel, loud enough that perhaps the whole town might have heard them.

At last Aitor's words trailed into helpless sobs, and Jacob stopped, too, breathing ragged.

Aitor convulsed silently on his bed of stone: a pitiful old man before his beloved, pathetic, lost, grieving. He no longer had care for what anyone thought of him but for his God, who had left him, and had taken away everything.

He felt a hand on his cheek, suddenly. He opened his eyes then and saw Jacob drawing him close, tears rolling down his pallid face too, tracking trails through the grime.

"Aitor, I'm sorry," he whispered. "I only want you to understand."

Aitor did not answer, could not answer. Jacob's thumb ran over his old, tired skin, found the wrinkles, traced them gently.

"I used to pray for salvation every day," Jacob said. "I had a vision of a dark monster that would consume the world. I was ten. So I prayed, and prayed. I entered the seminary because of it. I saw it coming, and I made it my life's work to pray that we would be spared."

He sounded distant, faraway now, as if he were telling a story to a child, as if he confessed to a mother.

"Even in the box I prayed, at first," he said. "I tried to count the days. I imagined them passing, for a while. Aitor, I have prayed for salvation and for goodness my whole life, and they have never come. You must understand that they will never come. I tell you this because I love you."

Aitor did not know how long Jacob stayed there with him. After a while, he got up, and Aitor felt the light of the torch flicker away, heard the sound of footsteps leaving the chapel. A little while later, footsteps came close to replace Jacob, to take up the guard position at the door.

Then again the night was the only sound.

Lying stiffly on his makeshift bed, Aitor wrestled the cancer that gnawed at him, the secret places of his soul which he was afraid to examine. He turned his thoughts over and over in his head until they grew blurry and faint, and at last he slept a troubled and nightmare-laden sleep.

Several hours later he woke to complete silence and a crippling, heart-thudding anxiety.

The night was black and empty, but filled with an anticipation now, a tenseness that felt as if the air were strung with wires pulled tight, on the verge of breaking.

He sat upright with great effort. Hunger clawed at his stomach and made his limbs weak, a familiar friend, and he ached from his walk up the ridge and his night spent on the hard, cold altar. His body felt as if it belonged not to him, but a wretch whom he watched from above, puppeted by fear and hate and great desire.

He walked to the entrance of the chapel. Only one man guarded it now; he recognized Pascal, who had once been a postgraduate student in finance, and who was one of the youngest of the Travelers. The boy was asleep, sitting against the wall. His club lay on the ground beside him, his fingers curled loosely around the wrong end.

He passed Pascal's sleeping figure and into the streets of the city the Travelers had built. It was very still. All the smoke from the fires had long dissipated; the little buildings they had constructed seemed empty. The night chill seemed to have frozen their tiny town into a single moment, which he disturbed by merely looking at it.

He looked up, towards the ridge where the beasts' bodies must lie. First he saw the small, vague figures of the Travelers on lookout duty on the watchtowers, fewer than they had been, slouched against scaffolding and dozing gently.

Then he saw the black shapes of creatures pouring down from the ridge.

They moved noiselessly, as if they were an extension of the desert, their scabbed and tortured flesh belying a startling grace. They did not make any war cries; they did not call for blood or shout to each other as the Travelers had. They moved with a singular purpose, in the complete darkness, a thick and shifting line on the horizon.

Aitor did not think that the lookouts had seen them, and if they had, they did not have a chance to cry out.

The beasts swept through the city of the Travelers like floodwater, breaking through the main entrance as if the guards that stood there were chaff in wind. Aitor stood in the center of the street, frozen, and watched those men die without a sound.

He could not force himself to call out for help; anguish had paralyzed him.

The beasts streamed toward him, and parted, as if around a sea, as if he were no more than a tree in their path. They bounded toward the dwellings of the Travelers, moving with that unstoppable, voiceless wrath. No wall or door or barricade could hold them back.

They held crude weapons, thought Aitor, weapons that looked like the Travelers' own.

Screams began to rise from the Travelers' homes. Aitor had not been touched, yet it felt as if each cry pierced his skin.

Then the first gunshots shattered the air.

He broke into a shambling run for the first time in many years. The hard-packed dirt of the streets jarred his joints and sent agony shooting up his legs. "Wake up," he shouted, voice hoarse. "Wake up, wake up, wake up."

The beasts, if they heard, did not seem to take notice. They moved from dwelling to dwelling, and in each one Aitor heard the sound of a terrible fight taking place.

The town had woken. The clamor filled the air, sharp and jolting in the dark. The Travelers raced through the streets, half-dressed in the armor they had been making for themselves, brandishing weapons, shouting for their loved ones.

Aitor found himself staggering blindly, panicked, breath gone. The world seemed to be closing around him in a tiny, dark vacuum.

The Travelers were fighting back—he saw blurs of movement, and new voices lifted now in anger, not fear. He saw blood in spattered beads across the dirt, saw torn bodies on the ground, broken or discarded weapons beside them.

Aitor was not brave or strong. He ran.

He passed Pascal, who had kept watch over him, the prisoner. The boy lay dead where he had slept, his throat slashed wide.

He passed Gisele, howling incoherently as she beheaded an Other messily with a club, her gun discarded and useless. She struck at the lifeless body again and again until it was unrecognizable, a pulp at her feet. She did not stop until another came from behind her and rent her apart.

In the center of a little dusty square, stripped of his armor, he found a small knot of Others, dead and tangled in a heap where they had died fighting together, and surrounded by the bodies of the Travelers who had killed them.

At the heart of that knot, he saw Noah.

His friend and protector lay, long-limbed and red-haired and pale against the bruised dark flesh of the Others, his body twisted and broken like a doll's. It was plain that he had fought against his own kin, and had been rent by bullets and punished by Travelers' clubs. Even at a glance Aitor saw how he had suffered for his betrayal.

His gun was limp in his hand, his eyes closed. His cheek was split wide from his chin to the corner of his eye, so that his teeth lay bare and bone-white beneath. And yet strangely, on his face was a strangely lovely smile.

It was Travelers who came running, who saw Aitor frozen and grieving at the edge of the square, unable to understand, unable to comprehend what Noah had done and the price that he had paid.

It was the sight of God's chosen people, bloody and enraged and suffused with lust for death, that woke Aitor.

He did not have time to say goodbye to Noah. He fled. And as he ran, the sight of Noah—ghastly, joyous, perhaps dead or dying—remained emblazoned in his sight, blocking out all else until his mind screamed with it.

Aitor came to the rectory building. The animal-skin which had covered its door had been ripped aside, and there was no one inside, the lights extinguished. There, he stumbled haphazardly through the dark until he could press himself into a corner and huddle into it, trembling, while the din of man killing man faded into terrible silence.

CHAPTER 20

T ALIT HAD EXPECTED THAT THERE would be Sazers there to greet her as she came to the city. A part of her had believed that they would line the ramparts, waving colored veils. Perhaps they would have sung, and their voices, un-Burdened, healthy and whole, would shake the hills to their foundations.

The statues lining the path had grown monolithic now, four times the size of any ordinary being. They no longer chanted; their stone faces looked straight ahead, and the song of the Sazers had long ago faded. Still she felt the presence of her people, though, waiting for her to discover their secret.

The gate of the city stood wide and unbarred. She entered to the sound of rowling wind curving round stone edges, to the sound of her own pattering feet on hard-packed dust and stone.

No voices called out to greet her; there was no sign of life. She saw shards of pottery on the ground, faded and sun-bleached. The drifts of sand seemed untouched by time. There were no smells of cooking meat, of smoke, of the everyday sweat of many bodies mingling with spices or perfumes. There was only the wind, thin and light and heady.

She slowed to a walk just within the gates, her ribs aching from the effort, her whole body quivering as it sought for breath and found very little. The road stretched before her—what must have been a main causeway—lined with tall buildings.

The faces of each structure were carved so intricately that it was hard to believe that any hand had made them. There were curling plants and blossoms she had never seen before, the faces of winged and staring people. There were pillars of stone which stretched as high as her belltower, and supported peaked shelves of stone inlaid with man-sized scenes of dancing, singing beings, just like the ones from the images from the Church of Prophet.

Talit sensed that there were people watching her as she made her way down the main road, following an invisible leyline which drew her further into the ancient city.

They appeared as flashes of color at the edge of her sight, color more brilliant than any she had ever seen in nature; they were flickers of shadow which escaped her as she turned her good eye to look at them. Sometimes she thought she heard a voice, words indistinguishable, but when she turned to wait and listen, there was no one.

Onward.

The main road took a gentle turn, and suddenly the buildings fell away from her. She found herself at the heart the city, the axis of a dozen smaller streets which spread away into the maze of impossible buildings and watchful stone faces.

Before her stood a Church. It was massive, larger again than the Church of Prophet by at least five times. The size of it stretched her mind, and it seemed to shimmer in the lazy light like a living thing, its stone breathing, humming, peaceful. Up and up it went; its roof was tiled with a glittering, hard material that caught light like water.

Its door stood wide, dusty, gaping. She could not see inside.

Her attention was caught, though, not as much by the beautiful Church as it was by the footsteps she saw trailing through the middle of the square, leading from one of the smaller streets and into the open mouth of the Church's opening. The footsteps were marked by blood, uneven, crusted and freshly pressed into the grit of the street.

Ghostly citizens passed close to her, brushing at her sides, tugging at her tattered tunic. But she did not care. She turned toward the prints and followed them. If someone had passed this way—if anyone were to dwell in a place so magnificent, so forbidding—it must surely be the Lord.

She passed into the Church. As though she stepped into another world, her vision adjusted itself to the dim lighting.

Where the rest of the city lay building upon building upon building, this construction stood the height of many layers combined. The ceilings vaulted high above her, lost in shadows above the tall open windows which sent streams of yellow light in long, dusty ribbons to the stone floor.

The door opened upon an enormous hallway supported by huge pillars lining an aisle as wide as a road. There had once, perhaps, been places to sit or kneel, but age and weather had collapsed them to be little more than heaps of rubble.

The Church of Prophet possessed weight, but this place possessed so much that it seemed to be all the heaviness of the world focused into the roots of the building. This was the anchor against which all things pulled. There were no enormous statues, no glittering, shining trimmings, only stark stone. But the simplicity gave it a gravity and sense of timelessness, of presence.

It was so easy to imagine the calling of bells in this place, the stern chanting of night prayer echoing against the bare walls, the intonations of Prophet a deep and round thunder which moved the hidden things within the soul.

Talit kept close to the walls, uneasy. To step into the openness of the aisles—even after a life spent under the open, unwelcoming sky—felt sacrilegious, as if something might strike her down if she entered. The footprints, too, meandered along the edge, as if the person before her had gone just as gingerly.

As she moved down the perimeter of the huge building, her steps whispered through the empty space and lifted a glittering wake of dust. She walked for many lengths, until she felt that she walked in a fever-dream.

Wake up, she told herself, and gripped her knife tight in her fist. She crept now with a growing fierceness along the edge of the Church towards its far end, too distant and shadowed for her to see.

When she fought the Lord, she would die. She knew this with a conviction that gave her yet one more step—again one more, and then yet one more still. Even her knife against his might was pitiful, nothing at all. But she would give it her everything; she would be her own small justice for her people.

And if she must die, at least she could say that she had tried to free Prophet; that she had tried to free them all. And so she could die the death of a hero, not that of a foolish cripple.

The dais of the main Church came into her view, three times as grand and high as the dais of the alcove. The altar which stood upon it was canopied with fluted pillars of stone, and a covering of stone which had been carved to look like cloth.

She ascended the altar stairs, her feet carrying her in an awkward shuffle. The knife felt cold, cold as night in her hand.

At the top of the stairs, she stopped. There, upon a dais which ascended the height of several Sazers standing atop one another, was something she did not understand.

There had never been anything like it in the city of Saze. It appeared to be a part of a shell of something which had once been much bigger, like a broken half of an egg. Despite its size, the sweeping height of the Church made the dais seem small.

Talit approached. She saw now that the thing was made from the same hard and polished stuff that could be found in the Church of Prophet, in some of the benches and in delicate curlicues that would not bend, no matter how hard they were pressed.

This thing had been badly burnt and warped; someone had tried to clean it, but the blackness of fire seemed to have become a part of it. Its sleek edges had been deformed beyond repair, curling like ragged claws.

At last she came close enough to see that upon a raised portion of the wreckage was a person.

His eyes were closed, and he lay flat on his back. He wore ragged clothes which perhaps had once been black, but had faded with time until they were pale and gray. On his chest he wore two gray, shining medallions that were marked with the same symbols which covered the inside of Saze's Holy Archive. His arms, crossed over his chest, clutched at a large tattered bundle which was black and sodden from grime and fire.

He was not a Sazer. Talit recognized his features immediately. This was a being like the ones depicted on the walls of the Church of Prophet, smooth, strangely lean and with that same perfect symmetry with which the church itself was built. He was very tall, far taller than a Sazer—had he stood, he would have loomed over any of them.

He was not the same as the towering statues and faded paintings, though. The face of this being was lined, and heavily creased in the same weather-worn way of all Sazers who worked beneath the ceaseless sun. He was marked with imperfections and scars—many large and raised and red, in the way of warriors, several which must have come from injuries grave enough to threaten death. One crossed his face from cheek to chin, so deep that it had twisted his mouth up to one side in a gnarled rope. Prophet had suffered greatly in his lifetime, she saw, in the pinched lines of his face, the deep grooves around his eyes and mouth.

Despite the marks of pain and hard work and exhaustion, though, he smiled.

Talit felt her heart pumping fast. It was all real, then. If the beings from the Church of Prophet were real, if this was one of them—

But this was not just one of them, she realized. This could not be—not in such a place of honor.

For generations, Storytellers had told the tale of a man who had sacrificed everything to save his people from the Lord. Of he who had given up his body so that his soul could spend every hour in communion with the Lord, pleading for the souls of the Sazers, the damned. He who spoke in his sleep every three hours upon the hour, to call them to prayer and atonement.

They had believed that he had four shining heads—that while his soul bore the brunt of the curse, his body had been cursed, too.

But Talit knew now that those were only stories; that they were not true.

This was him. This was Prophet.

Talit lay her knife and her mother's pack aside on the hard shelf on which the strange person slept. Then she reached out, and touched Prophet's face.

It was warm and soft, the flesh of a living person, and when she took her fingers away, blood flushed beneath his skin where she had pressed.

Yet he did not move, not even so much as to breathe.

"Talit," said a voice from just behind her, and she turned, and saw Ziek.

He stood slightly to one side; had she missed him, or had he been there, watching? It did not matter—he was here now—he stood alive before her, his face swollen. His eyes were faraway and wandering, full of something else. "He is here."

She closed the distance between them in a heartbeat, wrapped her single arm around him. He rocked as she embraced him, his now-unfamiliar body wracked and shaking, steadied only by her grip.

"He is here," she agreed, tears stinging at her eyes. And Ziek was here, too. For that moment, that was all that mattered.

Ziek let her pull back and then hug him again, but she sensed that even as he put his arms around her, he was not truly present.

"He is here," he repeated, insistently, now, and pointed. She followed the slant of his finger to Prophet.

"Yes," Talit said again. She stepped closer to Prophet once more; she put her hand on his cheek. "Wake up," she whispered, and then louder. "Wake up. Save Ziek; save us all. Please help us."

Prophet did not respond to her, though his skin warmed her cold hand. There was no breath, no movement.

"Wake up," she repeated, and as Ziek stood behind her with that distant, bemused expression on his face, she found herself growing more frantic. If the Lord was close by, perhaps if Prophet woke he would help her to fight him. He could do something, anything to end this terrible cycle. "Wake up—wake up—wake up—we are dying, why do you sleep!"

Anger rose up in her as he did not answer, and she raised her arm and struck him across his face. First lightly, and she trembled with sudden fear the blasphemy of it; but he did not stir, and then again she struck him—again and again—and again he did not move.

Should he not have risen up against her? she thought; he, who had the power to hold back the punishment of the Lord with the weight of his prayer and favor, should be able to kill her as she stood.

Perhaps it was nothing, then, she thought, and she realized that she sobbed in anger, that he had betrayed her; that it had all been a lie.

And Talit understood that there would be no movement from him, not so long as the sky held firm and the sun turned around the world: that even as she and Ziek died, he would sleep forever.

She shoved him then, haphazard and crooked, and Prophet's body slid askew over his resting place, arms flying wide to let the bundle in his hands come loose, where it toppled to the ground behind the altar with a clatter that resounded like thunder in the deep corners of the church.

Spent, Talit stood and let tears slide down her face. She had lied to Ziek, and now she realized she had lied to herself, too.

She did not want to kill the Lord. The knife she carried was too small for the magnitude of this weight she carried within her. Prophet could have helped her to find him—Prophet could have come with her.

But she would not have killed him. No—if he were only here, then she would have begged him for help, for him to lay aside the curse of the Burdening and end the death of her people. Perhaps she would even have asked for forgiveness for all those years ago—she would even have groveled—

If he were here, she could have at least asked where Lanon had gone; if he yet lived; if he had died peacefully.

If the Lord were here—

She looked at Ziek, where he stood rapt and staring at the body of Prophet where it had fallen. There was a new expression on his face now; he seemed disturbed, sad.

Perhaps now he understood, she thought, that she had lied, that she had failed, that they would both die now. Perhaps he would leave her.

Prophet did not watch them, she knew now. Did anyone?

Why had they come here? What had Ziek hoped to find?

"I'm sorry," she told him.

She had just stepped around the side of the altar, her sandals scrabbling for purchase on the shining material of the wreckage, when something on the ground caught her eye, its color moody and solemn against the yellow and russet of the church.

Her heart knew what it was before her thoughts could register. It was a fold of filmy, faded cloth; it had been woven thinly with great care, decorated with the patterns of the Sazers. She caught it up in trembling fingers and unfolded it to see the Sazer marks that meant a prayer for farewell, a blessing for travel.

Father had woven those marks into the purple sash with his own hands, sitting long hours into the night, his eyes burning with exhaustion and with tears. Mother had wept as this shroud was laid upon Lanon's shoulders on the day of his Ceremony, as he was committed to the Lord, to suffer forever.

It had lain on the ground haphazardly and crumpled, as if it had been shed in haste. Beyond it, Talit saw that there were more sashes: the whole of the wreckage behind the body of Prophet was covered in them. Some lay folded in neat squares; others were hung draped from sharp corners.

The shadows had hidden them, but now Talit stepped into the belly of the broken shell, and in its scorched blackness she saw a tapestry of Sazer art: hundreds and hundreds of sashes, of burial shrouds for the yet-living. Here hung the work of countless grieving hands, marked with the patterns for grieving, for steadfastness, for resolve of heart, for comfort and for memory.

Here lay a legacy of her people.

"Where are you?" Talit said, her voice echoing in the church again and again until it seemed that someone else whispered to her from all sides. "Lanon?"

And then she shouted it, until her ears rang; she ran from the wreckage to hunt through the church in a frenzy. Her brother, her brother, Lanon had been here.

When she did not find him there, she raced out into the silent square, into the empty city. The whispering she had heard earlier taunted her now; in every dusty and wind-worn home she thought she would throw wide the door and see him, and with every corner she turned, it was his arms into which she imagined throwing herself.

Lanon, she cried out again and again, but there were no other foot-steps, and at last when she had circled the city what felt like a dozen times and stood alone in the empty square, the silvery sun offering no warmth, the empty city no longer whispered. The hilltop and its immense stone tomb were filled with the same silence that pressed against Talit's corners, a waterskin filled to bursting.

He is not here, she thought, and fell quiet. The emptiness of the place swelled to fill the place of her voice, resounding and final.

Ziek came out into the square behind her, his shuffle slow but steady. Somehow he had picked up her pack and slung it over his own narrow shoulders.

For a precious moment, the film which covered his eyes these days had fallen away: he did not see whatever strange visions had been trou-bling him, but instead saw Talit, his best friend, who had lied to him, and taken him into a strange place to die at the hands of monsters. But in his gaze she saw neither anger nor rebuke, but joy, a peace that she could not understand.

"How?" she asked him, expecting no answer, and there was none, but he put his hand out to her.

She made herself stop crying, wiped her nose with the back of her wrist.

He took her single hand in his swollen, deformed one. And as he traced it once with his thumb, the sweetness of his gesture told her that for these few and precious moments he was wholly Ziek again, not just a fading stranger.

And with that sweetness, the warmth of his eyes as he turned to the path to start again on whatever strange mission he walked, Talit felt a seed of light within her: a tremor of faith, defying all impossibility.

Lanon was alive, she thought. He was not here, but somewhere he was, and he was alive. He must be, and he had found already what it was that they sought; if they went a little further—just another step, and then another—they would find it, too.

Ziek sees it, she thought. He knows where it is. And whether the thought was desperation or faith, she no longer cared, for what was there to lose?

She, too, would go anywhere to follow this senseless light, this hope-less hope.

Lanon lives. Lanon lives. We will live too. And if he did not—and if they died here in this alien wasteland—then at last she would put her face to the earth and admit defeat, but not until that moment came.

They left the abandoned city slowly.

And as they turned from the hills, she no longer led Ziek, but turned her feet to the light he carried, for the rest of her world was darkness.

CHAPTER 21

T HE SILENCE LASTED FOR MANY minutes. For as long as Aitor
strained, he heard nothing: not even the howling of the strange animals that patrolled the desert at night, no calls of survivors hunting for
other survivors.

Perhaps, Aitor thought, he was finally alone again. And the thought
brought him no peace.

He waited, and as he did, drifted in and out of consciousness, waiting for someone to find him. They would punish him then. Perhaps they
would execute him. Or it would be a creature of the desert, come to deliver the same justice that they had given the rest of the Travelers.

He no longer prayed for mercy, and yet no one came to end him.

At last, his bones stiff and aching, he crawled from his hiding place,
and came out into the pale light of the moon.

The city stank of death. In the emptiness now he saw the fight clearly
as it had happened; the chaos and terror spilling into blood which had
soaked the hard-packed sand and turned it rust-brown, the scattered
belongings which the Travelers so carefully protected.

The buildings they had worked so hard to reinforce had been damaged; there were half-walls standing tremulously upright and unsup-
ported, rubble lying in the streets which they had so carefully cleared.

Bodies lay crumpled in small dark heaps along the walls—not as
many as he had thought, but enough, humans and beasts alike. Over each
one he stopped, and out of habit, he offered a prayer.

There were others in the streets, congregated in small groups. They
did not weep, or if they did, they wept silently. Their hard faces were instead grim and tight and cold; they bandaged their wounds, and collected
their dead even as he prayed over them.

Aitor did not see any of the Others alive. Against the guns of the Travelers they had not truly stood a chance, even in overwhelming numbers.

His feet carried him by instinct to his chapel.

What had been once a house of hopeful prayer—and then the lonely haunt of an ill and obsolete old man—was now destroyed. A fight had taken place there, an ugly fight from which no victors had emerged.

Man and beast lay tangled in a gruesome mess, spattered blood and brains dried and darkening and stinking like a slaughterhouse. There were several bodies there, unrecognizable. On one side, the wall, weakened by time and age and weather, had given way, leaving the building to lean awkwardly on three legs. The altar had been knocked askew, the paltry decorations and the contents of the sacristy scattered and soaked in charnel.

Very clearly Aitor could see it as it had stood that first night when the Travelers had brought their woven mats and flower garlands. Facing away from the congregation and his face upturned to the cross of Knurów, he had offered Mass with Jacob to the light of two blessed candles brought from the chapterhouse of his Order. That night a small matching flame had lit his heart, too.

He found that he could not weep. Whether it was because his body did not hold enough water or that his soul was as dry as his tongue, he did not know.

Aitor turned his back on the destruction. Perhaps there was a prayer he might have said to somehow undo the foulness of the death that lingered within; a prayer to forgive the Others, or perhaps the Travelers. None came to him that he could think of.

He walked on, avoiding the groups of Travelers he saw. They pretended not to see him, too. Better that they grieve now, and worry about him later. An old man could not run far in this wasteland. He would be there and waiting for their judgment when they were ready.

The main square lay abandoned. There was no one there; the people had fled from it, seeking shelter in the warren of small pathways between makeshift buildings, away from open ground.

The large altar they had built to replace the chapel had survived the attack. Bloodied by the sacrifices they had offered, it looked no different from the rest of the city. It stood upright and desolate in the night.

Aitor stopped before it, and a chill washed over him. Where the crucifix of Knurów had once stood guard over the firepit, a witness to the sacrifices of the people, there was only emptiness, and the broken remnant of the pole on which the crucifix had hung.

The loss of the Traveler people was great, and he knew that he was being selfish. But the absence of the staring and afflicted Christ left him feeling more gutted than the sight of the chaotic deaths, the gore smeared through the streets.

The last thing he had left of his time aboard *La Trascendencia* was gone; his last connection to a life where he had been young and strong, and once, full of hope. Aboard his ship, adrift in the stars, Aitor had walked lighter not just because of the lesser gravity, but because of something which had drawn him upwards even when there was no longer any concept of up.

God might have been there, with hands outstretched one last time, waiting for the moment when humanity would reach back—

If this had been a test, then they had failed; Aitor had failed. Now they must surely be alone, unforgiven for the last time.

Aitor felt his mouth stretch wide. He cried soundlessly, his skin pulled tight as a mask. He fell to his knees before the broken pole. He was weighted there; he felt his soul sinking down to grow roots in the dirt.

At last he fell quiet, his face buried in his hands. The stench of bodies was so pervasive that his nose had grown accustomed to it. Now there was only the stink of his unwashed body as he tucked his nose into his sleeves.

Aitor listened. He heard the sound of the open sky above him, the harsh cries of circling carrion birds arriving, the sound of whispering footsteps padding closer.

"It is finished," said Jacob's voice, and Aitor sat up, because the voice was not the calm and commanding bass which seemed as if it could silence storms, could demand the presence of a god over bloody, thrashing sacrifices. No: this was the voice of a man on the brink of falling apart.

Jacob stood over him, his shoulders low, his cassock torn to expose a gashed shoulder. In his arms he carried the corpse of Gisele. He had wrapped her in a blanket of coarse cloth, so that only the top of her head was visible, cradled against his chest, but the blanket was soaked through already.

"It is finished," Jacob said, and this time he laughed, a choking, grating sound.

Aitor looked at the chaotic light in Jacob's eyes, at the way his hands were coated in gore and filth, how he clutched at Gisele's body and made no effort to clean them. There he saw the same Jacob who had awoken, wild, from sixteen hundred years of isolation; he saw that there was madness in his eyes, a heathen fire of retribution that could not be quenched.

Jacob carried Gisele past Aitor, then, up the massive altar, and lay her at the foot of the broken pole. Her body huddled there beneath its blanket gave no indication of the disease that had begun to eat at her flesh.

Jacob descended the stairs slowly. Aitor waited, motionless, unable to hold his gaze without trembling, unable to look away.

"For this and all that came before it, I will not forgive Him," Jacob said. "I will never forgive Him, for He knows what He has done."

"Please," Aitor whispered. He could not stand to hear it, but neither could he deny it, the raw and gaping pain which Jacob felt and which he felt, too. "Please."

Jacob sank to his knees then, beside Aitor, and he huddled there like a child who could not face the world, his face in his hands. "Nothing matters. There is no hope."

Aitor did not answer him. There was a void yawning inside him, one that ached and swelled and which he did not want to face. To repeat those words, to give them life himself, would have been to give in to despair.

"We are God's playthings," Jacob said, his voice muffled. "He made us in His image, it is said. Did He get bored? Were we not faithful, until the end? Was this what He meant when he would not destroy the city, for the sake of the just? What did we do wrong?"

Laughter, then. A high-pitched giggle broke free, and when he lowered his hands, his expression had lost its accusation, had grown feral and unfocused. That mania Aitor had seen within him burned bright. There was blood in the tears that stood unshed in his eyes.

"I will burn them," Jacob said. "I will take God's toys away. The poor sons of bitches out there, and us. He will have no one left to mock."

Aitor still did not speak, but Jacob turned to him, and took him by the shoulders with ungentle hands. "Then we at least might die alone, in peace," he said, pleading. "Then we will be free."

And suddenly the thought came to Aitor that he should kill Jacob, to take a knife and twist it deep into his throat. It would be so easy for him to take control now, to end this pretender and his false prophecies. The people would believe that the creatures had killed Jacob; they would mourn him, and that would be the end.

At the expense of his own soul, he could lead them back to truth.

But even then, he thought, what would he say?

"The people will know it is hopeless." A last resort, a weak plea.

That same thin, stretched laugh from Jacob, again. "And they will go," he said. "They will die in bitter and glorious defiance, and they will die happy because they will choose to be deluded. It is better than to die alone and cowering from the truth, like rats."

A violent image came to Aitor then of his hands encircling Jacob's thin neck; he imagined finding the thin and delicate windpipe, crushing it.

But he could not do it. How could he take away a last hope—even when it was a lie—from a people who were slowly losing everything? And if he did, what words could he speak to comfort them?

"There is no hope," Jacob repeated, and he pulled his cassock from his shoulders then, tore it wide and exposed his skin to the chill of early morning. "Soon it will be over."

There, standing out from his chest and stomach and hips, Aitor saw the telltale disfigurations, worse than Gisele's, worse than Conor's.

Jacob was mutilated, disfigured; his body swelled and press out in strange ways which had been hidden by the baggy folds of his cassock on his shrunken frame. His skin was no longer the color of human flesh; it flaked and oozed black.

Aitor stared at Jacob as he stood bare-chested before him. Beneath the deformations he was emaciated, made of jutting bone and lean, desperate muscle. No longer did he wear his iron mask of authority; he no longer exuded boundless and unbridled youth. And he was no longer lovely.

"If God spoke to me today," Jacob said, "I would curse Him with every breath. Look around you, Aitor. Tell me that you see the hand of the Lord. Of unending love."

And Aitor closed his eyes against the sight of the death around him, his sorrow and love and hate a leaden thing. He held in his mind the image of the Other, holding up its hand, blessing him, marking him with the sign of Christ in this cruel and evil world.

"I will not yield," he said once more. "You will not break me. I will believe."

Jacob's face flushed heavily. He lifted his head high, his eyes like black stones in his face. "Leave, then," he said. "You who love God so much, then, see if He will save you in the end."

But this time he did not turn his back on Aitor, waiting for him to go; instead he watched him, as a beast watches its prey. It was the first time that Aitor had truly felt that Jacob hated him. But now feeling it, he understood, and accepted it.

"Please do not do this," Aitor said at last, thinking of the creatures, of their human eyes in their deformed and terrible faces. "Do not end it like this." For looking at Jacob he saw that despite their small numbers and their weakness he was already planning something of great magnitude, that nothing could stop the self-designated Prophet of the Lord from wreaking revenge. He would sow and reap blood until the world was soaked again.

Beyond Jacob, the sounds of the Travelers were beginning to stir in the town; people crying out for one another, low sobbing, rubble being scraped away to search for survivors.

But Jacob did not answer him.

"I will tell them the truth," Aitor said. "I will tell them you only want revenge."

Jacob smiled, then, no warmth in it. "Then tell them," he said. And Aitor, thinking of Gisele, that night he had confronted her—despairing calmly, glad for placating lies, laughing at him in that casually cruel way—knew that Jacob was right.

Aitor turned to look again at the ghost-image of the cross of Knurów, for even stolen, he had felt that its shadow was still with them. Now, though, there was nothing.

Where shall I go? he asked the broken pole.

O Lord, I know that I have failed you.

He began to walk towards the entrance of the Travelers' city, where a few of the Travelers had begun to gather, carrying bodies to be buried, salvage to be rebuilt.

Jacob called after him, his voice rasping harshly. "Where will you go?"

Aitor thought of his lost sketchbook, how he had so naively dreamed of building a place for God to find, the way a child builds a perch for a bird to rest. He thought of the last tangible piece of Christ he knew in this world, its ugly and frightening face. "I will go to find my Lord," he said, his voice dull.

Jacob sneered, then; Aitor heard it thick in his voice, knew that Jacob had somehow read his most secret thoughts. "Do you truly believe God was in that piece of wood?" he said. "Do not mourn for it, Aitor.

Mourn for yourself, and mourn for us all. For we are lost from Him, and even you cannot find us. We are a mistake. He has not been stolen. He has deserted us forever."

Aitor turned to answer him, but he had already walked away.

One last time Aitor wandered through the streets of their little town, once the hope of humanity, once a promise of life, a new world.

The Travelers made way for him. None of them would come near him, nor even look at him. Some of them had heard the exchange in the square, he knew. But if they knew that Jacob's plan would kill them, they gave no indication. Their expressions were as cold as tombstones.

Once again he passed Noah's body, but his heart was sick, and he could not make himself stop for fear of what he might see.

In leaving, he took nothing. There was no reason to do so. He would go quietly—perhaps to his death, and in that way perhaps he could atone.

If he did not die—then what?

The sun was rising as he labored his way for the last time up the hill to the place where he had once slept, overlooking the square where they had feasted and sacrificed.

On a whim he walked up to his old sleeping place, where once he had kept a lonely watch on the people he had rescued.

At the very top of the hill, where he had spread his bedroll, there was only a dark stain on the rock where the smaller of the two creatures had lain; the bodies had been taken away.

Time would erase this place, he thought; soon the Travelers would be gone, and there would be nothing left of their story, nothing left of the foolhardy survivors who had set off into the stars all those years ago. No church, no city.

Aitor looked back over the city of the Travelers. A tail of smoke rose from a place hidden from his sight, and he knew that they were burning the bodies.

The square itself lay empty, entirely deserted now. There was nothing left for him.

He turned his gaze to the horizon. The humming wind had already shifted the sands, but he had seen which way the Other had looked, as it thought of a home it would never see again. He thought of how it had beckoned to him, tried to draw him away into the desert wilderness.

He began to walk.

He did not know how long he walked, or why he bothered to stand up again when he had fallen. The warm dunes cradled him and the wind sang beautiful, distant songs, but still he got up and walked yet further.

He did not know how long it had been since he had eaten or drank. A thought grew in his mind, an understanding of why he pushed forward: if I keep walking, perhaps I will find Him. I will bring Him back to my people. I will bring Him to Jacob.

And in answer to that thought, Jacob's own voice speaking from where it had nestled in his thoughts: do you truly believe God is in that piece of wood?

Did he go, then, in search for the crucifix, or something more?

The thought grew and thundered now with every beat of his heart, which now filled his ears, the swelling roar of a beast. And he saw the beast sometimes, flickering shadows at the corners of his eyes which resolved themselves into nothing when he looked directly at them. He found himself imagining, too, that the sky, which hung heavily and painfully blue, was a vast pool into which he might plunge his head and drink for hours until he burst.

A new hallucination came into view, hazy on the horizon, then; a city of stone and earth houses, all hung with small colorful cloths and mats, a bustling metropolis in the midst of the waste like the remnants of some city from the ancient histories. Smoke twisted up from between its roofs, and he dreamed that he heard the voices of its many people, saw small dark shapes moving about its streets. It stood surrounded by a wall made of high-piled stone and sharpened stakes facing outwards.

As he drew nearer Aitor smelled cooking meat, and realized suddenly that it was not a dream at all. And just as he understood, the shapes of a dozen creatures appeared at the gates and approached him.

They surrounded him smoothly and swiftly, closing around their prey. He saw in their eyes that they knew of the deaths of their brethren, and also of the slaughter of the Travelers.

Aitor stumbled before them, nearly pitching into their knees as he skidded forward in the soft sand. The world rolled violently, like the heaving of a ship.

He saw the sand before him, churned by many heavy feet, and his hands scrabbling for purchase as he tried to right himself; he saw also himself as if from above—an old man, emaciated and wild, his face streaked with dirt and tears; more creature than human.

"He will kill you," he told them. "He will destroy you for what you have done."

The creatures looked down at him and did not make a move. Perhaps, he thought desperately, they pitied him.

In a final effort, he raised himself up and, trembling, traced the Sign of the Cross in the air before them: both a statement and a question.

Then they were speaking to him, pulling him upwards, their voices rising with questions in a language he did not understand—but Aitor fell forward and into deep sleep, and he could not hear them.

CHAPTER 22

Talit and Ziek descended the hills slowly.

They could not move faster than a shamble, for Talit had little balance with only one arm and eye, and Ziek was growing worse by the day.

He no longer possessed the clarity he had shown her in those brief minutes outside the church. He smiled often, and stared at the horizon ahead at something unseen, which seemed to hang some distance above the ground. Sometimes he hummed, in the tunes of the Sazers' chant, but he no longer spoke the words. She did not know if there were thoughts left behind his eyes.

And that was only part of him that was still recognizable to her as Ziek; the rest of him had bloated and rotted beyond recognition. He lumbered as a beast would. If the weight of the pack bothered him—if it bothered him that his flesh sloughed from him in patches as it rubbed at him with every step—he gave no indication.

But he led them now. Talit did not keep track any longer. The hilltops all blurred together; the orange-blue rocks were all the same. The skies were blue, or they were pink or yellow or gray or bone white. It did not matter.

She followed Ziek. Where he went, she would go also, and that was the only thought left for which her mind had space.

Any hopes of returning to Saze were gone, now. Sometimes she wondered dimly what destination drew Ziek, for surely they were growing closer, and other times she was convinced they went in circles. All her steps felt the same. That small hope she had felt now stuck in her throat, and ached.

On the third day, though, they found a thin trickle of running water. There they plunged their faces into the water like dogs, and drank until their stomachs were distended and aching.

That day they huddled in the shelter of a rock overhang, holding each other, and did not journey farther for the day. Ziek drifted in and out of wakefulness, shuddering with the pain of his deformations, and then again with the pain of his own movement.

While he was asleep, Talit kept watch over the world far below them. By turns she imagined that the sun was spinning around the earth, and then that it was the world which spun round the sun. From here everything was so small. Even the river below them which fueled the life of Saze seemed a motionless crystal catching light, and throwing it up in little twinkles.

When Ziek was awake, he was aware only a little of that time.

"Where are we going?" she asked him, once.

He blinked up at her, and turned his stare down along the invisible path they had been following. They had long left the tall statues of the smooth people behind, and now Talit did not recognize their surroundings.

"Where we have to go," he told her.

"Where is that?" Talit asked.

"Where we can see."

Finally, she gave up. The cryptic answers meant nothing to her, and she had already resigned herself: it did not matter where she went. The world had fallen away, and something else was closer now. She felt it as a strange pressure from both outside and inside her, moving them: where?

In that day of respite, they slept, and it was a blessing that gave them the strength the next morning to stand up and try again.

On the fourth day, they found plants again, small tough things that gave her stomach cramps and were awful to the taste. Ziek ate when he was fed, but if the food was not held to his torn lips, he would only stare dreamily over the horizon.

As they left the hills behind, the heat grew unbearable, and their fevers were no longer cooled by the high winds. Delirium returned, and Talit found herself dreaming as often as Ziek did, her mind slipping away from her once again.

It was more peaceful this way, to travel numbly and to imagine a million birds spilling over the sky in rivers, sloughing light from their wings; to see strange symbols hovering in the sky, staring and brilliant eyes which stirred among the clouds and blinked down at them. It was only for Ziek that she forced her mind to come back from its wanderings, to try and see the world as she knew it.

To mark the time, Talit began to chant in a monotone. She chanted all of the words she remembered from the Songs of Prophet, which Ziek had told her were hymns of praise and petition and lamentation from long ago. Her voice was whipped away by the vastness of the wilds around them, but it gave her something to hold onto in the long stretches of silence.

Sometimes Ziek's voice joined hers, wavering and small. He harmonized even though he could not speak, as if the songs were pulled from some other place in him that could not be removed.

If only they could have learned what the songs meant, Talit thought, dully, hopelessly. If only they could have learned some ancient secret hidden within them.

On the fifth day, Talit realized that the sun had risen and set since Ziek had last spoken or even sang. There were no more moments of clarity, and his distant smile had no recognition for her. His eyes bore the blankness of the Burdened; his feet shuffled forward, but his mind was no longer there.

It grew hotter and hotter. The stone of the hills burnt their feet and they walked with blisters which opened and left a wake of blood and pus behind them. The wind rose until it was a constant keening, and it battered them until they were chapped and covered in filth.

Talit cried for Ziek as she walked, her tears tracking trails down the dirt on her face. She held his hand, but it no longer really felt like his.

On the seventh day, they left the hills behind them and found themselves once more among scarce trees and the cover of immense rocks stacked atop each other, as if giant children had placed them there.

They were still near water, but it was unfamiliar to Talit, and she could not tell if they followed the river which would lead them to Saze, or if this were a branch which took them yet farther away. If Ziek knew, he did not say.

On that day, the winds kicked even higher, and the edge of the sky darkened to a deep red-orange, as if a giant had spilled the contents of his bowl into the heavens. Talit, startled from her vacant daydreaming, looked up and saw that a storm was coming.

The storms came rarely to Saze, rarely enough that Talit had only heard of them. At the time of their last passing, Lanon had been healthy, she very young.

The storms were the reason that the Sazers lived so plainly. Storyteller told many tales of the people before the Yellow Year, who had lived and worked in grand shining towers. They had created beasts that served them and did much of their work for them; they had had time to ponder the mysteries of the earth, and to discover its underlying magic.

But they had grown proud, Storyteller had said; the storms were the Lord's way of keeping his people simple, and close to him.

The storms were known as cleansings: renewal, rebirth. Many Sazers were lost to the dusts, flayed by biting sand carried with the force of a god's smiting hand. Buried alive. The Sazers stayed within their homes— sometimes for weeks—and there they prayed, their water containers full of grime, their food grit between their teeth, dying of starvation, of thirst.

But always, there was someone left to rebuild from the wind-picked bones of their city, to begin again.

And always, always the Church of Prophet remained standing.

Now as Talit squinted with her good eye through the erratic landscape, the dusts hung in the air heavily in thick orange-brown clouds, pluming like smoke. Ziek did not look up to follow her gaze.

"We have to find shelter," Talit told him, and she tugged at his arm insistently. When she had come to a halt to look, he had walked on, and now he pulled back, his gaze focused on the invisible path that lay open to him. It was not very hard to hold him.

"No," she told him, and she repeated herself three more times, each time louder than before.

At last she finally yanked him to her. She was angry with this body that had been Ziek, this body that was stupid and mindless now and could not hear what she wanted to tell him. He fell, snuffling and whimpering as he caught the ground with an awkward wrist, and at once she helped him up.

"I'm sorry," she told him, her eyes burning. "I'm sorry. I'm sorry."

They took shelter in a grove of trees backed by several tall rock formations, and there Talit held him to her.

She must stay awake, she told herself; awake long enough to make sure he did not try to pull free from her, long enough that perhaps he would sleep first.

The dusts rolled over them.

The world became orange with the cleansing—a living, angry thing. It swept bare the face of the land, throwing debris, tearing branches, levelling ground. Their meager shelter offered little protection, and the world seethed with hot stinging dust that felt as if a thousand small fires tore at her skin.

For hours she huddled there, her eyes squeezed shut, her hand cramping as she clung to Ziek, who at last did not struggle. She listened to the hum and roar and whine of the storm as it moved around them. As she listened, she heard other things, too, as her mind drifted through exhaustion and hunger and pain.

She imagined that she heard the voice of Prophet, calling them all to morning prayer; she heard the greeting calls of Sazers as they went to their daily work; very distantly, the stomping and clapping of a celebration, the cheery piping of a flute and the bang of a tambour.

She thought she heard her beloved bells, calling her from not too far away.

At last the sound of the storm around her joined these other things, and settled into the rhythm of a cruel song, and she lay comforted by it, her pain long settled into numbness.

When she woke without realizing she had been sleeping, her hand was empty, and she knew that Ziek had gone.

CHAPTER 23

THEY DID NOT KILL AITOR, but instead lay him somewhere soft, and there were blankets arranged around him. Something hot and warm was spooned into his mouth, and then he slept again.

When he woke, time began to pass very quickly and very slowly all at once, and he lay suspended half living, half dead. The world was pieced from shimmers of color and smells, sounds and faces.

The faces that came and went were those of nightmares, and though their hands were soft as they tended to him, he could not shake the image of Gisele, made a terrible thing in death, from his mind, could not stop hearing the screaming of his people. As they came to him, he cried out and whimpered and tossed and turned until they left him in blessed darkness.

In that darkness he found himself once more in his cryobox aboard *La Trascendencia*. He was peaceful, asleep. Here he was secure knowing that he was safe, prepared to make his sacrifice for God's people. His years in seminary were not long behind him; his head was full of the grand sermons of the Superior General as they readied themselves to depart the earth.

There were no deserts, no wastelands. God wheeled always above them, a comfortable unknown.

Let me sleep, he thought, for unconsciousness was easier.

And so he slept; when he came close to waking, they gave him food and drink until his eyes closed heavily once more, his body trembling and aching with the long-forgotten sensation of fullness and nourishment.

But at last he did wake, and he opened his eyes to see that he was in a small house—a single room, built of stones and hard-packed earth. In the corners there were crude wooden chairs draped in patterned cloths, a small table on which sat an earthenware jar. The air was strangely heavy and smelled of oncoming rain.

Aitor struggled to stand from where he lay, swathed in blankets, and found that his hands and feet were bound with crude shackles of thick-twisted rope.

They had not killed him, he thought dumbly; the sign of his faith had saved him, just as it had not saved the creature who had died outside the walls of the Travelers' town. They had had mercy.

They came to him then, two of them; perhaps they had heard his struggling, and had been waiting for this moment. They were creatures like the ones he had seen come to destroy their city, and the sight of their mutated limbs and puckered flesh filled him with instinctive fear and loathing.

But they did not slaver; did not raise hands against him. They gently lifted him to his feet, and with a small stone knife produced from the folds of their ragged clothes they cut the ropes binding his feet. He found now that with their ministrations, he was strong enough to stand, to straighten his back a little, to lean on them without faltering.

Neither of them spoke, and he was too surprised to do anything but stare. Instead they stood near him expectantly, waiting.

Aitor followed them out into the street.

The city of the creatures was massive. It was as large even as one of the cities which had existed before the Departure, large enough to hold tens of thousands. It was an enormous sprawl of small stone dwellings, all of them thick and fortified on one side with walls and tall overhangs. Many of these walls shadowed porches, upon which there were piles of woven and dyed mats. Nearly every stone surface had been painted with colorful patterns, or inlaid with mosaic made from colored stones and shards of what Aitor recognized as scrap metal.

The dwellings stacked upon themselves in some places, becoming a mound much like an anthill, backed by a troubled purple-orange sky thick with heavy clouds.

From this anthill spilled the creatures, many hundreds of them, calling out to each other, talking in groups, many carrying baskets full of food or heaps of collected reeds and grasses. Many wore only the simple tunics which Aitor had already seen; many more wore heavy indigo veils which covered their faces, and they drifted among the others slowly, speaking to no one, avoided by all.

The Others who had ministered to him ushered him down the street. He did not know if they were his guides or his guards, but while they made no effort to unbind his hands, neither were they rough as they pushed him forward.

There were eyes on him as he passed amongst the creatures, but no one moved to harm him, nor to spit, nor even to speak to him. Rather, the creatures seemed to move aside for him, creating a small path for him to walk in peace. Those who escorted him allowed him to linger, to stare.

They walked toward the heart of the city, and the dwellings became more elaborate, multi-roomed; the streets were wider, and the clothing which the creatures wore was of a finer weave, and more colorful.

The murals on the ever-present walls were no longer only patterns and collections of color, but were pictures now, and as they passed, Aitor saw that the pictures made up parts of stories. There were images of the same creatures—depicted faithfully with their lesions and growths—hunting, and fishing, and traveling in groups with cloths draped over their heads to shield them from the sun. In the pictures, they gardened and wove and built and sang in groups.

The walls, he realized, recounted a history of the city, played in reverse as they walked further inwards. Here was a depiction of the city much smaller, surrounded by a group of the creatures hand in hand, observing their handiwork from afar beneath a painted sun. There, a scene of workers laboring over what looked like green-and-yellow river-gardens against a vast expanse of desert. There were images of battles, too, and privation, and what seemed to be great dust storms tearing apart the city, leaving devastation in their wake.

One of the murals caught his attention in particular, and he paused to look at it. The creatures flanking him paused, too, waiting. They had been watching him look at their pictures, their attitude grave.

The mural he looked at was of a cloud rising from a depiction of a tiny landscape, so small that the outlines of what must be tall buildings were marked by rectangular shapes only as long as his thumb. The cloud swelled in a bloated mushroom to fill the entirety of the wall, heavy-bellied and sinister. Made of orange and yellow and gray, Aitor knew it immediately as the thing which had destroyed the world as he slept, unknowing and peaceful, in a dark box circling amidst impassive stars.

He looked up, shaken. They had come to the center of a wide square, a space whose earth had been trampled flat and hard by the passage of many feet over many years. It, too, was walled all round, and each wall bore the same images of spreading clouds, of cities aflame, of wreckage and chaos.

Aitor saw it with a sort of numbness; what he saw here was divorced from what he had understood of these creatures. It was not real. It could not be. But he knew, also, that the truth had been there for as long as they had known of Others among them on this terrible new Earth, and that they had ignored it.

At the center of the square was a building, and its shape was familiar to Aitor's eyes although he had never laid eyes on it before in his life. It was a church, and from within it came the sounds of singing.

The creatures—the Others; the remnants—who watched Aitor no longer needed to shepherd him forward. They held the door for him as on weary feet he returned to a place he thought he would never see again.

The church was small; it had been no grand basilica, and it had been devastated by war and weather and time. Parts of it had been blasted away and then crudely patched with clay and rock and scavenged timber. There was little art visible within it; any statues had long been destroyed or had crumbled away, and the paintings which once had covered the walls were blackened with age.

But it was the first recognizable building Aitor had seen since the Travelers' arrival, and stepping inside was like coming home.

It hurt him to see it, a part of him which had half healed now ripped open again. But while it hurt, he loved it. Let there be more salvaged. O God, let there be a shadow of beauty and truth left in this world, so that he might look at it, even if he could no longer understand it.

The church was packed with Others; all of them were veiled, and they knelt before the altar in orderly rows. Aitor looked to the sanctuary and saw that there was a crude bier there, and upon it were the bodies of the two Others that had been slain by the Travelers at the settlement, lying with their arms crossed over their chests. Crosses had been painted upon their foreheads; their eyes were covered by the same decorated stones that they had left for Aitor and Noah.

Aitor could not tear his gaze from the deformed remnants of humanity who mourned them, bent low before the altar. With their obscene bodies hidden beneath swaths of cloth, they looked like ancient saints giving homage, faceless, holy.

How could they pray, he thought, when they looked as they did, when God had abandoned them here on this Earth to suffer? And to whom did they cry out?

It struck him then, what they were singing.

Aitor was suddenly eight years old again, spraddled on hot and grimy concrete in southern Andalucía. He listened, bored and wistful and sleepy, to the voice of Padre Aguilera resounding over the timid voices of the elderly and the very young.

The words which the Others sang were pronounced as clearly and carefully as if the singers read from a book of chant, the swell and harmony of it as intricate and precise as a choir:

> *Miserére nostri, Dómine, miserére nostri.*
> *Fiat misericórdia tua, Dómine, super nos,*
> *quemádmodum sperávimus in te.*
> *In te, Dómine, sperávi: non confúndar in aetérnum.*

And Aitor whispered the translation to himself in Spanish, words he had memorized and chanted to himself many times in seminary, as he prepared to take the steps that would seal him in perpetuity as a priest of God:

Have mercy on us, O Lord, have mercy. Let your mercy be upon us, Lord, for we have hoped in you. In you, Lord, have I hoped: let me never be confounded.

He shuddered with a sudden wakening of closeness, of a presence which he had not felt for a long time. And yet that presence was not with him, but with this people that prayed and hoped and waited for so many centuries. He was there only as a listener, on the outside, observing something he had lost long ago.

What had they seen all these years, as they looked at an altar filled with nothing at all?

But Aitor thought he knew, even as he wondered.

Perhaps these people had glimpsed beyond the veil, just as he had that first time in the theatre, gazing deep into the hidden heart of the universe: perhaps they had seen, from the corner of their eyes, the Watcher.

And alone in the desert, they waited for the moment when at last they would come before its face.

AMEN, whispered the voices which had been his companions all the fifty years of his lonely exile; but they were not speaking to him, but with the congregation of Others. And the ancient, ever-sorrowing voice of the Father Superior was the first among them.

AMEN. ALLELUIA.

Outside, the sound of deep and ponderous thunder shook the air.

The men—for they were men—who had brought Aitor here came in, and veiled themselves, too. The others who knelt moved aside to allow them to pass. But they did not enter further into the church. The two of them faced Aitor, and they seemed to wait, to see what he would do.

As if he dreamed, Aitor passed through the people, and walked to the altar. No one stopped him as he ascended the stone stairs, felt his feet slip in grooves where feet had trodden many thousands of times before. He stood before a simple altar, decorated with a plain cloth of simple weave; there was nothing on it.

His eyes were drawn upward then to the shadowy alcove behind the altar, where once candelabra or soft electric lights might have illumined the darkness.

And it stood there on a new pole, as if it had been waiting for him all this time, its bloodied arms outstretched, neck twisted and mouth stretched in its gruesome scream, looming from the shadows. The crucifix of Knurów.

Its eyes bore into him, and they saw him—they knew him and what he carried within.

His first thought was that he must have it; he must escape, he must take it to the Travelers. For it was theirs, and it had been stolen from them—and perhaps if they returned it, something of the Christ would be returned to them too. Perhaps if he gave it to Jacob they could come to an understanding; they could talk, he could make Jacob understand.

But he could not, now that it stood here and listened to these ancient songs of praise and thanksgiving. It stood here proudly as if it had stood here a thousand years. Just as once before, many worshippers sank before it, giving it homage.

He knew then that these people had watched the Travelers. They had seen them offering Masses, praying and working, building to create human life once more amidst the wreckage of civilization.

And before that, perhaps there had been men of Christ who had walked among these ruins, praying, giving Communion, whispering Vespers in the ashes of ravaged cities. Perhaps they had sat alone beneath the night sky, sick and dying, and had prayed for the safe travel of *La Trascendencia*, before the memory of it was lost at last to them, except for myth and legend.

Perhaps this was all that was left of them now.

Had these people watched Aitor alone in agony before the crucifix in the small hours of the night, begging for some sign, for some small hope, laid gently aside by his people?

Had they seen the bloody killings, the deaths, and the emptying of the chapel until it was a forgotten and abandoned place?

Had they witnessed all this, and judged the Travelers, and found them unworthy?

Aitor sank stiffly to his knees before the crucifix, as if the force of its gaze bore him to the ground. *My God,* he thought, *Do you see them?* And he put his face in his hands, as if it might hide him from the stare of the crucifix's carved eyes, its widespread, tormented arms driven through with holy nails.

But as he knelt, the humiliation and disgust which filled him drained away, and he felt himself left hollowed out, suspended. Here before the face of this nonsensical, ancient faith, he felt a strange tranquility in contemplating everything he did not know. Around him, ignorant, unaware of the absurdity, the people lifted their voices in harmony, drawing the mystery closer to them, growing it in them, consumed by the beauty of their song.

And then the song was over, leaving a quiet that was deafening. Aitor wept.

When at last he stood again, his escort stood close to him, watching him solemnly. The rest of the mourners had left, leaving the church barren once again.

The taller of the two extended a hand towards the crucifix. He said something then, and Aitor did not understand him; at least to his knowledge, it was no language of Old Earth.

"I do not understand," Aitor told him.

The man shook his head, then, and lifted his own discolored hand, placed it upon the bier which carried the bodies of his brethren.

Non intellego, Aitor repeated. *No te comprendo.* And he could not meet the other man's eyes.

But the stranger put his hand out slowly. A peace offering; a reconciliation; a gesture that was hauntingly human. And this time, Aitor took it.

His escort took him then away from the church, and out into the city again. The people in the streets no longer tried to conceal that they were watching; those with unveiled faces stood in rows and watched solemnly as Aitor and the other passed through their ranks.

They came then to a host of soldiers lining the street, carrying clubs and rods and hammered stone swords, a great many of them. The murder at the Travelers' city had hardly thinned their ranks—there were many hundreds, filling the side streets which opened away from the one Aitor walked. They, too, made no move, and there was no hostility in their eyes.

One by one, they laid down their weapons before him. They knelt, and pressed their foreheads to the ground.

The man who had drawn Aitor along with him let go Aitor's hand then, and bent down, and in the thin fine layer of dirt above the hard-packed ground, he sketched a tiny city with walls, with watchtowers; he drew outside it small figures, holding crude representations of guns, knives, bows, walking from the city towards a snaking river.

The hunters, Aitor thought; Simon, Amir. "Yes," he whispered, and waited.

The man walked a little way forward, then, until he stood at a mural painted on the side of one of their buildings; this building was larger than many, perhaps a gathering place of some kind.

The mural itself depicted many of the strange people, dancing and singing in a circle, their hands joined. The strange flowers of the waste were bright spangles of color around their feet.

Aitor's guide pointed at the mural, and then back towards the church they had left behind. He made the motion several times, his gestures becoming more and more insistent each time.

Aitor stared at the image, at the small deformed figures capering amidst sunshine, at the joy on their faces. He strained to see what it was that they wished him to see.

There were larger figures, others like them, in the background, he saw, sketched in less detail around the outsides of the circle. They watched the little dancing figures with baskets and tools in their hands, paused in their work, their crudely sketched smiles offering peaceful benediction.

Children, Aitor thought, and his body felt numb and bloodless as he realized it. The creatures which had attacked the Travelers at first, who had stolen from them, had been children.

He could see it now: stupid children, full of bravado, approaching the hunting party. They had seen these people, so different from them, and had been afraid, and then full of the prideful stupidity of youth—

He looked at the people who stood arrayed before him, bowed down before him, pleading for mercy.

But they asked the wrong man. Despair filled him. Already that the city was a tomb, and they all walked dead.

Even as he thought it, the wind shifted to bring a sharp, acrid scent to them, and on the horizon arose plumes of smoke.

For Jacob came seeking vengeance, and there was no room for mercy left in him at all.

CHAPTER 24

TALIT DID NOT WANT TO move; she did not want to live.

The storm had settled heavy drifts of sand around her until she lay buried to her waist in debris. The low-hanging sun lit the world with an eerie pink haze which surged with thick curling currents, as if she drowned in a vast sea of light.

Fate had been laughing at her for so many days now, and now again it spat in her face. That she had been able to find Ziek—that she should have him again, if only for a little while—and then he should be torn away from her again—that she should find a piece of Lanon, only to realize she would not live to see him again—it was too much to bear. Her heart was as a dead thing inside her, and with it killed, she was dry and brittle.

Ziek had led her when she had no more will to go on. Reason said that without him, she should only curl up in the sand, and let it bury her until she found a deep and troubled forever-sleep.

Yet as she lay there as a corpse lay, Talit found that she could not be without him and what he meant. Whatever he had seen, she wanted it too.

And so one more time, she stood up, and shook the sand from her tunic, and pushed into the storm.

Silently, secretly, she cried out to anyone who was listening.

Let me find Ziek.

Forgive me.

Let us go home.

The wind pushed against her spitefully; sand bit against raw skin. She tried to shield her face with her arm, and then realized that the arm was no longer there, and she felt only a burning itch where it should be.

Where are you? she called out, but only in her thoughts, for when she opened her mouth it filled with sand, her words swallowed into the thundering winds.

Sometimes she thought that she walked not far behind Ziek: she saw him, a tiny shape wavering like a dark shadow far ahead of her. But then the winds would shift again and blow apart his figure into an eddy of dust that was lost.

She was never really truly alone, though, for her fevered mind built companions out of the streams of dusty light and shadow. But it was her dead eye that saw them, ghosts of vision that mocked her; images slipped by just at the edge of her sight as quickly as darting fish, flitting in and out of focus.

There to her right, a racing four-legged shadow trimmed with gold: a creature whose neck was ringed with thick hair, its body sleek and lean.

There, looming tall as four Sazers standing atop each other, a figure sat in a chair of green stone, looking down at her; where she should have seen a body, there was only a confusing tangle of many-colored light.

And all around her, a thousand others. Some had many eyes; others wore multiple heads facing different ways on their oddly-shaped bodies. There were shapes of creatures with many wings, which did not fly or walk so much as they were in one place in one moment and far ahead of her the next. Some wandered on four legs, but wore the faces of the smooth people from the churches, eerie and beautiful.

All of them watched her; they seemed to be traveling with her, streaming steadily in the same direction. Some of their mouths opened and they seemed to speak to her, but the howling of the storm devoured their voices.

The day waned and fell towards dusk, and Talit staggered onwards, tripping on rocks and desert weeds. Her illusory companions were deep blurs of shadow, now, glimpses only of faces turning towards her, of eyes glinting just before they closed.

She clung now to a determination she had not known she possessed, which came from a place inside her she had not known existed. A stupid and ridiculous determination, a laughing madness that told her there was reason to go on, that if she only kept walking, everything would be made well.

She could see the faces of her family waiting for her: Mother, her hands busy at her work as she skinned and tanned her latest kill, all the while whispering a prayer to bring her daughter home. Father, nurturing the sacred gardens, sowing and threshing and gathering up their precious contents, looking always to the distant hills in the west, his heart with her.

And Lanon, alive and camped in a bend in the river somewhere, waiting for her to discover that he was whole, that he lived, that he had always been waiting—that he had a great and wonderful secret to tell, when she was ready to find him and listen—

As the darkness came, and the blurry rose-gold light deepened to purple, there came also a familiar presence which she knew was no illusion. She saw it moving alongside her as a crawling many-legged shadow first, and then during a lull in the wind it was a spiked thing which stood perfectly motionless above her on a crest of land some distance from her, its eyes glinting sporadically in the changing light.

Then it was not just one, but two, and three; they moved alongside her, flanking her journey, jaws gaping lazily.

The dustwalkers had found her once again.

This time she had no torch to protect her, no resource. She did not even know if Ziek still carried her mother's knife with him in the pack, or if it lay near Prophet's splayed body in the ancient church, abandoned.

Awkwardly, her body clumsy and slow to respond, she began to run.

The dustwalkers trotted alongside her, closing in. Their bodies slid through the dust-shapes of her hallucinations as a knife through flesh; they dispersed the deepening golden-blue shadows noiselessly, vanishing first, and then bursting through each new cloud the storm kicked up. They dogged the edges of her vision tirelessly: not too close, not too far.

Waiting.

Why did they wait? she thought. Why do they not just kill me now? And the insane thought—the desperate hope—came to her that perhaps they recognized her as the Sazer who had killed one of their comrades.

That could not be true; dustwalkers slaughtered for sport, eviscerating anything they saw which moved and screamed and bled. But she could not explain in any other way how they ran in rank and file along her, their heads turned eerily to watch her, their jaws parted in slavering smiles. They only flanked her, an eerie escort, making no move to draw any closer.

She turned her face straight forward, fear jarring her pain-numbed, scorched skin alive and tingling. If Lanon was watching—if the Lord was watching—perhaps they would leave her alone, until she reached—

But she did not know what it was that she would reach.

Her body seethed with pain as she ran; every step sent the feeling of knives ramming into her legs, tearing her wounded side apart. But the force which propelled her forward was fear now, and she knew that she moved with the strength of the dying.

The sun had sunk below the horizon, but the winds raged on. Eyes watched her from the shadows; wings flickered in the spaces between eddies of dust.

Talit put her head down to watch her feet as they sloughed through drifts of sand and dust. They no longer felt like they belonged to her; they had not for a long time. Her lungs burned as if they would melt her from within.

She tripped and fell, skewing headlong into a rise in the ground. Skin tore from her cheek and her side and hung raw and chapped; her naked and burnt flesh felt now winter-cold under the buffeting wind.

The dustwalkers' cries ghosted faintly over the sandstorm, a guttural and ululating shriek.

Talit could not move; she could not even gather enough strength to lift her head from where it lay jammed at a wrong angle into the ground.

"Help me," she cried, though she could barely hear herself, and she sobbed into the sand, catching breath like shards that cut her throat. "Do not leave me here alone. I am coming."

The voices of the dustwalkers closed tight around her—distress? exhortation? exultance that their prey had fallen at last?—and the wind screamed.

And then came the tolling of a bell.

The sound cut pure, a wild jubilance of sweet song. Talit knew that voice as if it were her own.

She looked up, and in the maelstrom of dust and bracken and choking violence, she saw, from very far away, that the heavens had peeled back, and there stood the tall figures which had lined the road to the church in the hills. These figures, though, stood many thousands of paces high, and the dust storm in its majesty came only to their waists.

They extended their hands; their heads all pointed the same direction. Their mouths were open, and from many throats issued tremendous song—one single, unbroken phrase in rounds, which she could not understand, and yet which was so beautiful that it caused her pain.

So Talit followed their gaze, and in the distance, she saw a great light.

CHAPTER 25

THE FLAMES WERE VISIBLE WITHIN only moments, a wall which swept towards them, driven by the wind.

The people in the city streets scattered, shouting, and in moments Aitor was left nearly alone in the street.

Only one remained with him. It was his escort, one of the two who had brought him to show him the murals. Full of grief, Aitor did not know how to react as the man came close.

The man drew a small stone knife from his belt and cut through the ropes that hobbled Aitor's wrists and ankles, leaving him free. He said something then, meeting Aitor's eyes; in his gaze Aitor saw an apology. Then he turned his back and fled into the labyrinth of buildings.

Aitor watched the city burn with despair. He knew, though he did not see, what must be happening, just as it had happened on the day of the Exodus. Just as it had happened so many times before.

Jacob did not care that the stones of their buildings would stand when the fire had died out. Beyond the city, the plains burned; beyond that, the forest. He burned their resources: their weapons, their shelter and their tools, the meager crops they might have grown to sustain themselves, the animals and their shelters.

Even should the people survive the flames, even if their home remained intact, there would be little left for them here. They would starve in this barren place; if they left to seek fresh grounds, they might starve trying.

And this place which they had built—its murals would be gone, blackened by fire. The labor of the hands of the children of Earth, the survivors, would be erased with no remainder.

Aitor knew somehow that Jacob was close, that it was his hand which first readied the kindling and struck the flame.

Here was Jacob's final and desecrated offering, his challenge to God.

He looked upon the burning city and thought of the final desolation, the day of Departure. On this final day he had already been asleep, already circling the earth, frozen and safe. Many times he had imagined what it must have been like; he had read the broken, stilted accounts of his brothers; he had dreamed them to life many nights.

Now he thought, it is fitting that I should finally witness the end of mankind.

God, deliver us, he prayed, as eight billion souls might have prayed on that last day. *Kyrie eleison,* he whispered, and heard no answer.

But if God would not rescue them—if He merely watched, impassive; if He had walked away long ago to attend other things—even if He had never been there at all—Aitor chose defiance.

Let Him see that one remained faithful, he thought. That yet remained one who cried out for love, even when love was dead.

Let me rescue Him instead. Let Him be guilty, and weep for us, His children.

Aitor turned back toward the fire and its many lunging heads, to the air which blurred and warped in the distance until the desert hills shimmered, as in a dream. He began to walk once more—as fast as he could—into the heart of the city.

With each step he chanted the words he had heard Jacob shout so many times into the open sky as he gave prophecy to the Travelers, words that none of the Travelers had recognized, but which Aitor knew as intimately as a kiss.

Eloi, Eloi: lama sabachthani—

Smoke filled the streets, a blinding gray haze. The Travelers must have set the city ablaze from all sides, for the fire seemed to press in from everywhere, driving Aitor inward, ever inward.

As always, no one took notice of him; he saw shapes darting through the smoke, carrying precious possessions, carrying others, calling out for each other amid the growing crackle and roar of the flame. In the distance he heard the sharp rat-tat of gunfire: the Travelers shooting those who were trying to escape the city.

With every blind turn he made, he traced the lines of humanity's history, brushing the walls with his fingertips: partly so that he did not travel in circles, and partly as a good-bye.

He found the square with the church by following the story of the city backwards to its origin, the plaza painted full of destruction and sickness.

The church stood waiting solemnly, wreathed in smoke. The fire was not far. And he could have grieved for the church, this beautiful place which had lasted everything; he could have prayed a thousand prayers that somehow it, too, would be saved.

But there was not time for that now: Aitor could yet save one thing with his own hands. His steps sped until he was jogging, his old bones carrying him faster and faster.

There was no one in the church left now but for the Christ which awaited him at the head of the altar, fixed and unchanging. Aitor went to it and genuflected on aching knees. As Jacob had in the chapel many months ago at their arrival, he turned his face up to the agonized God-man on the cross, and stared. It looked back at him with its bulging wooden eyes.

He took the cross down from its place gently; it was warm in his palms. Already the fire was loud and growing louder. Through the long-broken windows of the church, its light spilled in and bathed the old stone with amber and honey.

The crucifix was large and heavy. Aitor settled it on his shoulder and slowly, his muscles trembling with the weight of it, he left the church behind.

The city was an inferno. The murals stood scorched and peeling from blackened walls. All of the peoples' belongings were surely ash by now. Thick black smoke plumed and curled, a living dragon, through the city, and muffled the shouts and cries of the people as they fled. A few of them lay trampled and suffocated at his feet, silent, staring.

Aitor was alone now, and he did not know where it was that he walked. The sand upon which he walked burnt his feet through the soles of his thin and ragged sandals.

He bowed his head against the heat that scorched his exposed flesh, drew ragged breaths in the smoke which battered him. He heard once more the whispers of the people, whose souls he had borne with him through fifty years adrift in space with only his Lord as company. Begging, praying, cursing, their voices beat against him as much as did the buffets of heat from the flames.

But he could not falter, for now he carried the last of Christ through the wilderness to witness the death of the world.

The streets of the city lay covered in smoldering soot: scattered belongings, buildings cracking and warping under tongues of flame, ashen heaps which had burnt themselves out, and smoldered in red-hot piles.

Where the path lay open to him, he took it without hesitation, forging slowly forward through the flames. Shapes moved around him in the smoke, and he was aware that many traveled near him, that they, too, sought exodus.

Aitor's cough slowed him as he fought to breathe the black air; his body at last was giving way to its age. But he was nearing the edge of the city now; the brilliant light of the fire washed it pale as it loomed closer and closer.

He stumbled then, and fell to his knees, felt his skin tear without protest. The cross fell awkwardly beneath him, one of its arms banging squarely into his side, driving the breath from him.

No, Aitor thought, and he struggled feebly. It is not finished. I will not let Him burn. I will not yield.

But his legs did not seem to obey his commands; his hands would not release from the cross. It felt as if he were bound to it, the immensity of the world contained in this single carving, as if it would bear him down into the center of the earth.

Aitor would have lain there willing his blistering and swollen body to move until the fire consumed him, had not a pair of hands borne him up from either side.

And when he blinked away the sweat and tears from his eyes, he saw that beside him were a man and a woman whom he did not recognize at all. As they helped him stand, they showed no anger towards him, an intruder who carried their holy symbol, only a reverence and respect that he did not understand.

Forward, slowly, but without ceasing.

They began to pass signs of a fight. Traveler and Other both lay slaughtered in the bloodied sand. In the careless indifference of death, they often were wrapped in a terrible embrace, their weapons forgotten.

Thus so many years ago, and thus now, Aitor thought, *Kyrie eleison.*

Once more he staggered as they walked, as they passed the bodies of those he had known and loved—even from afar—in their time in the Travelers' city. But he let the people of the desert bear him up and away, let them guide him when his tears blinded him too much to see.

And onward they walked as the fire tore apart the last of mankind's home, and tears streamed down his face, only to hiss into nothing, steamed away by the heat.

As the city fell at last into deathly silence, they passed at last through an unfamiliar city gate, and escaped into the deep-water blue of night.

They were on the far side of the city. Unfamiliar hills rose high around them, imposing and strange when he was so accustomed to the unyielding flat of the plains. The wind winding through the hills was as cold as ice to Aitor's fire-wrecked skin.

The desert folk bore Aitor up into the hills, where the sparse, tough vegetation grew into a thin blue grass, and there they paused to look back at their home.

But the city was no more, and there was only a conflagration left.

Beyond it, closer to the Travelers' home, fire swept across the grass-lands, where the wind had blown the sparks of destruction. The forest beyond it, too, burned. Birds wheeled, agitated, far distant under the heavy purple clouds, outlined in trails of pale smoke.

Aitor whispered the *requiem* for the dead, his voice too small to carry.

He turned, then, clinging to the hideous cross, and saw that the faces of those beside him were stained with tears, and that they wept openly.

"I am sorry," Aitor said to them, and the woman turned to look back at him. "Thank you. Thank you."

They did not need to share a language. Aitor saw that she knew his meaning, for she raised her hand, and once again, as another before her had done, marked the air between them, three-fingered, with a cross.

And then there was gunfire: two sharp reports one after the other, splintering the night.

And the people who had helped Aitor crumpled boneless to the ground. In all this time they had not made a single sound.

No, Aitor wanted to shout, but the word would not come to his lips.

Turning to see who had done this, he saw a figure standing atop a nearby hill, his gun cocked in his hand. The shadows from the fire in the city ate away the flesh of his face, turning it into a hollowed mask, and he hunched over himself so that he looked like a crooked wraith. But Aitor knew that there was only one person it could be.

No! he cried again into the darkness, and there was no response. *Will you take everything I have?*

Be not afraid, a friend had told him, so very long ago.

But where he had been brave then, Padre Aitor Gómez Gomarra was a coward now. He turned and found new energy, and weeping bitterly, he fled into the hills, bearing his God across his shoulders.

CHAPTER 26

TALIT FOLLOWED THE LIGHT.

The other shapes she had seen flitting through the dust and sand had been transient, changing; this one alone remained constant. As she focused on it, it seemed to grow—not just a light, but a pillar of white fire.

It moved, wavering, on the horizon, just out of reach, splitting the murky indigo of the night with gold. It lit the monolithic dream-figures which lined her path, bathing them in an eerie glow.

It is not real, she told herself, it cannot help me.

But she turned her head to it and ran, drawn to it as a moth to flame, even as she felt her muscles failing, her lungs filling with dust, her organs collapsing in on themselves.

She thought that the dustwalkers had seen the fire, too. They were behind her, still, but they had drawn nearer. The dust masked them, but they were close enough now that she heard feet thudding on sand, smelled their hellish stench.

Talit ran—and then suddenly she was running faster than she had ever gone before. One moment she was lost in a chaotic world of dust and fangs and endless wind; the next she was racing Ziek across the city of Saze.

It was not Ziek the Burdened, but *her* Ziek. He sprinted just ahead of her, his face alight with challenge. Even as he ran, he turned his head to call something taunting which the wind whipped away.

And neither was she a broken shell, but instead she ran whole and strong, both of her eyes clear, both her arms pumping her forward steadily through the shouting bedlam of Saze. There was no storm, only a clear sky of blue and orange. The bright-painted murals of their people were a blur of color as Ziek and Talit sped to the city center, to the Church of Prophet.

Talit laughed as she ran. She found in herself true joy, that which could not be pressed down or destroyed, for where the Church had stood once, there was instead the pillar of fire, and it lit the world from within.

The people of Saze had replaced the eerie tall figures which had lined the desert. They stood at the edges of the road to make way, and they cheered and sang songs of exultation in voices that shattered the sky. Lanon was among them, and her mother and father. There were a thousand other Burdened Sazers, unveiled, their faces bright and clear as the day they were born.

But even as the Sazers flickered and were blown to dust, the light remained before her, and Talit knew that she could not stop until she had thrown herself into it, infused herself from head to toe. So she ran with tears streaming down her face, blinding her until she saw nothing but that tower of light, waiting for her.

And as the shadow-shape of Ziek disintegrated before her, and the voice of her bell sounded once more as a clarion shout through the wasteland, she came to herself once more, and found that she had run through the gates of the city of Saze as the people hid from the wind and sand in their homes.

She stood alone before the Church of Prophet, where its doors stood open wide.

No one left their homes during sandstorms, yet someone had entered here.

Talit could no longer feel shock or surprise; the light was gone, but she felt it ahead of her, waiting. It had brought her here, and so now she must enter. Somehow, without knowing why, she understood that once she entered, she must surely change forever.

The dustwalkers were there behind her, once more. And strangely, they no longer pursued her. When she looked over her shoulder, she saw that they stood in a ring around the Church, motionless, as if paralyzed. They did not look at her, but up, in fear, at the great white flame which stretched above them, as far as the eye could follow.

Talit turned her back to them, and went inside.

The Church seemed small compared to the one atop the great hills to the west, but it was her home. The braziers were not lit, and the hall was very dark. Here, the stone figures of the smooth people did not move or grow, only stood peaceful in their places, their eyes turned toward the empty hollow before the altar where a small figure lay crumpled there at its base.

Talit knew immediately that it must be Ziek.

He did not move as she drew closer. His tunic had slipped up over his shoulder to cover his face; his feet were bloodied and torn.

In a way, she thought dully as she knelt by him, she was glad, and she could not cry for him any more.

The pack her mother had given her lay open at his side, empty. But in his hand, he clutched something large, wrapped in faded cloths. Lost in the swaths of his dirtied tunic, she almost missed it.

As she reached down and pried it from his swollen hands, she knew at once that he had taken it from the arms of Prophet on his bier.

I killed you for this, Ziek, she thought as she lay it awkwardly across her knees to unwrap it. My lies drove you and all we have for it is this.

She pulled the thing free from its wrappings, and beheld a man.

He was carved with such skill that it took her a full moment to understand that he was made from wood, with a precision no Sazer had ever created, and not living and dying there in her arms.

He lay with his arms spread wide on beams fixed crosswise. His wrists and feet had been transfixed by spikes which had caused his flesh to burst like ripe fruit, dangling in ribbons that oozed thick streams. Where he had flesh, he was crisscrossed with deep crusted cuts, as if a dustwalker had scored him from head to toe and left him festering. Chunks of flesh had been pulled away from his skeleton to expose carved bone, carved organs which seemed almost to pulse beneath. Some of the wood had been blackened by fire, so that it seemed that his skin had been melted away from him in places.

Mouth agape, the man screamed silently, teeth broken, tongue swollen. But though he cried out, his eyes were stretched wide, the lids pulled back so that they bulged as if from great strain, and they swallowed her with a gaze that was endless and forever. In that gaze there was not only pain, but a stillness that was overwhelming. It enveloped her; it pulled her closer.

There was, in those eyes and that stillness, something more. She knew what it was: she had known it as she struggled up into the hills chased by dustwalkers, as the desert tore her body to shreds, starved and beat and killed her. She had known it as she looked on Ziek's face in the moments just before sleep, as he smiled and dreamed of salvation, even as the Burdening consumed him.

Talit stared at the carving, and then stared again. This man was one of the smooth people, like the statues in the Church of Prophet—but no, perhaps he had been, and was no longer. He was not even a Sazer, like her.

And Talit, looking at him, remembered the stories that had been told around Sazer cookfires, of the legends which spoke of ancient days. She beheld, as she had imagined it for so many days, the killing of the Lord.

This was the man who for so long the Sazers had worshiped and feared.

The Lord, this man, this being from ages before: he was Burdened, too.

She picked up the carving and held it high. And as she did, the wood warmed to her hand, and the Church of Prophet seemed to lean closer, to hold its breath.

Slowly, her feet carrying her the final steps of her journey, she took him to the mysterious darkness behind the altar which had stood empty for so long, and she found that there was a place waiting to receive him.

She stepped back to look on him for a long time. The darkness all around her pressed closer, a warm and gentle thing, speaking as softly as a mother. The sound of the dust storm outside was a lulling whisper.

Talit thought of Prophet, asleep in his faraway temple, and Lanon, she felt sure, who had already found what she had already gone seeking.

She thought of the tower with its four heads just outside, its crackling voice calling for hope; she thought of Leader, and all the Leaders who had gone before him, sending away her people into the wilderness for the sake of a sin long past, for the sake of a master long gone from this world. She thought of many things.

Nothing was certain, now. But for her, it was enough.

A hand slipped into hers, warm and smooth and strong. She took it in hers, and felt it close around her cold fingers.

As she turned to follow its owner, the Church of Prophet resounded with the tolling of bells.

CHAPTER 27

INTO THE NIGHT LAND AITOR went.

Away from the destroyed city, the world flickered before his eyes in a low indigo-violet light.

The roaring of the fire had dwindled to a distant rumble; when he dared look back, it looked now almost like an oil painting, smudged and blurred and unreal. It had swept across the desert, so that paired with the low-bellied storm clouds which gathered, it seemed that a shallow and sullen sea swallowed the world from both above and below.

Where he was going did not matter. He forced his feet into a mindless shuffle; he keened in desolation as he ascended.

An old man should not be doing this. And yet he was the only one who would.

Only one thing remained to him, not even the stars, which lay hidden from him behind the light of the fire from below: he must find a safe place for this remnant of his Christ, and only then could he sleep.

He would not be shot down like a dog; he would not let Jacob take the crucifix and defile it.

He did not even realize that his steps had grown slower and slower, that his heart was seizing, that his breaths were shallower and desperate, for he could no longer feel much of his body.

He did not realize even until he felt himself falling for the third and final time, until the ground rose up to meet him, and he lay with the cross fixed beneath him, its hard edges and points marking bruises into his flesh.

How many hours he might have lain there, drifting in and out of faded dreams, he did not know.

It was when footsteps found Aitor, slow and halting, that his thoughts surfaced again, holding to reality with a thread as thin and fine as spider silk.

The feet came closer to him, and then the person stood over him, unmoving.

Aitor knew the footsteps, the person who belonged to them, as well as he knew his own heart.

A long moment passed as the person looked down upon the last priest of the Order of Saint Joseph of Cupertino, the last soul which clung to the hope it had once found in the House at the End of the World.

There was the sound of something falling to the ground with a heavy thud. Then hands wrapped around Aitor, bore him up, even as he held to the Cross of Knurów with numb and nerveless fingers.

Jacob slung Aitor over his shoulder. The world rocked and swayed; Aitor closed his eyes, and smelled the heavy tang of blood mingled with smoke and fire.

As Jacob carried him through the night, Aitor caught glimpses of a world that seemed as if it were underwater. He saw that they ascended, and that the night was waning. The footsteps were uneven and ragged; Jacob's breathing was wet and raw.

At last they arrived at whatever destination it was that Jacob had chosen for them. Aitor was jostled roughly as he slid from Jacob's shoulders, as he was leaned sitting upright against a rock.

When he opened his eyes fully at last, what lay before him was a majestic beauty which he had thought long ago that he would never see again: they had come to a lookout point which gazed out on one side to the bones of the charred and smoking city they had left behind, and on the other, a panorama of towering mountains which lay painted with the colors of the breaking of the dawn.

Above, the storm clouds finally broke, and for the first time in over sixteen hundred years, Aitor watched as rain swept the land in a great curtain.

He lay motionless as it poured down on him. He was cold and wet and broken, but he did not notice.

Below, blue smoke billowed from the charred city, and dispersed to the skies. What greenery and bracken there had been around the city was charred to black ashes now. Shadowed by the deep blue purple of the storm, the world looked bruised and raw as flesh.

Soon the city would return to the earth, just as all the others had.

And yet still the mountains stood, and still the world turned, he thought, and perhaps it would turn for sixteen hundred years more. All this would fade, and there might be others who could live in it better, with more grace, with hearts that understood.

"Aitor," a voice whispered, and he looked upon its owner.

Jacob stood before him, caved in on himself. Aitor could see now that the blood that covered him was his own. He bore a wound which had torn him open from waist to collarbone; his cassock had stuck and dried over the wound, closing it where it might have lain open and pulsing.

He was no longer recognizable, was no longer beautiful. Over it all, his skin was charred and blackened and blistered, and the tumors which had begun to deform him were no longer visible beneath the burnt and melted skin.

But his eyes were Jacob's eyes, and his soul looked out of them. No longer were they full of death. He looked as an orphaned child did, now, a sad bewilderment to him, an unspeakable tragedy.

"This would have been a good place to build your church," he whispered, his words slurred and mangled by his torn face, his throat disfigured by smoke.

"Why?" Aitor said, his own voice almost as raw, and he did not mean the church.

Jacob turned away, looked down at the city, his back turned to the mountains. "I cannot stop wanting Him, Aitor," he said. "I cannot stop. All of it was for Him. Everything always has been. I know that now. I cannot escape, even when I am angry. I am sick with Him . . . "

"Yes," Aitor whispered. "I know."

Jacob reached down to take the cross from Aitor's hand. Aitor watched in silence as he ground the end of its short pole into the earth and, with agonizing slowness, supported it with stones, so that it looked out over the city, its arms spread wide to embrace the ruin.

Then he sank to sit by Aitor, his hands pressed against his wounded torso, propped on the same rock. There the two of them leaned together as if they had been at the other's side their entire lives, with nothing left for envy or enmity, as if nothing had ever come between them. As if they were drowsy at the House at the End of the World, looking out at the waves coming to break on the rocks.

Aitor closed his eyes against the rain. "Father," he said, "Will you hear my confession?"

Jacob was a long time in answering. When he did, it was only a laugh, a small and sad choking sound.

"Jacob," Aitor said. "Iakobos."

And after a pause, Jacob lifted his melted hand, and Aitor saw that he made a small, faltering sign of the cross.

Aitor confessed then, in a whisper broken by long silences he sometimes did not remember to fill. He told Jacob of his doubt and his bitterness. His anger; his selfishness, jealousy, and pride.

And I failed you, he told Jacob. Forgive me, forgive me, forgive me.

Jacob said nothing. He listened with his still-lovely, fathomless black eyes staring down at the burnt city, looking upon it unblinkingly. Aitor did not know if it was the landscape he saw, or if it was the faces of the dead.

At last Aitor's confession trailed off for so long that he forgot he had been making it. Above them, the thunder stirred restlessly in the bellies of the clouds, and the rain slacked a little.

Jacob's response came slowly, so soft that Aitor almost did not recognize it. He spoke the words of absolution: those words a priest would never forget, not even at death's door. And as he gave Aitor God's absolution, Aitor sensed that he gave his also.

Then, into the long moment that followed, Jacob said, "Bless me, Father—", and it was more than the opening to a confession; it was a question that hung between them.

Aitor only took Jacob's hand into his own, and kissed it with numb and blistered lips, and waited. And waiting, he saw a sort of peace come to Jacob, even as he looked upon the city he had destroyed.

His voice was weak, and he no longer spoke English, but his home tongue, so that Aitor understood nothing. But still he waited patiently, and tasted smoke in the rain as Jacob mumbled, unable to form his words, tears streaming down his ravaged face. He licked his lips with a blistered pink tongue many times, as if it might heal what was ruined beyond repair.

For a long time Aitor listened, and was at peace. It was only after long minutes had passed in silence that he realized that Jacob must have finished, or could not finish, for his eyes remained open, but his mouth lay slack, his fingers limp.

The rain had nearly stopped now. Far below them, the peak of the church of the Others stood tall amidst the growing light which had begun to wax as the clouds thinned, and moved on to other places.

"Aitor," Jacob whispered suddenly, very clearly. "Everything I have done—" Turning his head to look at Aitor, he was again the Jacob of the seminary: always thinking of God a little more than the rest of them, always a little more grave, a little more afraid. "What would He say to me?"

Aitor looked up at the wooden Christ in agony above them, unmoving, unchanging. It watched over them now, just as it had aboard *La Trascendencia* for so long, always and forever suspended above the world and its people, embracing them with its tortured arms. "Beloved," he breathed.

Jacob did not answer him, and when Aitor finally turned his head to look at him, his eyes were open and staring at the brightening sky.

Side by side, the last two priests of Old Earth contemplated the heavens. When he tried to speak again, Aitor found that his lips and tongue did not obey him, and so he prayed the prayer of absolution in silence.

The two of them remained together, unmoving, as the rain dissipated and the clouds drifted away, leaving the paling dawn sky as clear and translucent as a forest lake.

They were there as the day passed under the familiar orange-blue sky, and as the sun descended again and orange-blue bled into pink and scarlet and gold, and was washed away by night.

When the moon arrived, it was huge, a giant white eye which blazed like a small sun, and at last the stars came out to arrange themselves in the heavens.

Aitor felt a small warmth return to him. Old friends, he thought.

He looked down from his contemplation then, into the land far below them, where the city of the Others was soaked in ash and shadows. It seemed now that it was merely asleep beneath the vast ocean of stars, resting for a new day.

Near the outskirts of the city, Aitor could see that on the blackened plain, smaller lights mirrored the sky. There were many of them, little wavering dots of fires, each with a tame tail of smoke, spread in small constellations along the horizon.

Even from far away, he heard their voices, clear and unearthly, as they sang.

Aitor turned his gaze further, following the patches of light far westwards, where the land lay untouched by flame. Here the fires ringed at a distance around square patches of land which looked as if they were covered in little seas of pale gold, washed white in the moonlight.

Wheat—it is wheat, he thought, turning his eyes back to the heavens.

Look, he wanted to tell Jacob. Now, truly: you can bring Christ to the world. There may one day again be bread. Somewhere in the world, perhaps there are vineyards, too.

And at last he smiled.

The sky was so lovely, more lovely than it had ever been in the history of the world, and closer than ever before.

But he no longer looked at the brilliance of the stars, for they seemed to shrink until they were unimaginably intense pinpoints of light, searing the fabric of the world.

No: just as he had as a boy, Aitor looked deep into the hollows between them, seeking, as he always had sought, what might lie between.

This time, as he did, the skies unfurled to receive him.

www.ingramcontent.com/pod-product-compliance
Lightning Source LLC
Chambersburg PA
CBHW061504030726
47503CB00005B/1811